"Go to hell, Zach!"

Attorney Amanda Shaw was surprised to hear that her voice was crystal clear. In fact, she could hardly breathe. In just five minutes with Zach, she'd lost her hard-won control—as usual.

A shadow crossed his face. "I'm here to take you home," he repeated.

"Zach, I can't just leave. Something big is going to happen for me at the firm. It's about to be announced."

"Congratulations," he said without missing a beat. "With all that clout, you can take some time off. Your boss was smart enough to pick the best, and he's not going to risk losing you."

Zach thought she was the best? His unexpected praise warmed her.

"But I can't believe you're having a hard time choosing between your job and your family's needs."

Scratch the praise.

Dear Reader,

Have you ever experienced a perfect moment? A moment so exquisite you wanted to stop time? Several years ago, it happened to me.

I was skiing on a gentle and beautiful four-mile beginner's trail on Okemo Mountain in Vermont. In gorgeous wooded surroundings, the sun shone brightly in a clear blue sky, dappling the snow-covered trail ahead of me. The air was crisp, but not freezing.

On that perfect day, I snowplowed to a complete stop and closed my eyes for a moment. The sun warmed my face; the sparrows and starlings sang their songs. I tasted gentle pine-scented breezes on my tongue and inhaled more deeply while listening as the thickly branched pines and firs whispered to each other.

I enjoyed all that before I finally opened my eyes and beheld the beauty of our world, the perfect tapestry of land and air and sky. I had truly found heaven on earth, and for that moment, all was right with my world.

In my story, Amanda Shaw needs to find the ingredients that will make her world right. She has many choices, many decisions. A powerhouse career in New York City, a ski resort in Vermont, a young sister who needs her and a determined hero who offers Amanda her dreams—his world.

I hope you enjoy watching Amanda figure it all out. And I hope you're lucky enough to experience a perfect moment in your own life.

Happy reading!

Linda Barrett

P.S. I'd love to hear from you! Please write me at P.O. Box 741395, Houston, TX 77274-1395.

Love, Money and Amanda Shaw

Linda Barrett

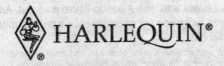

HARLEQUIN®

TORONTO • NEW YORK • LONDON
AMSTERDAM • PARIS • SYDNEY • HAMBURG
STOCKHOLM • ATHENS • TOKYO • MILAN • MADRID
PRAGUE • WARSAW • BUDAPEST • AUCKLAND

ISBN 0-373-70971-4

LOVE, MONEY AND AMANDA SHAW

Visit us at www.eHarlequin.com

Printed in U.S.A.

This first one's in memory of my dad, Emanuel Cohen,
who would have been so proud.
A girl never forgets her first hero.

And to my husband, Michael,
who definitely measures up.

And to West Houston RWA for providing the programs
and support...in particular to Patricia O'Dea Rosen
for her thoughtful critiques and friendship.

An aspiring author needs them all.

CHAPTER ONE

ATTORNEY AMANDA SHAW stood at her thirty-ninth-floor office window and looked out at the most powerful city in the world. In the first week of January, Park Avenue was still dressed for the holiday season with twinkling lights adorning the trees on its center islands. In other buildings, myriad lighted offices held the evening at bay. She never tired of admiring the city. Amanda never took its opportunities for granted, and most important, she never looked back. Her years in Vermont were history.

Reluctantly abandoning the view, she scanned the surface of her desk. Her current case files were neatly stacked and color-coded the way she liked them. Corporate law. Clean, neat, intellectual. All business with no messy emotions. Just like her life.

She sighed with satisfaction at her accomplishments to date. An excellent career, a growing financial portfolio and an independent lifestyle. Everything was falling into place perfectly.

The Finley case required a visit to the law library on the next floor. She picked up the folder and started walking to the door when her phone rang.

"Mr. Garroway wants to see you, Ms. Shaw," said

the ever-efficient secretary she shared with two other associates. "As soon as possible."

ASAP means now. Amanda replaced the file on her desk and buttoned the jacket of her Evan Picone navy-blue suit. Thick Berber carpeting cushioned her feet as she hurried down the corridor. Despite the urgency, however, she admired the lithographs on the walls as she usually did. She nodded to herself. Yes, she belonged here.

"Come in, Ms. Shaw. Come in."

Mr. Garroway stood behind his desk, a smile on his patrician face. He waved her to a seat.

"Ms. Shaw...Amanda...I hope you're planning to attend the company's annual postholiday party tomorrow at the Hilton."

She responded to the hint of a question in his voice with a nod.

"Good. Very good." He paused and steepled his fingers before meeting her gaze. "You'll have more to celebrate than most."

She sat up straighter, ears almost twitching to hear every single word he said. She'd been hoping, of course, that her abilities would continue to be recognized. No one in the firm had ever denied her brain power or her willingness to work hard. But there were no guarantees in life. She'd learned long ago to depend on herself and to always have a backup plan. But how sweet it would be not to have to use it!

"In essence, Stanhope Jones and MacGregor is offering to make you a junior partner in the firm. And if you're in agreement after we discuss the responsibilities, the announcement will be made tomorrow at the hotel. Until then, everything's confidential, and that includes family.''

Her heart went *ka-boom*. She couldn't speak for a moment, but finally felt her smile break through. From her boss's wide-eyed reaction, she knew it was her famous smile, from the old days of doing fashion shoots.

''Thank you, Mr. Garroway. You won't be sorry. I know I can handle the work.'' Sitting still was impossible. She jumped from her seat and shook her supervisor's hand. ''Thank you, thank you again.'' She repeated herself three times, still pumping his hand. So much for the sophistication she'd worked so hard to acquire!

He chuckled. ''Don't you want to hear about the salary and other remuneration?''

She thought of her growing portfolio. ''I'm all ears, Mr. Garroway.''

In the privacy of her office a few minutes later, Amanda pirouetted around her desk. Happiness, she decided, was climbing each rung of her ladder. She could have all the security she wanted if she depended only on herself.

TRYING TO IGNORE the concern clawing at his gut, Zachary Porter watched Amanda wend her way around the crowded New York hotel suite. More polished and beautiful than ever, Amanda fitted right in to the culture of the prestigious law firm.

She circulated among her peers as though she had

been born to wealth and power. A word here, a smile there, the barest tinkle of a laugh. She had mastered the social graces until they were as much a part of her as breathing. Zach knew she'd hone any skill necessary to achieve her goals, just as she had done in school to achieve all A's.

He eased his way into the room, identifying the power holders and the sycophants with a skilled glance. Stanhope Jones and MacGregor was no different from any other organization in that respect. The smell of money and power lured the wanna-bes as strongly as the year's first heavy snowfall lured skiers to Vermont. Zach laughed quietly to himself. Human nature never changed. Money, power, success, fame. And Amanda was caught up in the quest as much as anyone he'd ever known.

He watched her share a toast with an associate at this late-afternoon gathering, and mentally conceded defeat. With her gorgeous smile and designer dress, she seemed happy. Her thick blond hair was shorter than when he'd last seen her, now stylish and tamed. The shy youngster who had joined his family fourteen years ago had evolved into a beautiful jungle cat with an appetite for the big city, a powerhouse career and a near-obsession for wealth. It would be a miracle if he could get her to leave now.

Thoughts of his uncle's illness propelled Zach forward. He ignored the Armani suits and the uniformed caterers with their delicate offerings of baby lamb chops and stuffed mushroom caps, and continued into the room with renewed determination.

No one stopped him, and he laughed to himself again. Scruffy whiskers, jeans and a leather bomber jacket must have added the right touch of interest. He approached Amanda from the side, planted himself just within her peripheral vision and waited silently. *Come on, sweetheart, look at me.*

Amanda whirled as though he'd spoken out loud. And there, in her glorious blue eyes and delighted smile was the warmth of a woman happy to see him. Then, a second later, her professional mask reappeared. But that one moment encouraged Zach to revise his opinion. He'd not concede defeat yet.

AMANDA DETECTED Zach's presence shortly after he stepped into the room. Her sensitivity to him caused an ironic smile to curve her lips. She was as aware of him now as she'd been years ago, when her mom had married his uncle, and Zach had taken on the role of big brother. She'd gotten used to his eyes searching for her in a roomful of youngsters, gotten used to him giving her rides when he was old enough to drive and gotten used to him being part of unexpected girlhood fantasies.

Zach. His imprint on her soul was as sharp as the imprint of her own ambitions. But he was part of her other life, the emotionally demanding part that made her feel inadequate.

His appearance in New York could only mean more trouble. But what now? Pops was in stable condition, wasn't he? Was there some other family trouble? Or Zach and Amanda trouble? She caught herself. No, not that. He'd stopped playing big brother a long time ago, but could still manage to get under her skin—the only man who ever could. She'd always been afraid to analyze her feelings for him; she'd just known she had to fight them.

But she *was* glad to see him. She looked up, way up, into his familiar gray eyes, her heart beating more quickly than a moment ago, and smiled.

"What are you doing here, Zach?" she asked as she raised her face for a kiss. "How's everything at home? How are you?"

"One at a time, please," he replied, giving her a bone-crushing hug. "I'm a lot better now that I've found you. Late on a Thursday afternoon, I expected you to be working hard in your office, but now I see all you do is party!"

"Exactly right!" She laughed. She'd never tell him about the long hours, working weekends and utter weariness she sometimes felt. He'd just tell her to quit. He didn't understand. No one in the family really understood her need for independence. For security. "So why are you in the city the week after Christmas when Diamond Ridge needs you more than ever to keep things going?"

A shadow crossed his face, and Amanda braced herself.

"I'm here to take you home. Now. Tonight—"

"Tonight? But why? What's wrong? I told Mom I'd be home in a few days to see Pops. I can't leave yet!"

"But Ben wants to see you now," Zach replied.

"He *asked* to see you. Your mother's been sleeping at the hospital ever since he had the stroke. And Molly...the poor kid's a mess. They need you now."

Amanda needed a minute to think. It didn't compute...Ben, her hale and hearty stepfather...reduced to needing her. Ben, the man she considered her *real* father. Her stomach churned and she pressed her hand over it to control the rising nausea.

"Come on, Amanda. I'll tell you more on the way." Zach took her arm and started to lead her from the room.

"Wait a moment. Do you think I can just leave?" Amanda pulled back and spoke in a horrified whisper. "First, tell me what's going on now."

Zach stopped in his tracks, puzzlement on his face. "What do you mean, you can't leave?" His voice was low and controlled, but Amanda saw the effort he exerted to remain patient.

"Zach, I can't discuss it. It's confidential. Something great is happening to me. Something big. And they're announcing it tonight at this party."

"Congratulations," he said without missing a beat. "With all that clout, you can take some time off. Now, let's go."

She always forgot about his sharp mind and quick responses. Her own mind needed a jump start to function again.

"Just a minute. I have to think!"

He took her arm in a firm grip. "There's nothing to think about. Let's go tell your boss."

"Wait, Zach. I can take the bus tomorrow or rent a car..."

His lips tightened, lines bracketed his mouth. "But what if there is no tomorrow, Amanda?" he asked slowly, distinctly. "Now, once again, let's find your boss so we can leave."

Her nausea intensified and she felt like throwing up. What kind of a person was she? How could she think about her job when the best man in the world lay in a hospital in danger of losing his life? But without her job, she had nothing. No safety, no secure future. She couldn't jeopardize her promotion. What if they changed their minds? What if they gave the responsibilities to someone else? Sarah Wilcox would grab the opportunity if she had the chance. And Ben did have her mother and Zach for comfort.

Her thoughts came to an abrupt halt. Pitiful. She was pitiful and selfish. Full of rationalizations. Ben needed her. She had to go. She turned to Zach.

"I'll tell Mr. Garroway now."

"Good. I'll be right behind you."

She glared at him, but he didn't budge.

Pasting a smile on her face, she found her boss, introduced Zach and explained the situation.

"I'm sorry for your troubles, Amanda. We'll just postpone the announcement, shall we, until you're back with us in a few days."

"At this point," Zach interjected, "we're not sure how long Amanda will be needed at home."

His benign smile would have fooled anyone—anyone except Amanda. "I'll call you, Mr. Garroway," she said quickly, "as soon as I have a better grasp of my dad's condition. Thank you for your understanding."

"Not at all," her boss replied. "I'll be out of town for a few days myself, but please keep in touch with me through my voice mail. I check my messages several times a day."

"Will do," she replied quickly. "And, of course, I have my cell phone. I can be reached at any time."

"Good. I'll personally review your cases before I leave. And if you're not back by Monday, I might ask Sarah Wilcox to take them." He paused significantly, before adding, "She's quite a talented attorney, also, so your clients will be in good hands."

Amanda understood his meaning and forced a smile. "I'm sure they will," she murmured in agreement, while a big knot congealed in her belly.

"Time to go, Mandy." Zach grabbed her hand again and started to lead her to the door. She rushed to keep up with him, missed stepping on people's feet purely by luck. Once they reached the hall, she didn't have a chance.

"Slow down, Zach. Your legs are too long for me."

"You're lucky I'm moving too fast to do any damage. I was debating whether to give Garroway a black eye or shake some sense into you." He looked over his shoulder at her. "I hope you realize he was just rattling your chain back there. You're the one they want, Mandy. Your boss is smart enough to pick the best, and he's not going to settle for a runner-up."

Zach thought she was the best? His unexpected praise warmed her.

"But you had a hard time choosing between your job and Uncle Ben's needs in there."

Scratch the praise.

"You're still running scared, aren't you? Don't you know how to set priorities? Or," he continued thoughtfully, "is it that you just don't care? You're really something, you know that?"

Yes, she knew. She had just admitted the same thing to herself, but she didn't welcome his condemnation. She clenched her hands in frustration. Same old story, nothing new. She could handle any crisis at work without flinching, yet couldn't begin to handle personal ones. They required too much emotion, too much commitment.

"Damn!" Zach continued as he punched the button for the elevator. "You're twenty-eight years old and nothing's changed since you started college. What happened to the sweet kid Lily brought with her when she nursed my uncle and his broken leg way back when? Where did that warm heart go?"

She'd disappointed him. She heard it in his voice, saw it in his eyes. Those wonderful gray, glinting eyes, usually alight with humor, were now creased with pain. The pain she caused.

She winced with the knowledge, but pushed it aside. Zach knew almost nothing about the real Amanda. The warm heart that he remembered from years ago, had beaten inside the body of a scared young teen whose innocence had been destroyed long before he met her. He was ignorant about her early life, and she planned to keep it that way.

Amanda raised herself to her full five and a half feet and again buried the pain of the girl she once was. "Sorry to disappoint you, Zach. I am who I am."

"And that's not good enough for me and the people I love—and the people who love you."

For a moment, she couldn't breathe. Then in crystal clear tones, she said, "Go to hell, Zach."

FIVE MINUTES. In just five minutes with Zach, she had lost her hard-won control—as usual. It hadn't always been like that, just since they'd grown up and become adults. How she hated allowing him to get the better of her! She sighed. For the few days she'd be in Vermont, she'd grow a thicker skin and keep her mouth shut.

She fidgeted with the handles of her purse and stole a glance at him during the taxi ride to her apartment. He scanned the traffic in all directions and looked at his watch for the tenth time since they'd started.

"How do you tolerate traveling at a snail's pace every day?"

She laughed. "I rarely commute during the rush hour. The company's car service takes me home at night."

He turned toward her then. "How many nights, Amanda?"

She met his glance but refused to answer. Arguing with Zach was not her favorite form of recreation.

He must have read the truth in her eyes. "Every

night, Amanda? Are you in that office late enough every night to warrant a private taxi service?''

"I'm doing what I want to do, Zach." That was true enough, but lately, she'd been exhausted.

"That's some life you lead. When do you have fun? When do you have time to enjoy the fruits of your labor?''

The fun would come later, she thought, after she crashed through some glass ceilings. She knew what she wanted. Her goal had been clear since she was old enough to figure out what life was all about. Her path was clear, too. If she worked hard, she'd get everything she planned.

"Just let it go, Zach," she said. "Look, we're at my new place. Come on.''

"Just a minute." Zach turned to the driver, passed him a bill and said, "We'll be down in ten minutes. Get us to Newark in time for the evening flight to Rutland, Vermont, and you'll be having another Christmas.''

"Okay, pal. But ya only got the ten minutes or I'm goin'.''

"Step on it, Mandy. You heard the man.''

She opened the cab door, rushed ahead of Zach, said "Hi" to the doorman, rang for the elevator and got her mail. Ten minutes! No problem, she realized. Packing for two days didn't take that long. She'd cram her overnight bag with a couple of sweaters, wool slacks, lots of socks and a sweatsuit to sleep in.

But damn! Her laptop was still in the office. They'd have to go back and get it.

She ushered Zach into her apartment and spared a moment to see his reaction to her chosen decor. White carpeting lay throughout the foyer and living room. A white leather couch with strategically placed throw pillows, a glass coffee table sporting a book of modern art, and a white-lacquered entertainment center completed the furnishings. Tied-back floor-length drapes framed French doors that opened onto a terrace.

"It's very, hmm…impressive, Amanda, professional-looking. Very upscale." The polite words were just what she'd expected and what she wanted to hear. The front of the suite was for entertaining—high-style functional and very modern. An extension of her professional self. The bedroom and den were different, and for her eyes only. Her retreat. Not even for Zach to see.

"But I guess you miss all the snow at home," he added with a smile, nodding at the white floors.

"Well, it's not quite finished, yet. The decorator's scouting out some accent pieces and wall hangings…"

His face cleared. "Ah, the decorator… I was wondering where the family pictures were and the crocheted afghans that you always cuddled under—not decorator material, no doubt."

She shrugged. "Doesn't matter. There's fresh-squeezed juice in the fridge, the kind you like. So help yourself while I pack my bag. I won't take long."

She crossed in front of him and headed down the hall, trying to remember where she stored her overnight bag. She closed the bedroom door softly behind her and walked to her closet. As she reached for the carryall, she intuitively glanced back toward the doorway. Zach stood on the threshold, quietly examining this room, so different from the rest of the apartment.

She had searched every antique shop in Manhattan to reproduce the warmth of the home she'd left in Vermont. Not that she ever wanted to go back, but rather to remember that time as a special page in the scrapbook of her life. She'd planned the bedroom as her personal space, a safe haven that no one in the city would ever see unless invited. So far, no one had. Until now.

She watched him visually absorb the cherry four-poster rope bed covered by a wedding-ring-pattern quilt. The bed rested on a large pastel rag rug framed on three sides by the white-painted wood floor. On the wall above the headboard hung pictures of the family—her mother and Ben, Molly, Zach and herself. A crocheted blanket lay across the arm of her maple rocking chair, while a nineteenth-century oak mirrored dresser graced the far wall.

"Yes." Zach nodded. "Much better." His smile said it all, and despite herself, she was warmed by his approval. For about thirty seconds. That was when he took note of her packing efforts.

"Where are you going to put your boots?" he asked when he saw the small leather case she had chosen. "There's a forty-inch base at Diamond Ridge. The roads have been plowed, but snow's everywhere. Where's your ski jacket? Gloves? Hat? Sunglasses?"

He walked to her closet, looked up and yanked her large valise from the high shelf.

She should have known he'd try to take over. With supreme confidence, he ran Diamond Ridge Resort with Ben. He was used to giving orders, but she wasn't used to taking them. This was just the kind of male dominance she had guarded herself against since graduate school.

"I don't need much for just a few days. And I have some stuff at the house."

Her protest fell on deaf ears. Zach calmly began to empty her drawers and fill her suitcase. "Don't put a time limit on this visit. I haven't gotten any answers yet, and I don't know if the doctors have any, either." His voice trailed away on a whisper.

But then he turned to her suddenly, his voice now hard, his face stern. "Amanda, if you cause problems after we get home…if Lily thinks you resent coming home early, then you might as well not go. I'll think of some story she'll believe. So make up your mind. Will you come home willingly, or not come at all?" He paused and checked his watch. "The ball, Counselor, is in your court. You have five seconds."

The familiar sense of inadequacy swept through her. Her life in New York was safe, under control in a well-ordered universe. Her life in Vermont was fraught with emotions and turmoil, and she had never handled emotions well. She almost moaned aloud. Oh, God, she didn't really want to go back.

But suddenly Ben's image flashed through her mind. Ben, the man who had sheltered her and nur-

tured her. At the ripe old age of fourteen, she had
started to learn what a father's love was really about.
There could only be one answer.

"The taxi's waiting, Zach. Let's go. First to the
office to get my laptop and then to the airport."

"Forget the office. Diamond Ridge has all the con-
veniences, including computers. You'll use mine."

AMANDA COLLAPSED into her seat on the plane, relieved but not amazed that they were on time for their
flight. Surely the plane could not fly faster than their
cab had been driven! Darting in and out of traffic, their
eager driver got them to the airport with enough time
to check her bag and get a seat assignment. She hoped
the plane ride would be smoother.

She turned to make such a comment to Zach, but
he had already closed his eyes and tipped his seat
back. She started to do the same, then noticed the
pallor under his heavy five-o'clock shadow. For the
first time since he'd appeared at the party, she took
the opportunity to study him. His brow was furrowed
even in repose, and his pale complexion emphasized
the dark circles under his eyes. He shifted his position
again and again, his legs restless, despite his obvious
desire to nap. She began to appreciate the strain he'd
been under.

He'd told her Ben hadn't been feeling well for several days before the stroke. And obviously Zach had
been going nonstop ever since. Why had he taken the
time to fetch her? Zach hadn't known about the pro-

motion, but Zach knew her. Seemed he knew her well enough not to trust her.

She thought for a moment and faced the truth. She might have put the trip off if Ben was doing okay. What with her promotion and her new responsibilities, she really might have postponed going home. But then, if Ben had taken a turn for the worse, she never would have forgiven herself.

She sighed. Life offered hard choices sometimes. Her brain said one thing; her heart said another. And her actions reflected only her fears. Fears that were fostered in her earliest years.

She tried never to think about the old days—her father's drunken rages, his constant belittling, her mother's placating tones—or at least never to talk about them. Her mom never spoke about them, either. It was the time before Ben and Zach and the Vermont mountains. Days that for Amanda stretched into fourteen years, half her current age. She was truly grateful that her little sister had never known that life.

Her hands hurt. Amanda looked down and saw her fingers tightly interlocked. The pressure she exerted had turned her knuckles white. One by one, she deliberately loosened the digits and stretched them out. Disappointed at how powerful her unwanted memories still were, she resolved once again to strive for total independence. She would not count on anyone— man or woman, father or mother or husband—for the quality or the happiness in her life. Her education and ambition would secure those for her.

With her philosophy reaffirmed, she settled back and allowed herself to doze.

"Wake up, Mandy. We're getting ready to land."

"Mmm…"

"Tighten your seat belt."

"Always wear it," she mumbled as she twisted to find a more comfortable position. Her head dropped until it rested on Zach's shoulder, her arm curled on his chest. "Better," she continued.

As though from a distance, she heard his deep chuckle blend with the changing vibrations of the plane as it started to descend. Then she felt a butterfly kiss on her brow.

"Come on, sweetheart. Time to get up."

She opened her eyes slowly and saw a broad expanse of dark blue sweater. Zach's sweater. She felt her cheeks burn as she sat upright in one swift motion. "I'm sorry. Why'd you let me sleep on you like that?"

His eyes twinkled. "You can sleep on me anytime, Amanda, if you continue to blush so adorably—"

"Adorably!" she interrupted. "Babies are adorable, Zachary. Lawyers are not."

He laughed. "Whatever you say, Counselor. Look, we're almost at the gate. Get ready to go. We've got thirty-odd miles ahead of us to Diamond Ridge. It'll be midnight before we get home."

Amanda bit her lip. Home. What would await them there?

They retrieved her luggage and walked to the door of the small terminal. Snow fell gently outside. The airport lights illuminated a fresh accumulation on the few cars, the pavement and on the mounds of old snow that had been plowed to the sides of the road. The familiarity of the scene telescoped in Amanda's mind to her teenage years with Ben, Zach and her mom. The second part of her childhood had been good. But the world she had chosen to live in now was very different.

"Maybe I should have worn my boots, instead of packing them in the big valise." Amanda looked in dismay at the high-heeled pumps she still wore.

Zach grunted. "Wait here. I'll bring the pickup around." He walked swiftly into the cold night air before she could respond.

What happened to the fatigue that had worn him down earlier? Admiring his powers of recovery, Amanda stared at the tall, surefooted figure as he disappeared into the night. A complex man—familiar and yet intriguing. Tough but gentle, confident but caring…and with a body to entice the imagination. She let herself relax and instantly her imagination took over. Broad shoulders, flat stomach and strong, well-defined hands tenderly caressing her cheek, her neck… She shivered deep inside; her breath caught in her throat. Finally, finally, she remembered to exhale.

She struggled for control, for rationality. She was tired. Too much had happened that day, first at work, and then with Zach. He had dominated the past several hours. No wonder he dominated her thoughts. Just like he had when they were younger. Damn! She should have outgrown those fantasies.

"No big deal," she muttered to herself as she forced her mind to leapfrog ahead to Diamond Ridge. The resort comprised a hotel, a base lodge, chalet, ski school, cottages and condos, lifts, day care and ski patrol. The business catered to thousands of skiers during the season, and with Ben so ill, all the responsibilities would now be shouldered by Zach.

She knew what he faced. She knew the business well because she had worked it every day during her high-school years. Ben had taught Lily and Amanda everything about it. Of course, the business had been much smaller then, with guest accommodations in the small hotel only.

Expansion started five years ago when Zach returned to Vermont from Chicago to work with his uncle. They'd expanded the ground floor and added a second floor to the hotel, more than doubling guest capacity. They'd also erected a dozen individual cottages at the base of the mountain. New trails were constructed to accommodate more guests. And the guests had come! City dwellers from New York, eager for a piece of country, came back year after year. Southern New Englanders from Massachusetts and Connecticut chose Diamond Ridge, as well.

There was a lot at stake, Amanda thought as she spotted Zach's truck. A lot of money. She opened the door and stepped outside. The sharp, cold air stole her breath for a moment and she stood still.

"Wait there, Amanda," Zach called as he slammed the door. "I'll get you."

She nodded, thinking it would be safer to hold on

to his arm as she made her precarious journey over the snow-covered pavement.

She smiled as he approached and extended her hand.

"Thanks, Zach. I'll be fine…" Her words ended with a squeal as he scooped her up into his arms and carried her to the truck. He opened the passenger door and lifted her onto the seat.

"There. All safe and sound. We sure can't afford you to break your leg now."

"Both of us could have fallen and broken all our legs," she grumbled.

"Mandy, honey, you couldn't be in a safer place. I would never drop you, no matter what."

She glanced at him swiftly. His words might have been playful, but his tone of voice was deadly serious.

Zach walked to the driver's side and got into the truck. Amanda looked straight ahead as he shifted gears. The miles passed and she relaxed again. No hidden meanings here. Zach had automatically reverted to his protective-big-brother role, that was all. It made sense. Her unencumbered mind now drifted from Zach to the rest of the family.

"I wonder how Pops is doing," she said. "And Mom? Where's Molly now?"

"When I left this morning, Uncle Ben was responsive but still in the intensive-care unit being monitored by every machine known to man. Lily slept at the hospital last night, and Molly stayed home with me. I sent her off to school this morning and arranged for Mrs. O'Keefe to be in the family quarters at three o'clock. Twelve-year-olds seem to need more supervision than little kids. Or maybe it's just Molly.''

''Where's Mom tonight?''

''Probably at the house. Waiting for her daughter. She'll be very happy to see you.''

In the quiet of the car, in the quiet of a nocturnal snow on a beautiful alpine road, Stanhope Jones and MacGregor and New York City seemed very far away, like a half-remembered dream. Ahead lay the mountain and Amanda's other life. She felt the shift, felt it keenly, but for the moment, didn't resent the change.

This visit would be just that—a visit, a short interlude from reality. Soon she'd be back in the city where she belonged. She'd focus on her goals, increase her net worth and move ahead.

She would survive.

CHAPTER TWO

SNOW CONTINUED to fall as Zach drove to the back of the hotel. He looked at the building with satisfaction. They called it a hotel, but to him it was still a guest lodge. Despite its expanded size, it retained almost the same character and chalet flavor as in the old days. He parked as close to the private family entrance as possible. A light shone through the kitchen window and he nodded. Just as he'd expected, Lily was waiting up for them.

He glanced at Amanda, reclining in the seat next to him, sound asleep almost from the moment they'd left the airport thirty miles ago. Her features were more delicate in repose, her mouth softer, her expression unguarded, relaxed. Had he been wrong to bring her back? Maybe she didn't belong in the Green Mountains, despite her successful "transplant" as a teenager. City-bred girls never seemed to adapt to country living. Lisa never had.

He cut the engine and rubbed the back of his neck. Lisa. He hardly thought about her anymore. He'd met her in Chicago, a few years out of college when he worked for the Paradise Hotel chain. How young he had been. How in love. How arrogant!

That was her word. With Chicago at her feet, why would she up and move to the wilds of Vermont and a family business? He'd been stunned. After being with Lisa for more than a year, he realized he hadn't really known her at all. Maybe she was right about the arrogance. He didn't understand women then and he probably didn't understand them now. Hell, did any man understand women?

He looked at Amanda again. It should be so simple. He'd known her for years, but…nothing about her was simple. Who would have thought that timid young Amanda Shaw would have the gumption to do all that modeling in New York while she attended college? Amanda, earning A's at NYU and dollars in front of the camera, first appearing in that teen magazine and then in others. Unbelievable, even in retrospect. He shook his head at the memories.

Her gumption surprised him, but not her desire to amass significant earnings. Her investments had become her mantra, and that was when he knew that her dedication to modeling was not for the fame, not for the admiration and not for the lifestyle.

She'd done it for the money.

And then she'd surprised him again. Just when she was on the verge of becoming a superstar, she'd quit the glamour business. Walked away from it and concentrated on law school.

He got out of the cab and crunched through the snow to the back of the truck, blaming fatigue and the family crisis for his introspective mood tonight. Fatigue, crisis and Amanda. She was the source of discord in the household. A brief visit each summer was the most she'd bestowed on them in recent years, and last summer not even that. Clearly, her work and her big-city life came first.

He hoisted her large suitcase and grunted with satisfaction. In the pit of his stomach, he knew she'd need all the clothes they'd thrown together. She wasn't leaving anytime soon. Not this visit.

For the first time since the year his uncle had married Lily, they'd all be under one roof again. He shrugged and hoped Amanda survived the experience. He hoped she remembered how to ski! Or he'd have to teach her all over again.

He walked to the kitchen door and carried Amanda's bags inside. Lily's head was pillowed on her arms at the table, but she straightened quickly when she heard him enter the room. Zach immediately saw the question in her sleepy blue eyes.

"She's here, Lily," he replied softly. "Dozing in the truck. I'll bring her right in."

"How much trouble did she give you?"

He pasted a cocky grin on his face and gave her a thumbs-up. "Piece of cake, Lily. This time you worried for nothing. In fact, she packed a big suitcase. Look for yourself."

It was worth the half-truth to see the joy in Lily's face. His uncle was a lucky man. He was lucky, too. Lily had brought a woman's warmth and love to their all-male bastion. Until she came, Zach had believed he didn't need a mother anymore. And he didn't want one. They were too painful to lose. At eight years old, he'd become an expert on the subject. Both his parents—gone in seconds—victims of a drunk driver.

He turned on his heel and headed outside. Despite himself, he'd learned to love the woman who nurtured his young manhood, and he'd do whatever it took to make her happy. Handling Amanda was first on the list.

"I'M SO GLAD you're here." Her mother hugged her in a viselike grip, and instantly Amanda knew she'd been away too long. Much too long. A year and a half to be exact. She should have come up on weekends, but somehow there were always deadlines to meet, one more project to start...and finish...at work. Now she saw more than the normal joy of reunion in Lily's eyes. Now she saw a touch of desperation. Her mother needed her.

Suddenly she started to sweat. Her palms felt clammy, her stomach churned and a slight nausea rose in her throat as she felt the trap closing inch by inch. Her strong mother, who'd survived a rotten marriage and then put herself through nursing school, despite being a single mom, needed her here. But Amanda couldn't be in two places at once!

Her mind raced to find a quick solution. She'd come up every weekend; she'd bring all her work to Vermont, install her own computer and e-mail everything to New York; she'd hire a housekeeper and pay her salary or the salary of another ski instructor—whatever personnel Zach needed.

"You look tired and pale, honey," Lily said. "Sit down. I've got some hot cocoa for all of us."

Amanda smiled at the invitation and took a seat at the wide-planked oak table. Hot cocoa or coffee were always available in Lily's kitchen, the heart of their home. She glanced around the large familiar room, a warm country-style kitchen with nine-foot ceilings, dark wooden beams and a brick fireplace on the far wall. Family pictures were proudly displayed on the mantel. Blue delft tiles covered the countertops and backsplash, and tied-back simple tab curtains dressed the two large windows. Lily liked lots of sunshine in her kitchen.

Nothing had changed since last year, Amanda noted with satisfaction. Nothing, except that her beloved stepfather had had a stroke. Everything had changed.

"The good news is that Ben's doing well. He's actually in his own room," Lily said. "No more monitors, either."

"That's great news," Zach said. "What a difference since the stroke. Very encouraging."

"But," Lily continued, "we can't hide from the fact that *he's had a stroke*. His whole right side is affected. He's got a droopy eyelid, a droopy mouth, a weak arm and leg. And his speech…just barely understandable. Not very crisp. Not like his strong self."

Her mother's face crumbled, and Amanda felt Zach's intense scrutiny on her. What did he want? What was she supposed to do now? She wasn't good at this stuff. Not even with her own mother.

"But what about physical therapy, Mom?" A logical question.

Lily's expression brightened. "Yes. They'll be working out a schedule almost immediately, because the philosophy is the sooner, the better."

"See," Amanda said, as she turned toward Zach, "you were too anxious. Pops gave us a scare, but he's going to be fine." Her relief was almost palpable; all her inner tension oozed away and her body relaxed. Ben and her mom would be okay. She'd done her duty by making the trip. She'd help out for a few days. And then she could return to her own world knowing she had done the right thing.

She glanced at Zach again. A wry smile played on his lips and she knew he'd read her mind.

"Let's hear what the doctors have to say tomorrow," he said.

"Zach's right, dear. No one has made me any promises yet," Lily said.

"But it sounds very hopeful, Mom."

"I'm a nurse, sweetheart, remember? I've seen lots of stroke victims. It takes time, and then most people don't recover entirely and some get worse." Lily shook her arms in frustration. "If he weren't so sick already, I'd kill him myself!"

Zach explained quickly. "His blood-pressure medication. He rarely took it."

"And look what happened to him." Lily's voice trembled with emotion. "I'd nag and nag at him, and it worked for a while, but if I forgot to nag—"

"Lily, it's not your fault."

"I know, I know. But if only—"

"Forget the *if only's,*" Zach said sharply. "They're a waste of energy. Tell me about Molly, instead. Did she behave herself today?"

Lily rolled her eyes, but tension laced her voice. "She went to school, but the minute she came home, she disappeared. Mrs. O'Keefe said she didn't show up until after dark. She's worse than Amanda was. She skis off the marked trails and blazes her own. Then she winds up on real roads. Half the time, she walks home carrying her skis on her shoulders. You've seen her yourself.

"Poor Mrs. O'Keefe was worried sick today, knowing that we'd left her in charge. We can't give her that much responsibility anymore, Zach. She's elderly now. It's not fair to her."

"It certainly isn't, but today was an emergency." He looked at Amanda. "Tomorrow is the start of a new regime here. Molly needs some attention, Amanda. That'll be your job. But first I'll make sure that she won't disappear again. By the time we finish talking, she won't dare."

"She may need to, Zach," replied Amanda quickly. "I remember..." She remembered all too well needing her own space to figure things out. Like why her mother got married again after her father died. Why she was afraid of Ben and Zach—and when she wasn't afraid anymore, how that happened.

Girls needed spaces and places to think, and the long, gentle trails through sun-dappled woods were perfect for that. "Please, Zach, leave her alone."

Zach looked at her, and for the first time, she saw understanding in his eyes.

"She's only twelve years old, Mandy. I can't leave her alone," he replied softly. "It's too dangerous for her to be out until all hours, just like it was for you."

"But she was born on skis," Amanda protested. "Nothing will happen to her, and besides, you're not her parent, Zach—"

"Amanda!" Lily interrupted. "Don't be foolish. How will I be able to concentrate on Ben if I'm worrying about Molly?"

They were both right, of course, and Amanda could feel the heat of embarrassment creep up her neck to her cheeks. But she also knew that Molly needed her special times away from everybody.

"After we get back from the hospital tomorrow, I'll ski with her until there's no daylight left. Will that do, boss?" A mock salute accompanied the touch of sarcasm in her voice.

A grin slowly spread across Zach's face, humor lurked in his eyes, and Amanda's heart lurched into an aerobic beat. If he was flirting with her, he was doing a good job. But she immediately discarded that possibility just as she ignored her rapid heartbeat. "If you still remember how to ski, the answer is yes," Zach replied.

Amanda had already forgotten the question.

THE HOSPITAL was twenty miles from Diamond Ridge. At ten the next morning, Amanda sat behind the wheel of the family's Jeep Cherokee with Zach beside her, and Lily and Molly in the back.

She wished she were in the passenger seat. She hadn't owned a car in six years, and her experience driving in snow was almost nonexistent. Her mom, however, insisted that she take the wheel, "just to get used to country roads again." Lily seemed to forget that to do something again, meant that it had been done before. Amanda glanced sideways at Zach and caught him rechecking his seat-belt clasp.

"This wasn't my idea," she mumbled.

He turned toward her and winked. "But it's a good idea. You'll need to get around on your own while you're here."

How long did he think she was staying? All winter? She turned the key in the ignition and let the Jeep idle as she took a moment to assess the roads. The snow had stopped and the roads had been plowed before dawn. Excellent. The situation could have been worse.

"C'mon, Amanda," Zach said. "We'll get you through this. You're going to shift into first and slowly let out the clutch while you press the gas."

The situation had just gotten worse. No way was she sitting through a twenty-mile driving lesson with Zach. And no way was she going to argue about it in her usual forceful style. Not with her mother and Molly right there. Her brain cells went into overdrive as she searched for a way out. Suddenly an image of her law-school roommate—a very clever Georgia peach of a roommate—flashed through her mind, and she knew just what approach to use. If Ashley could melt men with her charming ways, so could she.

She peeked at Zach from under her lashes and flashed him the smile that had lit up photo shoots in her New York modeling days, a smile that made every man in her vicinity wish she was on his arm.

"Zachary, honey," she drawled, in a warm, golden voice reminiscent of sweet-smelling jasmine on a hot Southern night, "why don't you and I just change seats for a while right now?" She unbuckled her belt. "It'll take hardly any time at all, and before you know it, we'll be at the hospital."

She opened her door and twisted to the side, ready to exit the car, but instantly a strong arm held her as tightly as any seat belt ever had. She raised her eyes and blinked slowly once, twice, in innocent confusion, as she continued in her borrowed character.

"Oh, my goodness, Zachary. Whatever is the matter? I hope I haven't upset you. I'm sure I just don't understand."

"Now, you know better than that, sugar," Zach replied in a matching Southern drawl. His eyes twinkled and his lips twitched. "A gentleman always keeps his promises, and I promised you'd get a chance to drive today. Don't worry your pretty little head about it, sweet girl. I'll take good care of you." He chuckled.

It was the "I'll take good care of you," that blew her cover. She fastened her seat belt, placed her hands on the wheel and killed the accent.

"The day I need anyone to take care of me will be

the day I kiss the world goodbye. So you can stop laughing!''

But Zach shook his head and laughed harder. Soon Lily's gentle tones and Molly's light giggles formed a chorus for Zach's baritone. And Amanda knew she'd met her match. She looked at all their faces and started to laugh, too, until tears ran down her cheeks.

''Anyone have a tissue?'' She hiccupped.

Zach leaned over and pulled her toward him. ''You're full of surprises, Amanda. Great medicine to have around. We all needed a good laugh today.'' He gently wiped her face and looked into her eyes. ''I'm glad you're here, Mandy. Now start driving.''

FINALLY RELAXED behind the wheel, Amanda was able to admire the familiar scenery in the light of day. New England offered truly beautiful countryside. Every time she visited, she rediscovered nature's gifts. The Green Mountains of Vermont might be covered in white now, but their majesty shone through.

Skiers in their colorful jackets and leggings, dotted the slopes of Diamond Ridge. The snow gods had co-operated this year and business looked good.

''We've got seven lifts operating now,'' Lily said proudly, as though reading Amanda's mind. ''Ben and Zach decided to expand again this year. They put in another tough trail on the north face that meets up with Steeplechase run in the west. It's a two-mile chal-lenge for the expert skier, and so far, the guests are raving about it.''

Amanda turned her head to Zach and smiled. "You both must feel great about that."

"They do," Lily answered. "As well as the lifts, they upgraded the snowmaking system. So as long as we have cold weather, we'll have enough snow to cover every trail no matter how little natural stuff falls. And last year, for the summer guests, we put in two new tennis courts and a manmade lake for boating and swimming."

"Business must be terrific to invest so much," Amanda said, raising an inquiring brow in Zach's direction. Her mother's list translated into megabucks and for a moment, Amanda felt a chill run through her body.

Zach returned her inquiry with a bland look.

"We're doing a lot of new things, dear," Lily continued, "and doing them right. 'Diamond Ridge Resort,'" she quoted, "'where guests are family.' Many of our guests have truly become friends. People keep coming back." Then her voice broke as she whispered, "Ben had...has such plans." The rest of her thoughts were left unspoken.

"And we'll carry them out, Lily. You'll see." Zach's gentle reassurance caught Amanda's attention, and she prayed that his words proved true. For all their sakes, everything had to return to normal soon.

She glanced in the rearview mirror at her younger sister and frowned into the glass. Attitude was written all over her. Molly's world had turned upside down, too, but she'd made it clear she didn't want anyone's help to fix it. Especially not Amanda's. Their early-morning reunion had set the tone for the next few hours. Molly had seemed almost hostile as she stood in Amanda's doorway watching her get dressed.

"So how long are you staying this time?" she asked as she looked pointedly at her watch. "Should I set the alarm for your flight out? Oh, not today, I almost forgot. Zach said I should take you skiing this afternoon, so I guess you'll be staying until tomorrow."

"Zach said what?" Amanda asked in disbelief before she remembered her promise to stick with Molly on the slopes. "Oh, never mind, Molly. Just give me a little break here, will you? I got in late last night."

"Doesn't matter," Molly said matter-of-factly. "You'll be gone in a day. Just like always. We don't need you here, anyway. Zach and I can handle everything."

Sucker-punched, Amanda could hardly catch her breath as she heard her sister's words. Cold and to the point. Molly called things as she saw them.

What a twist! Finally, a person who was willing to allow Amanda the freedom to leave, who expected nothing from her, but whose directness bound her more tightly to the family than anyone else's appeals or threats.

She'd find time to speak with Molly later when they were skiing together. It shouldn't be too hard to reach her. After all, Molly had been partly her baby, too. Amanda, at sixteen, had taken over Molly's care after school so that Lily could concentrate on the business with Ben. Zach had been away at college during those years, so Amanda and Molly had been a pair. Ben's girls.

Amanda looked in the mirror again. Molly had been a beautiful baby, with Lily's blue eyes, just like Amanda's, and Ben's chestnut-brown hair. She had smiled with trusting delight every time Amanda came near her.

Now, at age twelve, she had the potential to become a knockout. Amanda's trained eye noted the high cheekbones, the defined mouth. Molly had the grace; maybe she'd get the height, as well. The missing ingredient, however, which nullified everything else, was her expression. No smile, no sparkle, no joy. Anger and sullenness did not sell.

Maybe that wasn't a fair assessment. None of them had anything to smile about yet. They were all under great stress, and until they spoke with the doctors, that stress level would remain constant.

Minutes later, Amanda amended that thought. As the miles passed and they approached the hospital, the tension in the car did not remain constant. It increased.

"I'm scared, Mommy."

Amanda heard the whispered confession as she and Zach followed Molly and Lily down the hospital corridor to Ben's room. Molly wasn't the only one scared. Amanda's jumpy stomach made her wish she had forfeited breakfast that morning. The antiseptic aromas, the uniformed nurses, the equipment that lined the walls, screamed their reality at her. The safety of her mother's kitchen could not cocoon her from the truth. Her big, strapping, gregarious step-father was in this place because he was sick.

She felt Zach's arm come around her and squeeze gently. "Hang tough, Mandy. Put a smile on that beautiful face even if it's hard. He loves that smile."

Smile? When she saw Ben for the first time as she stood in the doorway, she wanted to cry. He lay on the bed looking…fragile, small. When did he get so gray? Then he turned to face them, and suddenly Amanda caught a glimpse of the man she knew. He grinned a lopsided grin, waved one hand and tried to sit up. Action. Pops always wanted action.

Lily ran to him and covered his face with kisses.

"Get the…damn…chair…over…here, Lil. I want… to sit up and…see…my…girls." The fighting words were slurred and slow. Despite her best efforts, Amanda felt tears well up. She could see how hard he tried to enunciate. Sadly, she had to admit that his recovery would take a while.

"You're hooked up to an IV, Benjamin, so let's just take our time and move you the right way," Lily said. "Zach, you bring the wheelchair and hold it steady. Amanda, you get on his good side, so he can use you for balance as he gets into the chair."

"She's…already…on…my…good…side," Ben joked.

Amanda hugged him and blinked back the tears. "Hi, Pops." He patted her arm before she and Lily helped him into the wheelchair.

"Glad…you…came, Mandy. We…need…you on the…mountain now," Ben said slowly.

Amanda nodded. "No problem," she lied.

"Yeah, yeah, yeah." Molly's voice taunted behind her, and Amanda felt her blood heat at the sarcasm. Coping with Ben's condition presented enough challenge without Molly adding more.

"Where's...my...popcorn...girl?" Ben asked.

Molly ran forward and hugged her father. "I want you to come home, Daddy. I'll help you do everything until you get better."

Amanda heard the thickness in Molly's voice. And the hope. The girl was having a harder time than she'd let her sister see.

"I know, I know." Ben patted Molly's back with his good hand. "Doc's...coming...soon. We'll... discuss...things...today."

"That's enough talking, Ben. Save your energy for therapy later." Nurse Lily seemed to have found her strength.

A knock on the door preceded the entrance of a smiling young man dressed in green scrubs.

"Doc's...here," Ben announced. "You...know Zach...but...meet...my...girls, Tom."

Amanda looked at the physician, noticing his blond hair, brown eyes and amused smile. He looked familiar; she just couldn't place him.

"Hello, Amanda."

Her forehead crinkled in thought as she continued to stare at the handsome doctor. "Tom...Tom Hunter? The second-best ski racer on the boy's team? And you're Ben's doctor?"

"Yup. Downstate Medical School in New York.

And what do you mean 'second-best'? I beat Zach once!''

''I must have missed that race.'' Amanda laughed.

''Tom decided to set up his practice right here,'' Zach said, as he shook hands with the physician. ''And we're happy he did.''

''Some people don't move away forever,'' Molly added with a glance at Amanda.

''Hey, Miss Molly,'' Tom said, ''cheer up. Your beautiful sister might be hanging around for a while now.''

Amanda turned to him questioningly, but Tom walked toward the bed.

''I'm going to spend a few minutes with Ben, folks, so you can either wait outside in the hall or go get coffee.''

Amanda bit her lip and ushered Molly out the door. Zach followed on her heels, but Lily stayed inside.

''Want some coffee, Amanda? How about some hot chocolate, Molly?'' Zach asked as he started walking down the corridor.

''I'm staying right here.''

Amanda turned around to see Molly plant herself directly outside the door to Ben's room. The girl looked so determined that Amanda didn't try to argue with her. She waved Zach on with his errand and retraced her steps toward the youngster.

''Afraid you'll miss something?''

''Daddy might need me.''

''The doctor's with him.''

''So what? He might need me!''

"He'll be needing help from lots of people for a time—"

"But not from you!"

Slammed by her sister again, Amanda reeled back. How incredible that a twelve-year-old had the power to hurt her. She wouldn't have thought it possible. She placed a hand on Molly's shoulder.

"This isn't the time or the place to unload on me, Mol. But I promise when we go skiing this afternoon, we *will* talk. You can tell me anything you want."

Molly glared at her. "Anything?"

"Sure." She'd be able to handle her own little sister, wouldn't she?

Zach returned just as Lily opened Ben's door and motioned them all inside. Hope shone in her eyes.

"We've worked out a great plan," she said. "It's practical and will suit everyone." She glanced apologetically at Amanda. "Well, almost everyone."

Amanda groaned silently. Bad news was coming.

"Ben needs extensive rehabilitation, far more therapy than we can offer in this community hospital," said Dr. Hunter.

Amanda nodded. She figured there was a special rehab center nearby.

The doctor continued. "The two rehab facilities for stroke victims that have given us the best outcomes are located in Boston and New York City. Unfortunately, we have nothing in the area to match them." He paused for a moment. "I know you all want Ben to make the fullest recovery he can."

Everyone nodded. Amanda didn't miss the way he

made eye contact with each person as they responded to his statement. Including her.

"Then I need to make admission arrangements at one of the centers as soon as possible so Ben can start intensive therapy immediately."

Amanda turned to her mother quickly. "New York makes the most sense, Mom. You can stay with me and see Pops every day. It's almost the same distance to New York as it is to Boston."

"That's what I thought," Lily concurred. "I'm so glad you don't mind me using the apartment."

"Why should I mind? I'll even let you have my bed. I'll sleep on the couch."

"What about me?" demanded Molly. "Can I stay in New York, too?"

Amanda looked at Molly, then her mother. Lily's lips were pressed together, her brow furrowed.

Her eyes sought Zach and she found him leaning against the wall, sipping his coffee, observing them as though watching a one-act play. A raised eyebrow was his only comment.

Ben's slow but determined voice was the next one heard. "I want…to speak to…Mandy…alone. But Zach…you stay…by the…door."

Amanda sat beside Ben when the room cleared. He lay in bed again, now propped with pillows, and reached for her hand. He struggled to speak, and Amanda had to lean closer and concentrate to understand him.

"Molly…stays…here. You…stay here…too. Zach…

needs you...for...Molly...and for...the business. You...know...the business.''

She had negotiated dozens of contracts for her clients—union and employment contracts, real-estate leases and everything in between. She was focused and tough. But she felt like pudding with Ben.

"You do remember that I have a job, a big job, in the city, Pops," she said gently. "I can't be away for long." Despite her best efforts, her voice was tinged with anxiety.

Ben shook his head. "I...know...I...know, but the...business...is more...important. Zach...Zach... can't do it...alone. He...can't...do...everything."

"We can hire people. I'll pay for them."

"Hires...don't care...like family. Molly...needs you. Zach...needs you."

"Zach? Zach's the most self-reliant person I know. He doesn't need me. He doesn't need anybody. He can run that resort single-handedly and never miss a beat." She paused for breath. "Pops, he can also run Molly." If Ben had known Molly's opinion of her, he wouldn't be so anxious to have his girls stay together.

Ben waved his good left hand back and forth. "No," he said. "You're...too...independent. Too much...alone. You need...Zach. He needs...you."

What was he talking about? She didn't need anyone. She'd planned it that way. On purpose. And she hadn't changed her mind. She was happy the way she was.

"There's a big change waiting for me at the firm,"

Amanda went on. "More money, more responsibility…"

But Ben was shaking his head again. He looked frustrated. "Mandy, listen! I built…the…big… Diamond," he said.

"I know, Pops, I know." Why didn't the others return? Ben was getting too excited.

"Then…Zach…joined me…five years ago…as a partner. But before that…even as a…small boy…he helped. Then…you came…with Lily. And…you helped, Mandy. It's…yours, too."

"Pops, I was a fourteen-year-old kid. It's not mine."

Ben nodded. "The Diamond is a family business." He turned toward Zach. "Come…here…son."

Amanda studied Zach as he approached his uncle's bed. He'd been uncharacteristically quiet since they'd arrived at the hospital. When his gaze rested on Ben, she understood why. Pain lurked behind his eyes, pain and sadness, and…a touch of fear. No wonder, she thought. He'd lost parents before.

"Tell…Amanda…about…the business."

Zach took his uncle's hand and patted it. "I'll tell her everything she needs to know on the way home, Uncle Ben."

"Tell…her…about the…loans… About…the… competition. About…Snow Peak…expanding…Tell her…about the…rumors… We have…to…keep…up."

"Shh, Unc. We'll talk. You rest."

"We…had…to…grow, too, Mandy… Grow…or…

die. That's…the…way…it…works. We…owe…the bank…plenty.''

''I knew it, I just knew it. All the expansion.'' The chill she had experienced in the car earlier had a real basis in truth.

Ben yawned and closed his eyes for a fast moment. Then, ''So now…that you…understand…Amanda, will you…stay?''

She'd rather give him her entire bank account. But he didn't want her money. He wanted her. And she wanted her own life. Did that make her a bad person, an unnatural child?

''Pops, please… I don't know…''

''I can handle it without her, Uncle Ben. Don't work yourself up. We run a nice tight ship on the mountain. You know that. It won't be a problem.''

Zach's soft reassurance was for Ben, but the hard warning in his eyes was for Amanda. She complied with silence.

Ben closed his eyes again, this time for a longer period.

''Sleep, Pops,'' Amanda whispered as she stroked his arm.

''No!'' he exploded. ''No…sleeping. Maybe… you'll…understand…now.   Everything's…at…stake. We…have…to…keep going…or Lily…and Molly… and you…will…have…nothing… Is…that…what… you…want? Can…you…walk…away…from us?''

Amanda left the room with tears in her eyes, and quietly closed the door behind her. She needed a mo-

ment to compose herself. She was trying to understand
everyone's needs, but shouldn't they try to understand
hers, as well?

She reached into her purse for her cell phone. Auto-
dialing Mr. Garroway's number in New York, she
hoped her message would be coherent. Potential junior
partners should be able to think logically regardless of
circumstances.

At the tone, she said, "I have some good news. My
stepfather is being transferred to New York for rehab.
My mother will live at my apartment. Still a couple
of issues to put to bed. First, they need me to help run
the business. And second, my twelve-year-old sister
has to be considered. I'll try to find a way to have her
schooled in New York. If you can help me with this
part, I'll work on the business end of it. If all goes
well, I should be back at work in a week."

She flipped her phone off and sighed. The long trip,
the emotional reunions and the thorny issues had taken
their toll. She was exhausted, but needed to get her
life back on track.

CHAPTER THREE

"IT'S EMOTIONAL BLACKMAIL! Pure and simple! And Pops knew exactly what he was doing!"

Zach leaned against the desk in his office, the corners of his mouth twitching, as he watched Amanda pace the floor. It had only taken a few minutes after their return from the hospital for Amanda to let him know her true feelings. In constant motion, her hair swinging and her hands punctuating her speech, she was furious. It was obvious the situation called for discretion. He kept his mouth shut.

"You were there. You heard him. Tugging at my heartstrings and then giving me the old one-two punch. And you, Zach, have a lot to answer for, too." She glared at him, and if looks could truly kill, he would've been six feet under. But he had a momentary reprieve as her thoughts returned to his uncle.

"There is not a single thing wrong with that man's brain," she continued, "stroke or no stroke. Not one IQ cell was damaged."

"For which I'm thankful," Zach said.

"I suppose," she admitted grudgingly, but again she stared at him so intently he felt like a specimen on a petri dish. "When were you going to tell me about those rumors he alluded to? Or was that just a story he made up on the spot? Or did the two of you scheme together? What the hell am I supposed to believe around here?''

Her indignation and righteous anger were misplaced, but Amanda had never looked as alive to him, so vital and so human, as she did at that moment. As though in a trance, his eyes unblinkingly followed her expressive face, and his heart skipped a beat. Here was the real woman who lived underneath that professional, designer exterior. This woman showed feelings! She cared! Deep satisfaction took root in him, and Zach laughed heartily with relief.

He recognized his mistake the moment the first chuckle left his throat, but he couldn't stop.

''Funny? You think it's funny that my mother and sister are at such risk? And what about you? Why are they at risk and you're not?'' She put her hands on her hips and faced him. ''Zach, I promise you I'll examine every record—financial, legal and otherwise—in this business. I'll find whatever is going on. I'll go to court if I have to. If you think I'll do nothing…''

''Calm down, you crazy girl.'' He stood up and pulled her close. He put his arm around her, felt her resist for a moment, then surprisingly, she leaned into him. His blood coursed through his body at the speed of light before she stepped back again.

He took a calming breath. In fact, he breathed deeply three times before trusting himself to speak.

"Your imagination is running wild. There are no hidden schemes here. Get real, will you?"

Her eyes narrowed on him once more. "Are you willing to answer some questions, Zach?"

He heard the professional intonation and knew he was now speaking to Amanda Shaw, the lawyer. But matching wits with Amanda had always presented a challenge, and he grinned with anticipation.

"Fire away."

"Who owns the Diamond?"

He looked at her in surprise. A back-to-basics strategy? "Your stepfather and I are partners. We own the land, buildings and equipment."

"How is the partnership split? Fifty-fifty or something else?"

"I bought twenty-five percent of the business from him and Ben retained seventy-five percent."

"How is the responsibility split?"

"What do you mean?"

"The work, the mortgage. Do you do only a quarter of the work? Do you make only a quarter of the decisions?"

Zach reseated himself on the edge of his desk, the corner of his mouth lifting again. "Yup. That's me. If there's a mile of road to plow, I only do a quarter mile. I get off the tractor and make Ben do the rest."

She darted a piercing glance at him. "No need for sarcasm, Zach."

"No need for beating around the bush, Counselor. What do you really want to know?"

"I want to know how two intelligent men wind up

owing a fortune to the bank! Is that so hard a question?''

''The two intelligent men are investing for the future. We're competing at a high level here. You heard Ben say it—grow or die. That's the way it is. The independent resorts all over the mountains are slowly being approached by large hotel chains with major dollars behind them. We have to be able to hold our own.''

''So you'd go into debt?''

''It's the price of freedom.''

''But you're risking everything—my mom, Molly and yourselves. You could have nothing in the end.''

''We'd have nothing the other way.''

''You'd have jobs. An income. Something!''

''If all I wanted was a job, I'd have stayed in Chicago at Paradise.''

She looked so distressed he felt sorry for her.

''Sweetheart, could you really see Ben, after all these years, taking orders from someone who didn't know beans about a ski resort?'' He walked toward her and placed his hands on her shoulders. ''Ben and I make decisions equally here. The partnership split doesn't matter when it comes to that.''

''But why aren't you equal partners, Zach? If you share all the work, you should reap the benefits, too.''

''It's a family business, and Ben has more family than I do.''

She mulled his response over and he recognized the exact moment when the puzzle pieces fell into place.

"That's right, Mandy. Twenty-five percent for Lily, Molly and you. That's what he reserved."

"Oh, my God! What a mess." She collapsed onto a visitor's chair. "Now I'll have to protect their interests here. I'll never get ahead at my firm, and I'll lose everything I've built in the city. I'll never be able to leave."

Why had he ever thought she'd understand? That she cared? He and Ben were not only fighting for their business, they were fighting for their home, for the family. Which included her! Of course Amanda wished them well, as long as their plans didn't interfere with her life.

When she'd first struck out on her own, Ben was delighted and proud that she'd found her strengths, particularly her inner strength. But in the past year or so, he'd worried often that she'd become too removed from her family.

As he looked at her now, Zach saw only worry and sadness on her face and in her voice.

"Pack your bags, Amanda. You don't have to stay."

"What?" Her head snapped to attention.

"With Ben laid up, I'll make the decisions around here for now. You were right in the hospital. I can run the business single-handedly. And I can take care of Molly. There are people here who will help. So you're free to go. You're under no obligation."

Amanda rose slowly from her chair. He thought she would race away in delight, but all she did was gaze at him questioningly.

"First Ben tells me we could lose everything if I leave, then you tell me to pack my bags and not worry about it. So, Zachary, who's telling the truth?"

Every approach he took with this woman backfired! "You're the smart one here, Amanda, you figure it out."

An electric silence filled the room. Zach saw her expression change half-a-dozen times as she rose to his challenge, examining one idea after another.

"I know two truths," she said quietly. "Truth number one, Zach, is that you need my help. And I don't say that to squash your ego," she rushed on. "It's just that I know this business. It's hard work, and unless you want to kill yourself, you're going to need me."

She looked at him then, a little hesitantly, as if to gauge his reaction.

He nodded. "It's a lot of work, that's true," he replied noncommittally. He could survive the work if he didn't have Molly to contend with. But he'd figure something out, rather than have an unwilling Amanda stay on.

"And truth number two," she continued, "is that love can make people do awful things. Pops wants me here at any price, so he's manipulating me. He thinks he's saving me from my cold, lonely life in New York. He's got me back in the heart of the family where he thinks I belong, and he's milking the current situation for all its worth."

She glanced at him quickly. "Well, Zach? How am I doing so far?"

"You hit the jackpot, Mandy. So what? He loves you. Is that so bad?"

"In reality, I don't belong here," Amanda said. "And he's costing me a bloody fortune!"

"My uncle goes after what he wants."

"So what else is new?" Her brow creased in thought. "Most men go after what they want," she said sharply. "They want control and they don't care about the cost to their victims."

An old refrain. Every time Zach heard it, he knew she was thinking about her own father. She rarely mentioned him, but when she did, the same bitterness cloaked her voice.

"There are no victims in this family, Amanda. All men are not the same. You know that now. Ben and I are certainly not like your dad."

She didn't respond at first. "My dad? How much do you know about my dad?"

Surprised, defensive, curious. Her simple question was wrapped in layers of meaning and unspoken memories. After all these years, how could she think he didn't know about Charlie?

"I know enough, Mandy, to be very proud of you."

He held her gaze. She questioned him silently and he responded in the same language. *I know about him, but you can trust me, Amanda. You don't have to hide anything from me.*

"I was a little girl, five, maybe six, but I'll never forget," she blurted finally. "I'll never forget his roars, his rages, the meanness when he drank...." She spun around and then turned away again as if to dissipate her nervous energy. "God Almighty, Zach, he hit her! He hit Mom, while I hid under the bed and cried."

Her eyes glowed like hot coals on a chill winter's night. "But I learned. Do you know what I learned, Zach?" she asked, without giving him a chance to respond. "In this world, you either have money and power, or you're a victim. And I will never be a victim again!"

He heard the conviction in her voice. He saw it in her expression and in her stance before she went on. "I will figure out a way to protect Molly and Mom, and keep my job at the same time. And while I'm at it, I'll protect your investment, too. So don't pack my bags yet!"

Before he could reply, she ran out of the room. He watched her go and shook his head. Not that he blamed her for feeling the way she did. He wished he could change her past.

But now all he saw was a beautiful woman who had everything, and nothing. For a moment, earlier, he thought he had seen the real Amanda. A caring, loving girl. But he had been wrong. Money and power. Those were her goals, as they'd always been. Those were her substitutes for love and trust. Little comfort in a lonely bed.

He shook his head, then brought himself up short. Who was he to criticize? A serious relationship could never be on his agenda, either. Loving someone deeply held too much risk. Promised too much pain. And whenever he forgot it, images of his own mom and dad reminded him. Inside his grown-up self still lurked an eight-year-old boy sobbing for all he had lost.

Amanda was young and pretty, very much alive. It meant nothing that she managed to stir his senses and arouse a physical ache in him. She would arouse an ache in any normal, red-blooded male! He wouldn't give his heart to her. Not his grown-up heart. Much too risky.

Suddenly a picture book of Amanda opened in his mind. Amanda, laughing with excitement during a family snowball fight; Amanda, shyly giving him a handful of chocolate kisses to thank him for help with her homework after she'd been ill; Amanda, learning how to ski, following his every direction, frightened but trusting him with her life. That was a sweet one, precious and rare. He should hold on to that memory.

He had other remembrances, too. An older Amanda, bright and beautiful, at first, still confiding in him, asking for his opinion when she began modeling. And then, only occasional visits home, when they were both too busy for more, she in New York, he in Chicago. Each time, those reunions began awkwardly, as though they had to relearn each other. But only occasionally was there enough time to recapture the old relationship and get comfortable again.

Whew! Memories could be powerful, especially memories of Amanda. Now, however, he was forewarned. What with running the business, watching over Molly and handling Amanda, he had his work cut out.

JUST ONE DAY with the family reminded Amanda why she didn't return more often. She hadn't been pushed and pulled by so many emotions in years. She didn't like it. Too exhausting and unproductive. And the day wasn't over yet! She sighed as she pulled on her ski pants. Molly waited for her.

She owed Ben for all he had done for her as a teenager. Not that she thought Zach really needed her here. Or Molly, either, for that matter. Molly would adapt well after an initial adjustment period. And she probably knew almost as much about running the hotel as Zach.

She'd told Mr. Garroway on the phone that she'd be back in a week. But now it appeared she might have to extend that time until arrangements were made. Maybe an extra week. And then? Maybe she could return on weekends until Ben recovered. If she enrolled Molly in a New York school, there'd be more options. The girl could stay with Lily, or Amanda could take her back and forth on weekends. And Zach? Zach could devote all his energies to the business. She felt better immediately. Having backup plans provided some control.

"Come on, Amanda. Let's go. It'll be dark soon."

Molly spoke the truth about that, Amanda thought as she joined her sister at the ski lift nearest to the hotel. The days were short in January, dusk settling in as early as four o'clock. The lifts closed at five and reopened again at seven for night skiing under the lights.

Funny how one of the shortest days of the year

seemed to last forever, certainly longer and more exhausting to Amanda than any summer's day when the sun's light extended for hours. The hospital visit, the conversation with Zach and now skiing with Molly…and it was only three o'clock!

As she waited in line with her sister for their turn on the lift, she took note of the crowd. Saturdays were prime skiing days, and today was no different. This crowd comprised all ages and all types. And they'd all be hungry for dinner later. Perhaps she should have stayed with her mother to check on the kitchen and dining staff.

"Can you still ski, Amanda?" Molly interrupted her musings. "Because if you can't, I'm leaving you behind."

The girl threw up roadblocks with every sentence, and Amanda now focused her full attention on her sister.

"We'll soon find out how good I am, won't we? But whether I'm faster or slower than you, Molly, we stick together."

Molly began to respond, but Amanda cut her off. "How else can you tell me what's on your mind? And that's what you really want to do, isn't it?"

The younger girl didn't answer, but her smile of juicy anticipation confirmed Amanda's suspicions. Molly was going to take the opportunity to unload on her. In essence, she was going to tell Amanda off. And Amanda would listen…and then rebut.

But what kind of rebuttal could be used against a hurting child who finally allowed tears to fall?

None.

With each ride on the chairlift, Molly shared more of her feelings. On their first ride, Amanda listened to her sister exclaim about the beauty of the place and how she loved it.

"I'd never leave here. I'd never leave Mom and Dad, not like some other daughters I know."

"Molly, you're only twelve."

"So what? I know who my family is. I'd never desert them."

So maybe Molly *would* like to spend a semester in New York. Near both parents. A wave of excitement danced through Amanda. Her idea just might work out.

They reached the top of the mountain just then, and Amanda scrambled off the lift, concentrating on her balance and direction. When she looked up, Molly's bright orange jacket was a quarter of the way down the slope.

"Okay, kiddo, you want a challenge? You got it," Amanda muttered before pushing off with her heart pounding, her blood racing. It had been a long time since she was on skis, but her instincts had always been good and they didn't fail her now.

She waved to Molly when she caught up and then paced herself to match her sister. The girl was good. Very good. They weren't on the most challenging hill, but Molly's form, style and confidence showed. She barely used her poles, she shifted her weight automatically, and Amanda could tell that Molly felt the exhilaration and poetry of the sport. She knew the feeling well. She felt it herself, even now, on this very first run after a year away.

"It is wonderful, isn't it?" Amanda said when they reached the bottom of the hill and headed for the chairlift again.

"If it's so wonderful, why do you stay away? You can't ski in New York City!" Molly didn't need much invitation to attack.

"I have a big job there, Molly—"

"I know all about it. You think your job's so awesome, but it's not. Not when it takes you away from everyone. Lots of people have real awesome jobs, and they still come home."

They settled into the chairlift again.

"You don't understand, Molly. I don't have a lot of time."

Molly looked at her with eyes older than her years. "I got that message a long time ago. We weren't important anymore. And you know what, Amanda? You're not important to us, either. I don't even tell my friends I have a sister. I don't brag about you anymore. I saved all the magazines you were in, but I don't show them to anybody now."

The pain in Molly's voice matched the sudden pain in Amanda's heart. Molly felt betrayed by her own sister, and Amanda, with all her talents and skills, could think of nothing to say. Were there any words that could assuage the hurt?

"When you get older, Molly…"

They shoved off the chair together, but Molly turned to her sharply.

"When I get older, I'll never be like you. Never. Never." Her eyes glistened with unshed tears before she attacked the hill as if all the worries of the world were chasing her.

Amanda pushed off more leisurely, her thoughts whirling in confusion and sorrow. She had caused Molly pain. Right or wrong, there was no getting around the facts. She scanned the slope and spotted the orange parka streaking toward the base. The child was too full of anger to resolve anything today, but Amanda realized that if she wanted a loving relationship with her sister, she'd have to work at it, and work at it now.

She descended the hill swiftly, unconsciously shifting her weight and enjoying the freedom while her eyes remained glued on Molly. She'd figure something out later. At last, she caught up with her sister.

Darkness had fallen by the time they walked into the family's quarters and saw Zach waiting for them.

"We're short on time, ladies."

"All I want is a long, hot shower, a hot meal and lots of sleep," Amanda said, yawning, as she entered the room.

"Forget it. All you can have is a fast shower and a fast meal," Zach replied. "We've got a full house for dinner and beyond. You might as well get back into the routine as long as you're still here. You can start by working the dining room."

Zach could be somewhat forbidding in commando mode, but that didn't cause Amanda's stomach to tighten. Facing reality tightened it. No question. With every passing hour, her family responsibilities ensnared her more firmly. *Oh, God! What if I can't leave in a week?*

Zach couldn't run the whole enterprise by himself. Despite his opinion to the contrary. With Lily and Ben both out of the picture, who would help him? Amanda was the one with the experience; she was the logical choice. He needed her to get the job done, but staying on and working at Diamond Ridge demanded a huge commitment, a twenty-four-hour-a-day commitment.

What if she had to remain for the season? She'd be forced to tackle legal assignments electronically. And when would she have the time? She groaned. Working from home was not the way she'd planned her professional life.

And then there was Zach himself. Coping with him presented its own challenges. She closed her eyes.

"For someone who's been out in the fresh air, you're looking a bit pale, Amanda. Are you sick?"

Her lids lifted slowly. His gray eyes, now warm with concern, filled her vision.

"I'm fine."

He sighed impatiently. "Having second thoughts about your visit?"

"You know darn well I'm having second, third and fourth thoughts," she replied, "but I guess I'm here."

"Then be here in your mind, as well as your body," he snapped. "I don't need halfhearted help. You know it's a tough business, requiring a team effort and a hundred percent commitment."

"Tough? I can take tough. But a team? Not my

style. I've always been a loner. I like my independence."

"Just follow my lead for a while, Amanda, and you'll fit right in."

"You've got the wrong woman. I don't lead and I don't follow. I'm just myself."

He seemed larger than life as he faced her, his expression as serious as she'd ever seen it. "Then it's time you learned to play with the rest of us. You have a choice. I can run the whole show without you or you can run it with me...*together*. But it's got to be with your whole heart. Molly needs attention, but I can't baby-sit you, too. So think carefully. You're either in or you're out."

Baby-sit her? Who did he think he was to speak that way to her? Amanda squared her shoulders and stepped forward into Zach's space. He didn't budge.

"Don't threaten me, Zach. And don't talk to me as if I were a fool. I have never been afraid of hard work and I know what it takes to run this place. Just get out of my way."

She took a step around him, but he pivoted and blocked her path, standing casually with hands in pockets as though he had all the time in the world. Unwilling to play his game, she remained in place and queried him with a lift of her brow.

His gaze caught and held hers. Finally, he spoke softly. "What's your pleasure, Amanda? In or out? Are we a team or not?"

Hours seemed to pass. Zach's gray eyes glinted with challenge and an emotion she couldn't name.

Amanda was mesmerized by their fire. She expected anger, impatience, but instead, she saw...want. He wanted her to stay. Despite all his words to the contrary. Despite his bravado, he wanted her. Or needed her more than he cared to admit. Want or need. Did it really matter?

"I'll take the dining room." Her words floated on a tiny puff of air.

"Good. Very good," he replied softly.

Molly's voice shattered the moment.

"Well, if Amanda's taking the dining room, I'm staying at the front desk, and then I've got a baby-sitting job for one of the regulars. We don't need to work together." Molly quickly scampered out of the kitchen.

"Do I smell trouble?" Zach asked Amanda.

"Let it go, Zach. Just let it go," Amanda replied slowly. "It's been a long day."

By midnight, she couldn't have produced another smile if she was paid. She finally stumbled to her room, totally exhausted, and fell across her bed. Her job at Stanhope Jones was a snap compared to this! And tomorrow would be more of the same, including another visit to the hospital.

ZACH SAT BEHIND the wheel the next morning, with Lily and Molly in the back seat and Lily's luggage in the storage space. Amanda yawned widely as she joined Zach in the front. He looked fresh and ready to start the day. She closed her eyes resentfully, longing for another few hours of shut-eye.

Her thoughts drifted to her activities the previous evening, first working in the dining room where she'd circulated among the guests, answering questions and making sure everyone was satisfied with their stay at Diamond Ridge. Living up to the motto Where Guests Are Family required a dedicated staff, and now Amanda was part of that staff.

Then she'd gone to the chalet where the singles set was offered some country-friendly nightlife. Music, drinks, conversation. Night skiing came first for many, then they swarmed into the chalet. Here Amanda received a warm welcome from the staff, some of whom she knew, as well as from the guests, especially the male guests. She chatted with them all, recognizing that part of their high spirits came from enjoying their day and being on vacation.

She yawned again and heard Zach chuckle.

"Country life too much for our city girl?" he teased.

"Stow it, Porter," she replied. "I don't have the energy to fight this morning." She punctuated her statement with another jaw-cracking yawn.

"We may have disagreements, Mandy, but we don't fight."

She rolled her eyes heavenward. "Sure."

She felt his hand gently turn her head toward him. "You did a great job last night, sweetheart. Every other person I saw this morning asked me who you were. The guys in the chalet last night asked me *where* you were."

"And what did you tell them?" Intrigued about what he'd said, she looked at him expectantly.

He met her gaze. "I told them you were with me." He paused a moment. "You know, part of the team."

"Oh, of course." She'd need a blood-pressure kit if she spent more time with him. Was he trying to tell her something, or had he just chosen an unfortunate combination of words?

TOO MUCH TESTOSTERONE. Too long between relationships. Too big a mouth! Whatever had made him imply that Amanda was unavailable to any of those guys this morning? He wanted her to be friendly to their guests. He wanted her to take an equal part in managing the business. She was an adult, a sophisticated city gal. She could handle herself.

That was it! The reason for his idiocy. When the guys were on the prowl this morning, he'd forgotten that Amanda was all grown up, and he had automatically reverted to the big-brother mode. Naturally, his first reaction had been to protect her. But from now on, he'd remember that she was more than able to take care of herself. He grinned inwardly and relaxed. A sibling thing. It made sense.

THE TRIP TO THE HOSPITAL seemed to take only five minutes. Amanda grasped one of Lily's smaller suitcases, while Zach hoisted the large one from the Jeep. Molly and Lily handled an overnight case and another small valise. Amanda glanced at the troop. Ben would be happy to see them altogether before he and Lily were transported to New York by ambulance.

They were not Ben's first visitors. Amanda recognized their family lawyer, Sam Johnson, sitting in a chair, chatting with his client. But her attention focused on her stepfather. She'd been right. Ben's pleasure at seeing his whole family shone in his eyes and skewed his attention from the attorney. If he'd been able to control it, his crooked smile would have stretched across his face. Amanda grew hopeful at the life she saw in his eyes.

"Hello, Lily, Zach." The tall, stoop-shouldered attorney stood and greeted them. "It's been a long time, Amanda. How are you? Ready to take over and let me retire?"

"You've got a lot of years left, Mr. Johnson."

"And, Molly," the lawyer continued, "you're getting prettier every day, just as beautiful as your sister."

"Yuck."

"Molly!" Lily exclaimed. "That was uncalled for. You'll apologize to Amanda now."

Amanda recognized the stubborn look on Molly's face. "Don't worry about it, Mom. We'll work it out later."

"Indeed you will. And sooner than you think." Lily turned to the lawyer. "Is the paperwork ready, Sam?"

At his nod, Lily walked to her husband and took his hand. She leaned over the bed and Amanda saw her mother's forehead gently touch her stepfather's. She saw her lips form words of love and she turned away. She had forgotten how affectionate her mom and Ben had always been with each other. And why should they not be themselves just because they were in a hospital?

Her gaze collided with Zach's and she felt herself blush. His wink and grin caused her cheeks to burn. Annoyed at her reaction, she avoided his eyes. Zach simply appreciated Ben and Lily's relationship, just as she did. He was not flirting with her! Fortunately, her mother's voice saved her from conversation with anyone.

"Listen up, everyone. We have some issues to discuss. Well, not really discuss. It's all a done deal. Since Ben and I won't be around for a while, we had to make some changes. Some legal changes. And Sam's going to tell you about them."

What changes? Amanda immediately raised an eyebrow at Zach, her thoughts now only on the business of the moment. He surely must have known something and kept it from her. But he shrugged at her silent question, and looked as curious as she felt. She turned toward the attorney. Something big was going on and it involved all of them. What were her mother and Ben up to?

The lawyer stood, walked purposefully beyond the end of the bed and waited for all eyes to focus on him. Amanda recognized a pro when she saw one. She could picture him in a courtroom, commanding the attention of the jury, the spectators, the judge. He had consciously positioned himself at the head of their gathering and had drawn their attention away from

Ben and Lily. Amanda suspected that this was exactly what the older couple wanted him to do.

"At the request of my good friends and clients, there are two issues that have been legally addressed in the last few days. The paperwork has been completed for both." He looked meaningfully at Amanda. "Lock, stock and barrel—no loopholes."

Amanda stiffened slightly at the warning, now anticipating the worst. She probably wouldn't like what came next.

Mr. Johnson waited a moment. "It is sometimes touchy to combine family relationships with business arrangements, but I don't think that will be a problem with this family, because we're all on the same page here." He then turned to Molly. "We all want the best for Ben, don't we?"

Molly nodded.

"Well, Molly, your dad needs to know that you're being protected while he's away. That you're being well taken care of."

"But I'm fine, Mr. Johnson. I'm never sick. I can take care of myself."

"What would happen, Molly, if you were to ski into a tree tomorrow and break your arm? Who would get you to the hospital and allow the doctors to treat you?"

"Zach," was the immediate reply.

"The doctors wouldn't listen to Zach or anyone else unless they were your legal guardians. And that's why Zach and Amanda now have temporary joint custody of you, Molly, for a few months until your parents return.''

Her sister's face was so expressive Amanda could predict what was coming next.

''You mean they can tell me what to do?''

''They are *in loco parentis*. That means they stand in place of your parents for a while. They sign report cards, they give you your allowance, you ask them if a bunch of friends can sleep over. All the things that go on between parents and kids.''

But Molly was shaking her head. ''No way, Mr. Johnson. Here's the deal. Change it to Zach only, and I'll do it. There's no way I'm going to let Amanda tell me anything.''

''Excuse us, folks,'' Zach said before anyone could respond to Molly's demands. ''Molly doesn't understand that some things are not negotiable. I'm going to explain that to her right now…outside.'' He put his hand on the girl's shoulder and firmly guided her from the room.

Angry at Molly for complicating an already stressful time, but angrier at herself for being the cause, Amanda resorted to familiar territory to maintain her composure.

''Two guardians provide an extra measure of safety, Mom. No matter how she complains, your strategy was right.'' She blinked back incipient tears as she looked at the couple in front of her. ''I promise you both that Molly and I will live together in harmony. Don't concern yourself. She'll be fine.''

''But will you?'' asked Lily in a worried tone.

"Me? Why would you even ask? I know how to survive."

"You do, indeed. But I want more for you than that. I want—"

Zach and Molly reentered the room just then, and Amanda turned gratefully toward them. She wasn't up to listening to the dreams her mother envisioned for her, unrealistic dreams.

Lily was the romantic one; Amanda, the practical. She couldn't even remember weaving girlish fantasies about a Prince Charming and living happily ever after.

Zach gave her a thumbs-up and Amanda felt herself relax.

"Molly's fine with the arrangement now, Sam. She just needed to know some details about how it would work, and she needed to understand that her living in New York is not an option at this time. It's not what her folks want now. Isn't that right, Mol?"

"Yup." She glanced at Amanda and shrugged.

The gesture could have meant anything, but Amanda didn't care. It was the warmest communication she'd received from her sister so far. She shrugged back and winked. Molly smiled. It was a start, and Amanda could bring up her plan to have Molly with her in New York some other time.

"With that important issue resolved, we'll move on," Sam said. "The second item on the list is the corporation. Diamond Ridge Resort." He paused briefly to glance at Amanda and Zach. "Ben has made you both officers of the corporation with full power of attorney and full salaries. Amanda can sign checks just as you do, Zach. Both signatures are required for any large amount as detailed in the document. The bank is aware of these changes—they just need Amanda to fill out a signature form. You both can make any and all decisions from hiring a cook to buying more land. In essence, he's giving you a business to run together—with all the benefits and all the responsibilities.''

Amanda intercepted the surprise on Zach's face before he could hide it. A not-so-pleasant surprise if the scowl that followed was an indication. The phony! Last night he said he'd run the Diamond *with* her. Now it seemed he wanted to operate solo.

''Amanda's help aside, the facts are, I'm already running the business with Ben, and I also own a twenty-five percent share of the corporation.''

She had to give him credit. His calm voice was belied only by the throbbing vein in his temple.

''And that's why you're named as chief executive officer of Diamond Ridge Resort and will draw a higher salary, while Amanda is executive vice-president.'' Sam paused dramatically. ''Ben and Lily have removed themselves totally from the operation for the next six months. Think of your uncle as an absentee chairman of the board. And, by the way, that particular action was taken against my advice.''

''How so?'' Amanda asked. One part of her mind focused on Sam, while the other tried the absorb the implications of a *six*-month commitment. A totally impossible plan for her.

''New York isn't galaxies away,'' replied the law-

yer. "And no one runs a resort better than my friend,
Ben Porter. His mental faculties are intact and he
could give advice. But for some reason, he insists on
walking away from it entirely."

"It's…a…no-brainer, Sam." For the first time all
morning, Ben's voice joined the discussion. "My…
nephew and my…daughter…are…the…most…quali-
fied…to…run the…Diamond. Can't…just…let…any-
one…do it. And Mandy…won't…lose…money…get-
ting salary."

"Oh, Pops!" Amanda cried. "I don't want your
money. It belongs in the business."

"No…it's…better…this way…. Zach…"

"Here, Unc."

"You…make sure…she…gets…paid."

"I will."

"And, Zach…"

"Yes, sir?"

"You…take…care of…my girls."

Amanda shook her head in defeat. Pops didn't want
to understand. She could take care of herself. And that
included protecting her job in New York.

She stepped into the hall, extracted her cell phone
and called Mr. Garroway. As her mentor, he'd give
her some objective advice. She had to stay. She had
to go. She had to find a way to accomplish everything.

His answering machine was no help.

CHAPTER FOUR

TAKE CARE OF HIS GIRLS? Zach sat behind the wheel on the trip home, shaking his head. Despite what Sam Johnson said, his uncle's mental faculties may have been affected. Both "girls" needed him about as much as the ski season needed sixty-degree weather. The sisters, so alike in their outer beauty, also matched each other in their quest for independence. Molly's "I can take care of myself" could have been uttered by Amanda. They were mirror images of each other. And maybe that was the core of their problem.

He left his musings about sisterly relationships for another time and turned his mind toward the Diamond. He had a business to run and an unwilling partner to assist him. Amanda had been taciturn since leaving the hospital. She sat next to him now, quietly, hands in her lap, dark glasses hiding her deep-blue eyes. He might have thought she was as relaxed and calm as a sleepy house cat on a hot summer day if she hadn't been chewing her bottom lip. An old habit he'd thought she'd outgrown.

"Take it easy, Mandy," he said, reaching for her hand. "We're going to work things out."

She pulled away, removed the glasses and erupted

like a volcano. "Then let's get the rules straight right from the start. Number one—I don't need anyone taking care of me. Got that, Porter? Number two—I don't want Pops's money. Put it in trust for Molly if you want. And number three—"

"Number three is, Amanda grows up. Amanda tries to think about other people besides herself. Got that, Shaw?" Too bad dealing with Amanda required him to be almost brutal. It was the only way to get her attention. She had to be stopped before she created so many roadblocks they'd be living by Amanda's Rules of Order, instead of like a family.

Her eyes narrowed, her pulse throbbed in her neck, and he knew she was ready to explode again. "Stow it, Amanda," he intercepted, his voice hard, unyielding. "No one's giving you a handout. No one's trying to smother you. Just give us all a little break here. It's been a long day."

She surprised him with her silence. Maybe he'd gotten through to her. With hope, he glanced to his right. Amanda looked straight ahead, her lips pursed, anger simmering just below the surface. His hope dwindled.

He didn't anticipate one peaceful minute with Amanda around. Too bad. His thoughts turned to the younger Ms. I-can-take-care-of-myself Porter.

"How're you doing back there, Popcorn Girl?" he asked as he checked the rearview mirror. He couldn't see her from his angle of vision, but there was no response to his question. He glanced at Amanda. "She must have fallen asleep. Will you turn around and check?"

He felt, rather than saw, her comply. And then he heard her concern. "Oh, Zach. Can you pull over?"

He jerked his head around for a second and cursed under his breath in frustration. The child was a picture of misery. He should have expected it. Molly adored her father, and the day's events—the whole topsy-turvy situation—was bound to leave her frightened and miserable.

"There's no place to stop, Mandy. The shoulders are covered with mountains of snow."

He glanced sideways again. Amanda had already unsnapped her safety belt, lowered the back of her seat and turned on her stomach. She started wriggling to the back of the car, unknowingly providing Zach with a delightful view of a sweetly curved derriere encased in snug-fitting slacks.

He forgot about Molly. His hands tightened convulsively on the steering wheel. They itched to hold something else, something softer...rounder...something totally feminine. Perspiration beaded his upper lip, and he used all his willpower to concentrate on driving.

"Buckle up back there," he managed to growl. He refocused on Molly and took a deep breath, then another, before trusting himself to speak again. "What's happening, Mol? Talk to me. Amanda, what's going on?"

Then he heard the sobs. Deep, shuddering sobs coming from the child who had been left in his care. Ben's child, Zach's little cousin, his only living relative in the world besides Ben. Damn it! Why were these country roads so narrow? She needed him to hold her, to talk to her, to make her feel safe.

Then he heard Amanda's voice, or rather a variation of her voice he hadn't heard in years. A soft, gentle Amanda cooing over her sister. "Shh…let me wipe your face, Mol. Come closer. Cuddle with me. We'll both feel better…."

And in that moment, he knew. He knew as surely as he knew his own name that the real Amanda was alive and well and hiding inside herself.

"DADDY'S GOING to die, isn't he, Amanda?" Molly's words came out between her sobs. "And don't tell me I'm silly and everything will be all right. I'm not a little kid. I want to know."

"No, you're not a little kid, but you're still a young girl who shouldn't have such big worries. Pops is on the road to recovery. Isn't that what the doctor said?"

"But what if he's wrong? Your father died and Zach's parents died. Both of them! So Daddy could die, too. Manda, what happened to you when your father died?"

Amanda searched Molly's face. With all pretenses gone, her sister's vulnerability was apparent. There was no way Amanda could tell the truth—that she and her mother had lived a better life alone. Molly's situation and Amanda's weren't the same.

"I went to school just like always. We didn't have much money, but Mom went to college and became a nurse. She worked very hard to get her degree. After she graduated, she got a regular job in a hospital and things became easier. And then she met Pops.''

Amanda smiled. ''You know the rest of the story, Molly. How the hotshot New England skier came to the big city and for the first time in his life, broke his leg.''

''Yeah,'' Molly said. ''And Mommy was his nurse and he fell in love with her and made you both come home with him just until his leg healed.''

''But he didn't want Mom to leave, so he made the doctor keep the cast on longer,'' Amanda said.

Zach's deep voice joined in. ''I think I was the happiest one of all when she finally said yes and put him out of his misery. I was tired of doing all the work around the place. That stupid cast had me working extra hard for weeks.''

They all laughed at the memory, and the tension eased. Amanda leaned back in the seat, content with how she'd handled Molly and happy to see her laughing. But Molly had more to say.

''You're not like a real sister, Amanda. Not like my friends' sisters. You're never here. And when new people ask me if I have any sisters or brothers, I say, 'No, not really,' and I don't think I'm lying. Not really.''

So much for feeling content! Amanda forced herself to inhale. Molly's confession packed an unexpected punch, and breathing was surprisingly difficult. ''Well, I'm here now. So tell your friends, you *really* have a sister.''

''Will you stay until Mom and Dad get back?''

Molly's hopeful expression contradicted the challenge in her voice. Why did children see everything in black and white? Amanda thought. Why did they want exact measurements?

"Molly," she said slowly, "I want you to think about something. Something new." Her tone of voice must have registered. Molly looked at her intently.

"Would you consider going to school in New York, living with Mom and me at my place? We could get to know each other better, and you could see Dad as often as allowed."

She heard Zach inhale deeply. Molly said nothing.

"Well?" Amanda prodded.

"I can't go to New York and neither can you. Daddy wants us all to be here and run the business for him. He *needs* us to do it, Amanda."

Damn! What had seemed so simple earlier was suddenly complicated. Molly's priorities and her sense of family were going to get in the way.

Clearly, Amanda's taking a leave of absence would be best for the family, but would it be best for her? An extended absence could cost her the promotion, if not her job. Her reasons for remaining in Vermont might not be applicable under the Family Leave Act, but such a request had a basis in law. Asking for a personal leave would be much worse.

"It's the same old thing!" Molly cried. "You don't want to help. You don't want to be part of the family."

Amanda winced and looked away. God, her sister's

words hurt. But how could she be in two places at once?

Suddenly Molly's tone changed to excitement. "I have an idea. *I'll* talk to your boss," she said, "and I'll tell him how much we need you here, and he'll let you stay."

Amanda looked at her sister, the kid with the wet face and great ideas who now sported a grin. The Unsinkable Molly Porter. She felt her own tears gather and allowed them to fall. Underneath it all, Molly liked her! Molly wanted her. She was willing to fight for her.

Amanda raised her head, and another tear ran down her cheek. She glanced at Zach. His gray eyes softened, captured her blue ones in the mirror and wouldn't release them. A gentle warmth filled her as she met his gaze. A warmth that surprised her. Did she really need his understanding? His approval? Her reaction left her wondering. And then he winked at her and attended to his driving once again. So, what did that mean?

LIFE WITH AMANDA promised to be full of surprises, Zach thought as he pulled the car around to the back of the hotel and into the huge barnlike garage, which also housed plows and snowmaking equipment. He was prepared to handle all kinds of arguments with Amanda, but tears? Tears from Amanda were not on the agenda.

He ushered the two females into the large country kitchen, now silent and empty without Lily.

"How about some hot soup and a sandwich before we get to work? Today should be a busy Sunday with a lot of new guests." He started gathering the items they'd need and was happy to note that Molly immediately started to help.

"Yeah. I love checking out the check-ins. Fridays and Sundays."

"Molly!" said Amanda. "Don't tell me you're on the prowl for boys."

"Boys? Who said anything about boys? They're stupid. I'm looking for kids—rug rats. I make a lot of money baby-sitting and giving private skiing lessons after school. But not every Sunday has a lot of kids."

Amanda laughed. Her sister had a practical bent and was funny, too.

"You'll have to make a quick reconnaissance, Mol," Zach said. "I seem to recall your mom mentioning quite a bit of homework waiting for you."

"But I'm not in the mood for homework today. It's the first day without Mom and Dad, and besides, Amanda wants me with her, don't you, Manda?"

Molly looked imploringly at her sister. Amanda just looked plain startled.

"Well, maybe..." she started to say.

Zach had seen Molly play this game many times, the old one-parent-against-the-other routine. Of course, he didn't interfere when Ben and Lily were around, but they weren't here now. They were good parents, strong but flexible, and were astute enough to see through their daughter's ploys. If they gave in to her, it was a conscious choice.

He glanced at Amanda's confused face, and hoped that for once in her life, she'd just follow his lead without a fuss. Not that he was an expert, but Amanda hadn't been around children since she was a kid herself.

He could play hardball, softball or smartball with Molly. He opted for the last choice and hoped it worked.

"Amanda does want to spend time with you," he interrupted, "but she's not going to be happy if you skip your homework."

Molly spun to face him. "Why not? Just because you want me to do it doesn't mean she does. She never agrees with you about anything, anyway. You were even arguing in the car, so she'll be on my side, not yours."

He saw Amanda wince. Good. They'd present a united front. Molly's words contained some truth, but it was her tone of voice that made Zach, for the first time since she was born, angry with her.

He felt his smartball plan disintegrate with each passing second, and suddenly envisioned the next few months with both females banded together against him. He shivered at the thought.

"There are no sides here, Molly. Your sister and I may not agree on everything, but for as long as she's here, we're going to work together. Amanda's not the kind of person who skips out on responsibility. Amanda always did her homework. Even when she was sick. If she missed classes that first year, I had to collect the assignments from her teachers. In fact, when she didn't understand something, she asked for help. Always." He glanced at Amanda, curious to gauge her reaction.

She offered him an imperceptible nod of her head and looked...relieved? Amused? Maybe both. Zach smiled to himself. She probably didn't want to play the heavy this time. Her relationship with her sister was still too fragile. Not a problem. He didn't mind taking the heat today.

"Bummer!" Molly declared, making her disappointment too obvious to miss. "I can't have any fun if you two start agreeing about everything!"

"Fat chance of that," Amanda retorted with a laugh. "That's one thing you can count on, Molly. Zach and I are two different people with minds of our own. Homework, however, has to be done." She looked over Molly's head at Zach and lowered one eyelid slowly.

His heart skipped a beat. Like an endangered species, a rosy-cheeked, relaxed Amanda, armed with a sense of fun, rarely made an appearance. But, she was definitely worth the wait. The sparkling blue eyes, the megawatt smile, the playfulness and the wink. She stunned him. No wonder her modeling agency still wanted her. They'd lost a true cover girl when she opted for law school.

"Okay. I'll do my homework." Molly's resigned voice interrupted his musings. "See you later."

Zach watched Molly leave the kitchen, then looked at Amanda. "She's some kid."

"She is."

"So let's not mess up her life any more than necessary. What's the big idea of you suggesting she live in New York without first talking to me? It's a joint guardianship, Amanda. Not a solo one."

"But it's the perfect solution for all of us. We'd each be where we're supposed to be. And you could devote all your time to running the business."

He nodded. "What's perfect for you isn't perfect for the rest of us. Did you ever stop to think that Molly wouldn't want to go, or that I might need you here?"

If his voice hadn't softened, she would have taken his words at face value. But her heart fluttered. He used the word *need*, but his voice said *want*.

AMANDA HUMMED along with the radio Monday morning as she drove to the bank. Her phone call to Mr. Garroway had not been returned. Surprisingly, she wasn't as upset as she'd expected to be. Her job and New York suddenly seemed light-years away, and it was hard to be annoyed when surrounded by the majesty of the mountains. The clear, windless day and bright sunshine added to her contentment.

Working at the lodge again felt comfortable, too, except for the mingling part. Amanda always dreaded thrusting herself forward, introducing herself to strangers. But she'd learned to smile and extend a hand. Making sure the guests were happy was part of the business, and she'd do it.

Getting Molly off to school earlier and mixing with the breakfast crowd after putting in a long evening had presented a challenge. But now, she felt fine. The high spirits of the hotel guests as they anticipated their first run of the day had lifted her own spirits.

It was a matter of pride to her family to have happy guests. Happy guests returned and brought friends with them. A well-run business developed more business. Like the after-school ski clubs, the high-school competitive teams, the weekly "morning for moms" day when child care was provided free and the other events sponsored by Diamond Ridge throughout the season.

By the time Amanda reached town, she was convinced that Zach and Ben knew exactly what they were doing. She walked into the bank with a light heart.

She left with a heavy one.

Trying to keep panic at bay, she concentrated on her driving, carefully maneuvering around potholes and black ice as she made her way back to the hotel. There had to be a mistake, an explanation. Ben might have been carried away with dreams, but Zach couldn't have agreed to borrow so much money, even in view of the competition. He knew better than to pledge their personal assets. His Ivy League education in hotel and business management didn't teach students to become debt-ridden entrepreneurs.

Amanda wanted to make a beeline for Zach's office, but instead, stopped to chat with staff along the way. Touching base with the employees was as important as keeping up with guests. Karen Gallagher, a trim brunette and an old classmate of Amanda's, held sway over the reception area. Her flawless memory and excellent organizational skills made her a one-woman control center.

"Zach's out giving a group lesson on Steeplechase because the regular instructor called in sick. Then he's going to check out the new northwest trail that joins it."

"Must have some pretty skilled skiers this week," said Amanda. "Steeplechase isn't for beginners, and the new trail is way steeper than that. What are we calling it? The Risky Diamond?"

"Diamond in the Rough," Karen replied with a smile, "or the Rough, for short. When people ski the Rough, they come back feeling proud."

"I assume the patrol covers it?"

"Of course, Amanda, like we cover every trail. Nothing's changed."

"Good. We've got to provide the best facility there is, with emphasis on safety. We sure don't need any bad publicity."

Karen patted her arm. "You've been away too long, Amanda. Diamond Ridge has the best press around. Zach saw to that. He's doing a wonderful job with the place."

Amanda looked sharply at the attractive woman. Was there a certain proprietary tone to her voice when she mentioned Zach? Amanda studied Karen openly. Why shouldn't Zach be taken with her? She was pretty, cheerful and bright. Amanda shrugged. Not her business. But the thought nagged.

"What else is going on?"

"We're getting kitchen deliveries today. Cook's

changing the menu, so there might be some ruffled feathers in the kitchen." Karen leaned closer. "She's trying to get fancy with avocado salads and such. But you know, Amanda, when people stay here, they're hungry for stick-to-the-ribs food and lots of it. So good luck with her.

"And Zach said to let you know that Molly gets home exactly at three. Bus leaves her off at the door today because a ski club is coming. You might want to be around for that. And the real good news is that we have a full house every weekend this month with midweek bookings the highest we've ever had."

Karen's *we* had a mighty possessive sound, but Amanda felt a grin tug at her lips, anyway. After all, the woman had worked at the lodge for five years. She probably did feel part of the whole operation.

"Full occupancy all month? Now, that's good news." Better than Karen would ever know, Amanda thought. Her visit to the bank still made her shiver.

"Look who's walking toward us," said Karen a little breathlessly. "Tom Hunter."

Amanda glanced at her in surprise. And saw a slow blush stain her cheeks, saw her eyes soften.

Karen and Tom? Not Karen and Zach? Amanda could have laughed out loud in relief, an emotion she'd analyze later when alone. Feeling happy, she smiled warmly at Tom and was startled by his enthusiastic response. She stole a glance at Karen. The warm brown eyes were blank, her face a cool mask.

Shoot! Either this was a one-sided romance or Karen thought Amanda was going after her man.

Amanda had drawn the wrong conclusions. As usual. When it came to reading people, she was hopeless. But she could mend the situation. She retreated to formality.

"Dr. Hunter," she greeted him with a nod. "Of course, you know Karen. She virtually runs the place for us."

"Hi, Karen. Haven't seen you in a while."

"I've been working."

"So have I."

"Which is exactly what I have to do now," Amanda said. "Thanks for all your help, Karen." She started to walk away.

"Hang on a sec," Tom said. "I have news of Ben."

Amanda whirled around. "I spoke to my mother last night. Everything was fine."

"It is fine," he reassured her. "The doc from New York called this afternoon. Said Ben was one of the most determined patients he'd ever had."

Tears stung her eyes for a moment. "That's Pops. Always doing everything one hundred percent. And won't Molly be happy!"

She turned to Karen. "If you see her first, would you send her to me right away? She had a hard time yesterday."

Karen's smile was natural again. "Sure I will. She's Ben's little girl, after all."

"And Tom, the Diamond is yours. Ski whenever you want for as long as you like. I'll pass the word to the staff." She started to walk away, then turned back. "In fact, if you're free, stay for dinner tonight, but be prepared to answer Molly's questions!"

He grinned at her. "I never turn down dinner prepared by someone else. I'll be back after office hours. I only stopped off to tell you about Ben."

"You were lucky to find me at all. I just came back from town. Karen, would you…"

But she was talking to herself. Evidently, Karen had other plans at the moment. Amanda said goodbye to Tom and positioned herself behind the reception desk until Karen returned. She'd invite her for dinner when she got back, Amanda vowed. Karen gave a hundred percent of herself to her job. There was no way she wanted to alienate her now, not after the illuminating trip to the bank this morning. And besides, she liked Karen. She remembered her as a good-natured girl with an upbeat outlook. Always smiling. Well, usually smiling. It seemed Dr. Tom wasn't giving her anything to smile about.

AMANDA LIFTED her eyes from the paperwork in front of her and moaned softly. Everything she'd learned at the bank was true. She held a copy of the initial loan agreement and the repayment schedule in her hand and just stared. Diamond Ridge Resort was the collateral for a huge improvement loan. She knew that the money was actually being spent on the property, but the figures staggered her. What could have been in Zach's mind to allow Ben to expand on such a large scale?

The door to the office opened. Zach stood on the

threshold, bringing with him his unique fragrance of spice and fresh air. His black cable-knit sweater outlined his broad shoulders; his slow, sexy grin made her heart beat in double time. Red-hot fantasies floated at the edge of her mind.

"Come on out for a run. There's still time before dinner."

She glanced out the window. The sun was low in the sky, signaling the coming early dusk. The offer to ski tempted her, but business came first.

"We need to discuss this." She held up her reading material. "I have to understand what's been happening here."

He crossed the room until he stood in front of the desk and saw the papers. "That's easy to understand. We took out a loan. We're paying it back. Period. The end. Didn't we discuss this yesterday?"

Was this the business whiz she once knew? How could he be so cavalier about the amount?

"I didn't realize how much was involved. Why couldn't you have just borrowed a little at a time? Why didn't you stop Ben?"

Zach looked at her as though she spoke a foreign language. "Why do you think this was all Ben's idea?"

"Because he's married to the mountain."

"Mandy-girl, this is my home, too," Zach said with quiet emphasis. "I'm as committed as my uncle, but I don't know how to explain it to you." He paced in front of her desk. Finally, he stopped and leaned toward her.

"Remember what Ben said at the hospital? Without growth a business dies."

She nodded.

Zach reached for her hand. "Diamond Ridge was dying. That's why we took the plunge."

She couldn't believe it. "What do you mean? The Diamond is thriving. I could see it instantly."

"Ben and I have busted butt to turn the place around in the last two years. We needed the capital to build, or we would have been slowly choked by the competition. Ben maintained the place but hadn't improved it in years. I saw the whole picture five years ago, after I came back from Chicago."

Her jaw dropped. No words came forth. Zach had seen everything and she had seen nothing. She, with her straight A's and advanced degrees, had been oblivious because she'd left it all behind her.

"It took me that first year to assess the whole ski industry up here. We've always had competition— Stratton, Bromley, Sugarbush—and Ben wasn't keeping up. So we decided to renovate—and we knew it would cost, big time. In my second year, we drew up plans, spoke to contractors, got prices. The next year, we actually started the work. And then rumors began to fly."

She sat straighter in her chair. "Pops mentioned rumors at the hospital, but no one explained them."

"Rumors of legalized gambling have upped the ante on properties around here, Amanda. Smaller places than ours, like Snow Peak, have already been made option offers. If the legislation goes through, there will be such an infusion of money into these mountains that you won't recognize the place. And that scares me.''

Taken totally by surprise, Amanda barely heard his last statement. ''Gambling? Like in Atlantic City and Las Vegas? Big hotels, high rollers and famous entertainers? That kind of gambling?''

He nodded. ''Close your mouth, sweetie. Catching flies doesn't become you.''

''But that's fantastic,'' she replied, her mind racing in six different directions. ''Do you know what that means, Zach? You and Pops are home free! No more problems. No loans to pay off. You'll be rich! My God, you can even retire if you want.''

Zach stared at her unblinkingly, without saying a word. Time came to a stop, and the silence gradually permeated her psyche. She squirmed, looked at her hands, bit her bottom lip. What had she done? What had she said?

''Is that what you think I want, Amanda?'' Zach asked quietly. ''To sit back and count my cash? You mentioned problems, but I don't have any problems I can't handle. I went into this expansion with my eyes wide open. I'm part of the ski industry, not the gaming industry.''

Truth shone in his eyes. A man who knew who and what he was, he stood tall and confident as he looked at her. She wished, oh, how she wished, that she could feel the same confidence inside, way deep inside where the scared little girl hid.

Zach walked behind her desk with a slow, easy gait.

He leaned over and gently cupped her cheek with his hand. Suddenly, Amanda wanted to nuzzle into that large, strong hand. She wanted his tender caress, his gentle strength.

She tilted her head and gazed into his face. Was her imagination in overdrive, or was he sending her a message?

"This family is in the ski business, not the gaming business," he repeated. "If you have a problem with that, speak up now."

She shifted mental gears with difficulty, from Zach's touch to his conversation. She had to keep her wits about her. No emotional decisions. Gambling could be the answer. High return on investment. Buyouts. Soaring property values. Huge profits.

"But...but the property would be worth so much...."

Zach stepped a pace back and she instantly felt cool air replace the warmth of his hand on her face. She almost whimpered.

"Yes, it would. And what's more, the loan you're worrying about wouldn't create the smallest ripple in the negotiations. But we are not for sale, Amanda, at any price."

His words were evenly spaced, his voice soft, dangerously soft. She refocused on his face. Stern, glinting eyes replaced the warm ones of moments ago. He waited for her next move like a jungle cat studying his prey. She leaned back in her seat, effectively severing their touch.

"Don't be so naive, Zach. Everyone has a price.

But we don't have to argue—'' she waved her hand to ward off his retort ''—because right now reality is skiing. Rumors are just rumors. We're in the ski business, and until we get an offer for major dollars, we stay in the ski business.''

He rested his hip against the desk, a thoughtful smile on his face. ''Don't patronize me and don't dream about pie-in-the-sky profits. Despite all the speculation, legalized gambling will never be voted in—there's too much opposition.'' He paused and bent closer to her, his eyes once again tender.

''But if you want to dream, Amanda,'' he said softly, ''you're welcome to share mine.''

CHAPTER FIVE

NO ONE HAD EVER invited her to share a dream before. People like her never dreamed—they planned. People like her designed blueprints for life. They followed the *if…then…* approach. *If* she went to law school and did well, *then* she'd earn a lot of money. People like her set practical goals, but they did not indulge in daydreams.

She looked at Zach, big and tall like his treasured mountains. Outgoing. Self-assured. She'd never thought of him as a dreamer, but as a doer. A male version of her, actually. But she'd been wrong.

There were stars in his eyes right now. They glinted with warmth and humor and…hope.

"You put everything you have into this, didn't you? Your money, your heart. Everything. For your dream." She whispered the words, more to herself than him, and didn't expect an answer.

When she looked at him again, she readjusted her metaphoric lenses to focus clearly. The man who stood before her, who'd battled his way through Ben's stroke and a lousy trip to New York just to bring her home, who was sometimes tough and aggressive, sometimes quiet and gentle, who was always determined but willing to listen and who was listening to her now, this man who had organized their family into doing what he thought was right, this man was also a dreamer.

A dreamer with an enormous bank loan.

HE FELT HER MIND open to him, saw the understanding in her eyes and perhaps…admiration? No, couldn't be. Not Amanda. Not when it came to borrowing money.

But then a line furrowed her brow, and he knew his optimism was premature. He could almost read her thoughts. New objections, problems, worries, or whatever she wanted to call them, were being produced as quickly as she could think of them.

He leaned against the door frame, hands in his pockets and waited…eight, nine, ten seconds. Only ten seconds passed before she stood up and started pacing.

"We're walking a fine line here, Zachary. We have to meet monthly payments regardless of cash flow, regardless of guest flow."

He nodded.

"What if we have a warm winter? What if it thaws during the February school vacation? What do we do when people cancel their reservations? How do we make the payments then? You shouldn't have gotten such a large loan!"

Her voice rose as she finished her questions, her fingers threading through her silky blond hair repeatedly. A gesture he recognized from the old days, like biting her bottom lip, a giveaway to her nervousness.

He understood now that her anxiety went beyond a discussion of taking risk in business. It was all about losing control—about losing everything, about being so horribly poor she'd have nothing. The frightened child with no trust. No faith in anyone but herself. She couldn't control the world around her, but she could plan, act and control herself.

"In order to compete," he said, "I suggested we turn the Diamond into a year-round resort. That's why we borrowed the amount we did. Summer activities become just as important as winter ones when people put down their money for a vacation." He kept his voice soft, as calm as he could make it. For her sake and for his.

"I understand," she whispered. "But you've gambled everything on the weather! Winter and summer. The stupid, fickle weather. How could you do that? You can't control it! You could lose everything, Zach. You and Mom and Pops and Molly. You could wind up with nothing!"

Beautiful, vulnerable and so distraught. Zach walked to Amanda and gently took her arm.

"Come here for a moment." He turned them both toward the picture window covering the back wall of the office. "Look outside, Mandy. Look at all the people. The slopes are full, and that's the picture in my mind every time I think about the Diamond. You're right that I can't control the weather, but we've minimized the risks by converting to a year-round resort. A lot of research went into that decision. The benefits outweighed the risks and we forged ahead."

He turned her again, this time toward him, and put his hands on her shoulders. "But probably the deciding factor was that Ben and I had nothing to lose. Five years ago, we weren't keeping pace and we would have lost it all, anyway. Either to a buyer or to the bank. When you have nothing to lose, taking a chance is easy. Despite the weather."

He'd captured her full attention and held it. He needed her to understand what they'd done. To understand him.

"But the most important reason, Mandy, and this is a big one, Diamond Ridge is our home. People fight to save their homes. This fight just happened to be more elaborate."

She remained poised, her head cocked to the side, her focus totally on him as she listened to his words.

"I never knew, Zach, about the way things were here. It's hard to believe. Neither Mom nor Ben ever said anything."

"I guess parents don't share financial concerns with their kids," he replied.

"You knew all about it."

"I lived here."

"No," she replied slowly, "you lived in Chicago. You had a wonderful career with Paradise Hotels, but you returned. Why? Why did you give up an excellent opportunity when you were on your way up?"

She'd never understand the truth, but he didn't expect her to. Lots of people wouldn't. But that didn't matter. He'd done what he'd had to do. What he'd wanted to do. And had never regretted it.

"It's no mystery, Amanda," he said quietly. "My uncle needed me and—a long time ago—I needed him. Returning to the Diamond was no sacrifice."

Her eyes narrowed. "Baloney! It was payback time. Did Pops ask you to stay?"

"Of course not." His voice was hard, impatient. "He didn't have to ask. He'd never interfere in my life."

"Only mine," she muttered.

He smiled and tousled her hair. "Anyway, I stayed. In the beginning, Ben was scared. He needed time to face facts. But when he studied the competition, and when he believed we could continue to be the best innkeepers in the mountains, then he went in with gusto. And he hasn't looked back."

She nodded. "Okay, I understand sticking with a decision." She paused for a moment, blue eyes twinkling. "Confession time. On my first modeling job, I shivered so hard I could barely hold a pose. I was scared stiff and had to force myself to do it. But I had nothing to lose and everything to gain. And it worked. I made a lot of money."

He knew that. Her modeling career could have brought her scads more. "So why did you quit?"

Her mischievous grin lit up the room and caused his breath to catch in his throat. "Can't you figure it out, Zach? I wanted a long-term investment. Looks fade quickly. Brains don't. I guess I did what you did. I weighed the risks, and I bet on my brain."

He held her glance, couldn't look anywhere else, and watched the sparkle in her eyes turn to smoky heat as she met his gaze. His muscles tightened, and his breathing quickened. Her eyes remained on him, studying him intently, as though for the first time. Her lips parted slightly, the tip of her tongue peeping through. An invitation? Did she know what she was doing?

His heart hammered as he leaned toward her, the beat increasing when she didn't retreat. How long had he waited to kiss this woman? The girl he had first known, the co-ed in search of answers, the glamorous fashion model, the smart New York lawyer, and now his partner. How long didn't matter. What mattered was this moment.

He wanted to take it nice and slow, to savor the taste and texture of her mouth, her tongue, but his plan collapsed the moment his lips met hers. He felt the jolt, and when Amanda's arms twined tightly around his neck, he knew she did, too. He held her closely to him. A perfect fit. All rational thought deserted him as he became intoxicated with her kiss, her soft skin, her silky hair and hint of musky perfume, the kind that gets a man's attention.

He gentled the kiss, nibbled the corners of her mouth and traced her lips with his tongue.

"Mmm," she breathed. "More."

"Yes," he murmured, and proceeded to recapture her mouth, hungry for more, too.

She hadn't known it could be like this. A man and a woman creating their own world. She wanted the kiss to continue, she wanted to hold on and to be held. His warm breath fanned her ear, kisses nuzzled her neck and focused on the sensitive spot behind the lobe. If he continued to devour her, she would melt. But oh, it felt so good. So right. She shivered at his touch. Hot and cold all at once, a delicious fever. She leaned back to see his face. He released her instantly and met her gaze, his eyes smoldering.

She raised her hand slowly, her fingers stroking the planes of his cheek, his jaw, tracing his lips and the cleft in his chin. They traveled higher to his brow, a well arched brow, she noted absently, and down the straight line of his nose.

"Zach?" she whispered. "What's going on?"

"I'm not quite sure," he responded unsteadily. "But I want to find out."

Every part of her body tingled or throbbed. She'd never felt this way before, a little overwhelmed and a whole lot scared. And happy. A different kind of happy. Bigger, somehow. Better. And all because of Zach. She shook her head in confusion. How could Zach make her body pulse, make her heart race? She'd known him for years. There should have been no surprises.

She stepped back far enough to study the whole man. Zach stood absolutely still, accommodating her.

She saw a strong man. An honorable man. A loving man. A man who wasn't afraid of life. It would be so easy to connect with him. She stepped forward...and suddenly started shaking.

Loving Zach carried risk. Tremendous risk. His strength would overcome her. She'd suffocate. She'd become dependent. He'd want everything his way.

Every fear and doubt she'd ever had about life and people and love took shape in her imagination. They assaulted her like a battalion of furies chasing her soul. Cold. She felt cold inside. She had to save herself.

"No," she whispered, taking a giant step back. "No, I won't. I can't." Turning swiftly, she ran from the room.

"DID YOU SPEAK to Daddy, Dr. Tom," Molly asked, "or only to his doctor?"

Amanda blessed her sister for carrying the conversational ball around the dinner table in the lodge's dining room that evening. She'd bet she wasn't alone in her gratitude. Karen sat quietly, playing with her food, and Zach barely said a word. Fortunately, Molly chatted on.

"I spoke to his therapist," Tom replied. "It's only been a day, Molly, but your dad's already becoming a star patient. And your mom is learning how to help him do his exercises."

"Knowing Lily, she'll be back in her nursing uniform taking charge of the whole floor," Zach said.

Amanda glanced into his twinkling eyes and laughed, relaxing for the first time since she'd kissed him. The ordinary sounds of the dining room permeated her mind—muffled conversations from other tables, occasional laughter from high-spirited guests, the clink of silverware. She looked around the room, appreciating the normalcy of the moment, and then turned again to Zach.

"You know her well, Zachary."

"I've known her for a long time, Mandy, as long as I've known you."

She felt the heat rise from her neck to her face, couldn't stop it and didn't understand it. Was it his words? His glance? Why did she react with blushes?

She'd have to figure it out later. She purposely turned toward Karen. "How is your mom these days?"

"She'll be all right for the evening. I called her earlier."

"What do you mean?"

"Very bad arthritis. It's hard for her to get around."

"I'm so sorry, Karen. I remember your mother as an active woman."

"Yeah, well, things change. It's been a long time since you've lived here, ten years since we graduated high school, and a lot can happen in ten years."

"But Karen still looks like a kid, while Amanda looks like a sophisticated city woman," Tom said as he leaned sideways to tweak Karen's long French braid, while sending an admiring glance at Amanda.

Amanda winced at Tom's teasing. If he'd wanted to compliment Karen, he'd blown it. If he'd wanted to compliment her, he'd blown it, as well.

She looked at her old friend. Saw her sit up straighter.

"A kid, huh? Then I guess I'm the lucky one, Tom Hunter, MD," Karen said slowly, "because when you're old and gray, and sitting on the sidelines remembering when, this kid will still be dancing up a storm with the other eighteen-year-olds!"

Go for it, Karen! Amanda covered her grin as she watched the woman put the doctor in his place.

"Sidelines? Me, on the sidelines? No way."

Amanda glanced at Zach. He glanced at her. They burst out laughing at the same time and received surprised looks from the two combatants.

"Sorry, guys," Amanda said between laughs. "But talk is cheap. Put your feet where your mouths are and go on up to the chalet. There's a dance floor waiting for you."

"Good idea," Zach said.

Karen glanced at Tom, suddenly looking unsure.

"Amanda and I will join you as soon as we can. We'll make an evening of it," Zach said before he leaned toward Amanda and reached for a napkin. "Hold still a second, sweetie. You've got some sauce on your chin."

His fingers felt gentle as he tilted her head to wipe her skin clean. His eyes clung to hers, inviting a reaction. She returned his gaze and for a moment felt at one with him. Just for a moment, she glimpsed new possibilities and froze in place, her heart thumping wildly.

"I haven't danced with Amanda in too long," Zach continued as he shifted his gaze to the others.

Amanda barely managed a weak smile.

"I see," Tom replied slowly, turning toward Karen. "Want to take a chance with Methuselah?"

Karen looked directly at him and nodded. "One chance, Tommy. You've got one chance with me. Don't mess it up."

Amanda watched the pair walk out of the dining room and head toward the entrance of the hotel. Molly scampered after them on her way to a baby-sitting job. Amanda shook her head and tried to understand what had just happened.

"Tom looked a bit bewildered when Karen gave him her ultimatum," she said. "That took guts, if she's really interested in him."

"All due to you."

Amanda swiveled quickly toward Zach. "To me?"

"She's always admired Tom. They've been friends for a long time, but he's been too distracted for a personal life. First with medical school, then with setting up his practice and, finally, building it. Karen's just kinda been waiting on the sidelines."

"I noticed her eyes shine when she saw him earlier in the day. But still, what's that got to do with me?"

"You, my dear, caused her to act, instead of wait."

"But I didn't do anything!"

"You didn't have to. Tom's eyes were all over you tonight. And Karen isn't playing second fiddle to anyone. Nor should she."

"It didn't mean a thing," she protested, "at least, not to me." She'd felt only Zach's eyes. Tonight they'd teased, twinkled and maybe implored, but her blushing reaction was the same as if his glances had been sexy and hot.

"I'm glad," he said. "Now come closer. I see more sauce on your lip that I'd like to remove personally."

Amanda jumped from her seat as though her chair

was on fire. "I'm not that gullible. And we've got work to do, Mr. Porter, before we join the others."

SHE COULDN'T REMEMBER the last time she had danced with Zach. Had she ever danced with him? If not, she'd been a fool. They moved through the first slow numbers as though they'd rehearsed the steps a hundred times before.

She glanced at Karen and Tom, several feet away, swaying to the music and talking. Maybe they would discover each other now.

Despite her enjoyment of the moment, Amanda found herself assessing the chalet in terms of business. As she'd expected, the dance floor wasn't crowded on a weeknight, but still, many of their guests congregated in the chalet after dinner. She waved to some of the folks she recognized, and it wasn't long before she was again in demand as a partner.

"They come up here thinking only about skiing, and then they get other ideas," Zach grumbled as he released her. "Next time, let them bring their own girlfriends."

"Go commiserate with Tom," Amanda said with a laugh. "Karen's been partnering lots of guests, too."

But there was no comparison between her dances with Zach and with the others. Slow or fast. She smiled, chatted and found herself glancing at her watch, hoping Zach would cut back in.

It was almost an hour later before he did. "Sorry it took so long. Tom and I were talking. Now is there anyone left here who you haven't danced with to-night?" he complained.

"Just keeping the guests happy. And besides, there's safety in numbers," she explained with an ex-aggerated shiver. "I never focus on just one."

"Afraid you might get caught?" he asked, stopping in midstep to look at her. "But is it the wrong guy or the right one that scares you?"

She looked sharply at him. "If you're going to play psychologist, I'm leaving."

"You're safe right here, Ms. Prickly," he said as he gathered her in his arms again. "You're not going anywhere without me."

And for the moment, she didn't want to. She did feel safe. Safe and content. "Another dance, Zachary?"

"All night, if you want."

Dancing all night with Zach sounded intriguing, but impractical. "Sorry, Zach, I want to check my voice mail at Stanhope Jones and send an e-mail to Sarah Wilcox. When I spoke to my boss this morning, I learned that he'd given her several of my cases to handle temporarily."

"And you're scared." It wasn't a question, but a statement.

"The timing couldn't be worse, and you know it."

He held up his hands. "I promise I had nothing to do with it!"

"Yeah, I know." She paused. "I'll use vacation time to cover this week. And next. By then, we have to come up with a plan for me to either commute or work here—if Garroway will agree to that.''

Zach put his arm around her and pulled her close. ''We'll work something out, sweetheart. Don't worry.''

Her mouth curved into a wry smile. Famous last words.

WITHIN A FEW DAYS, Amanda felt quite confident that she and Zach were doing a good job of running Diamond Ridge. She'd readjusted to the rhythm of the place—the daily routines, the activities, the meals, the ski lessons—and was enjoying the work.

She sat in her chair behind Ben's desk early one morning in the middle of her second week, and looked at Zach over the rim of her coffee cup as she took a sip. He was perched on the corner of his own desk, his hands around his ceramic ski mug, his head bent to it before he inhaled deeply.

''I can never decide if it's the aroma or the taste that I love more,'' he commented as he raised the cup to his mouth.

''It's the warmth!'' Amanda joked. She knew his routine by now. The first one up every day, Zach walked the property for a half hour just as the sun rose. She wondered what he expected to find on his cold forays, but she never asked. She only knew that he brought back with him the familiar scent of the outdoors and a warm smile, which he bestowed on her every morning when they met in the office. Their morning meetings had become part of the rhythm she felt. In fact, they were the first beat of the entire march.

"Karen taught me the computerized reservation system yesterday. I love it. You chose well, Zach."

"We *are* part of the modern world here, Ms. Amanda. Beneath the Currier and Ives exterior beats the heart of a competitive American company. And don't you forget it."

She believed him now that she'd had a chance to be part of the operation. Zach had computerized as much as possible, from the accounting systems to the weather-forecasting system. If only they had no debt. If only costs were less. If only Ben had made improvements all through the years. If only, if only. She sighed. A total waste of time thinking about *if only*'s.

"So, what's on your agenda today, Mandy?"

She detected the smile beneath his words, but Amanda needed a system to keep on top of everything. A morning agenda worked just fine.

"Number one on the list is Molly. We've got to crack down, Zach. If she's not scheduled to teach after school, she pulls a disappearing act. She came home after dark last night, skis over her shoulder. Who knows where she went?"

"It's not so easy, kiddo, is it?" Zach said. "When you're the one responsible."

She knew what he meant. The past flashed back in a nanosecond, and it was she arguing with her mother and Ben about needing her freedom. And what had they done? Instituted a curfew. That didn't work. Grounded her. Only worked while she was grounded.

Took away her skis. She walked the woods on snow-shoes. Finally, finally, they worked out a compromise. At the end of the afternoon, when all the paying skiers were off the lifts, between the day session and the night session, Ben skied with her. They didn't talk much. Amanda was too busy thinking at that time, adjusting to a new school, a new life, a new family.

"One of us has to go with her, Zach. It's the only way that might work."

"All right," he said slowly. "We'll try that first. And if she still persists in disappearing, we'll try something else."

Amanda checked her list. "Second item, we need another weekend instructor." She smiled. "Lots of guests, Zach, and they want lessons."

"So give the problem to Pete. He's running the school."

"He's the one who told me. He needs us to recruit, run an ad or whatever we have to do."

"So run the ad. And make sure whoever we take is certified or eligible for the exam. Tell Pete to sched-ule instructor classes and arrange for exams. Next."

Amanda scribbled furiously. "Linen service. Prices are going up."

"So negotiate, Counselor. Do your best. Anything else?"

"One more item. And you're taking care of it."

She got his attention then. "The chef. She's buying fancy. Expensive. We need apple pies. Not water-melon from Central America in the winter. You hired her. You talk to her."

"Okay, boss. Are you finished?"

Amanda nodded and brushed some errant strands of hair out of her eyes. "I've got to cut this."

Zach walked to her and brushed his fingers through the escaping tendrils.

"What are you doing?"

"Shh. Just hold still a second."

She saw his face tilt to one side, then to the other as his hands played with her hair. She reached up to stop him, but he stepped back, his mouth curving into an infectious grin.

"There's just no hope for it, Mandy. No matter which way I style it, you're still beautiful."

He meant to tease her. She knew it, but his words caressed her, instead. They were so unexpected, it took her a moment to absorb them. And when she finally did, her tears were unexpected, too.

"Consider that the last compliment I'll ever give you." Zach grabbed a tissue from his desk, knelt down and wiped Amanda's eyes. "Come on, honey, stop crying. I'm sure you've been called beautiful before."

Of course she had. All her adult life. But that was business. Strictly external packaging. This sounded so different. Intimate. Personal. Zach used to call her "funny face" sometimes, but beautiful? Never. So what had changed? Why the tears? Why was his compliment so important to her?

She took the tissue and blew her nose. "I'm fine. Let's continue with the agenda." She noted gratefully that he returned to his own chair.

"I only have one item on my list today, Mandy. The weather service is forecasting the possibility of a big storm by the weekend."

"What?" she squealed. "That can't be. We're booked solid." Her voice became a horrified whisper. "We have a load of people coming."

He nodded. "Well, they might come and they might not. We'll have to see."

She closed her eyes and chewed on her bottom lip. This was just what she'd been afraid of. "How often are the weather forecasters right, Zach? Maybe the storm will blow itself out to sea."

"Maybe."

His expression revealed nothing.

"You're humoring me, aren't you."

He looked sharply at her then and she knew the truth.

"Please don't treat me like a kid, Zach."

"Then don't ask for an easy way out. You said yourself, we can't control the weather. We have to roll with it. You've been terrific so far, but sometimes I don't know how much to push on you before you'll break."

"I'll never break, Zach. I'll just work harder. No matter how much I might worry about the Diamond, I won't break."

He looked at her intently as though assessing her words. "No one's complaining about your work ethic. You've put in as much effort as Ben would have. The difference between us, Mandy, lies in our outlook. When you think of a storm, you think of the money we lose on paying guests. When I think of a storm, I think about our options for heat and food, the condition of our generators, how often to plow the roads, communication systems, electricity, radios and organizing the Diamond to take care of the guests we do have.''

She left her chair and crossed to Zach's desk. She leaned forward and looked him square in the face. ''This place needs both considerations. Physical and financial. So get your holier-than-thou nose out of the air, Zach. There's no difference between us. We're both thinking about the same thing. It's called survival. And don't you forget it.''

She turned on her heel, ready to make a magnificent exit, when his voice stopped her in her tracks.

''And you get your financially driven mind back to the reality of a nor'easter,'' he said forcefully, ''when the winds blow down from Canada howling like wolves lonesome for their mates, and bringing with them enough icy snow to block the roads and damage power lines. I am responsible for the well-being of everyone on this property, Amanda, including you. If and when a storm comes up, you'll follow my lead to the letter—unless, of course, you want to take charge of all the arrangements I mentioned before. Have you operated a snowplow recently?''

He lowered his voice before continuing. ''If we don't survive the natural climate, my love, we'll never have the chance to survive the business climate.''

The heat went out of her argument. Not because of

Zach's logic, which was sound, but because of his two little words, "my love."

She'd never heard people argue and still use love words. The loud voices in her memory were ugly, the arguments unprotected. That was why she'd wanted to escape from the room earlier. She and Zach had been arguing, and leaving was safer. Her automatic response. But she wasn't seven years old anymore; she didn't have to hide. And Zach never really got angry; annoyed maybe, exasperated, but never mean-tempered. She ought to know that by now.

"Why are we fighting?" she whispered.

"Because that's what lawyers do?" Zach answered with a jocular note in his voice. He rolled his eyes heavenward and added, "They like conflict and you're a very good lawyer. So I guess it's all your fault."

His grin left no room for uncertainty. He loved teasing her, she discovered, and he was doing it again.

She sank into a visitor's chair, feeling very safe but still confused. Why could she storm ahead in New York, kowtowing to no one, appearing in court when necessary and fighting on her clients' behalf? Why could she do all that without blinking an eye, and yet crumple over a small difference of opinion at home?

"It's the rules," she whispered.

"What rules?"

"There are no rules here. I have rules in New York. The law provides strict rules of conduct in court. I'm not afraid there. Everyone has to live by the rules, and you win if you are a little cleverer, or better prepared, or occasionally, a little luckier. But you don't win just because you yell louder.''

Zach walked to where she sat and crouched on his heels in front of her. He took her hands in his and gently squeezed them.

"Do you remember the first year you lived here when I was a senior in high school and stayed out late with my buddies? And the next day Uncle Ben and I had a shouting match that could probably be heard all over the mountains. I yelled about needing my freedom, and Uncle Ben bellowed that he'd put a curfew on me.''

Amanda closed her eyes at the memory. "Yeah. I remember the yelling.''

"Do you remember what you did?''

"I ran?'' she guessed.

"You sure did. Right between us, screaming like a banshee and telling us to stop it. Skinny little you, crying and trembling like a leaf. But you shouted at Pops not to hit me. You were the bravest girl I ever saw.''

"Are you sure that was me?'' It certainly didn't sound like her.

"I'm sure.''

"What happened next?''

"Uncle Ben and I were so startled we shut up. I remember the silence and the surprise. I think you were surprised, too.''

"Did Pops ever hit you?''

"Of course not, Mandy. He never had in the past. He wasn't going to then. He was just worried about an adolescent boy who could have gotten into trouble driving around late at night. When people live together, there's always going to be disagreements. That's normal.''

''I understand that up here,'' she said, pointing to her head. ''But in here,'' she continued with her hand over her heart, ''it's scary.''

Zach pulled her out of the chair and held her loosely in his arms. She leaned into him just a little, borrowing some of his confidence.

''We do have a house rule here that might help,'' he said as he caressed her shoulders. ''I know how you appreciate a rule or two.''

''Mmm? What rule is that?''

''The rule is that we never go to bed angry. No matter what happens during the day.''

''I've never heard of that one, but I think I like it.''

He shook his head in disbelief. ''It's practiced by millions of families all over America. Where have you been?''

She shrugged. ''Don't know, but I'm here now.''

''Yes, you are,'' he replied as he held her more snugly. ''And here you'll...''

He stopped. Maybe he'd thought twice about finishing the sentence. But that was all right. She didn't want to think about tomorrow. In this personal environment, where she felt like a pioneer exploring uncharted territory, she preferred to take each day as it came.

CHAPTER SIX

THIRTY-SIX HOURS LATER, Zach stood in front of the lodge looking at the densely clouded night sky. A frosty twenty degrees had him wearing insulated gloves, but his head was bare, his jacket zipped only halfway up, as usual. He inhaled through his nose, allowing the cold air to warm before reaching his lungs. Breathing deeply again, he savored the lingering scent of the pines and firs standing sentry around the resort. The sweet smell of freedom.

He turned slowly, taking pleasure in the panoramic nightscape, until finally, he began his nocturnal stroll around the property.

God, he loved this place.

Ben and he used to walk together every evening before they turned in. Lily laughingly called them the "masters of all they surveyed," but love colored her words, and he knew she delighted in the men's relationship. She was a good woman who believed in family ties.

The thought stilled him. Family ties. Was that the reason he found himself thinking about Amanda all day? She was family, and as his temporary partner, she shared a home and Molly's care with him. Heck, he felt responsible for both of them. Was that the basis of his attraction? Family ties and responsibility wrapped in a package too alluring to ignore?

He smiled as he pictured her. Beautiful and vivacious—that was how he viewed Amanda's outer layers. He'd spent many restless nights thinking about her long legs, the sway of her hips when she walked and her luminous skin, her cheeks awash with gentle color. His daydreams captured her in action, too—the shy smile, her grace on skis, her intensity when arguing an opinion. Those outer layers could make any man stand at attention. Including him.

But it was her inner layers that intrigued him, her intelligence and complexity. The delightful Amanda, the affectionate Amanda, the frightened and brave Amanda—he'd glimpsed them all, appearing sporadically, momentarily dislodging the professional armor she wore.

He resumed his pace toward the chalet. He liked women a lot. He liked dating them. He enjoyed light romance. Ben teased him about sowing his wild oats before settling down. Zach hadn't looked beyond the wild-oats part.

"Nah," he'd said to his uncle. "I'll leave the settling down to you." And he'd meant it with all of his being.

Real love promised terrible pain, and he'd had enough of that. More than enough. Memories of his parents visited him almost every day.

Annie and Howard Porter had died instantly in the head-on crash. Zach remembered his uncle's tears at the funeral. His aunt Rose kissed him, cried and embraced him. And for almost a year, they were a new family.

Then his aunt got sick.

"It's just you and me, Zach," Ben had whispered after the second funeral. "We're the Porter family now. We'll manage. We'll be fine, son." Ben picked him up and hugged him close. "And that's a promise."

Zach hadn't believed him. How could he? His whole world had gone haywire twice, so how could he and Ben ever be fine again?

Zach took a deep breath and thought about the quiet years that followed. That was what he called them. The quiet years. Ben called them what they were: the grieving years. Until one day, while skiing slowly down a four-mile beginner's trail, Zach noticed how the snow glistened like diamonds in the sun. He heard the sparrows squawking at one another in the trees, felt the cool wind against his cheeks and smelled the resiny pine forest surrounding him. He snowplowed to a stop, looked at the world around him and grinned.

"It was me but it wasn't me," he explained to his uncle that night. "It's like I saw things in Technicolor, instead of gray."

"Thank God," Ben replied. "A new beginning. I didn't know if you'd ever find joy again."

So, in the end, he and Ben found themselves together, a couple of bachelors trying to manage a business.

So how had he allowed Amanda to sneak into his

heart in less than two weeks? His heart? The frigid air suddenly caught in his throat as he forgot to breathe, and he coughed. Had she crept into his heart? Panic surged as the truth overcame his disbelief. Why else was he keenly aware of her as he went about his tasks during the day? Why else did his pulse race when he spotted a blond cap of hair? Why else did he admire her brain at work even if she contradicted everything he said? She thought he was bullying her half the time. He exhaled in a *whoosh*. He hadn't meant for it to happen, but she had a way of getting under his skin.

He was looking at hurt down the road. He knew it just as surely as he knew his name. But he also knew he'd not resist the siren song of Amanda. The soft spot she occupied in his heart from long ago had reappeared and grown larger every day. No one was more surprised than he. Or more frightened.

Zach turned toward the lodge, now anxious to get home. Home. Where Amanda was.

"A NOR'EASTER IS COMING," Zach said two mornings later, "and it's coming today."

Amanda looked out the office window. Dawn could have been mistaken for dusk. No sun, no horizon, just a steel-gray outdoor ceiling. It would be cold, of course, but so far the trees stood tall and unbending. The wind hadn't started yet. Later on, if this storm held a true course, the wind-chill factor would be unbearable, and every creature—human and otherwise—would want to snuggle up at home.

"By the time it hits this afternoon, we may get a

full-blown blizzard.'' Zach paced the room as he spoke.

Amanda listened, not offering a word. She held a pad in front of her, waiting for orders. Zach's intense concentration was reflected everywhere—on his face, in his restless energy. This was not the time to quibble about who led and who followed.

He turned to her. "Get Molly in here, please. I don't care if she's still in bed. She can put on a robe and join us."

Amanda stood up. It was Friday, but school had been canceled because of a teacher-training day. "Sure, I'll get her, but why?" *So much for silently following orders.*

"She's got to know what's going on and that I mean business when I speak with her. No disappearing acts today. Maybe being rousted out of bed will make an impression." His last words were rushed as he answered the ringing phone.

"Karen? Yes, the electricity will probably go before the day's over. Bring your mom. We need you here. Absolutely. See you soon."

Amanda raised her brow in question.

"Karen's mother can't stay in a cold house. They don't have a generator. When their electricity goes out, and it will, they'll be without heat..."

"...and Mrs. Gallagher will suffer with her arthritis." Amanda finished the sentence for him.

"Well, yeah, and we have a generator that will assure heat, and we need Karen here. So it works out. Give them a room on the first floor."

Amanda winked. "You're a softie, Zach."

"Nah, just a good businessman. Now, will you please get Molly?"

But Molly wasn't in her room. Amanda found a scrawled note on the kitchen table.

"We ate oatmeal and went skiing on Steeplechase."

A knot formed in the pit of her stomach as she hurried back to the office.

"Molly's gone on the mountain with her friends from the ski team. Her sleepover is tonight, but I didn't realize the girls would arrive this early. I guess I should have—with school being closed. Their parents must have dropped them off on their way to work, knowing we were expecting them."

Zach glanced at his watch. "The lifts aren't operating yet, and the patrol isn't out. What could that child have been thinking?"

Amanda looked out the window. The day had brightened slightly. "The lifts are working, Zach. She must have started them up herself."

Zach grimaced and started pacing. "Molly is going to be one very sorry young lady…"

"I'll go bring them in now," Amanda offered.

"Hold on a minute," Zach said. "I changed my mind. It's not snowing yet. You and I have a lot to do this morning, so let them ski while they still can. Molly will find her way back for lunch."

For Amanda, the morning passed in a blur of activity. She loaded wood for fireplaces in each guest room, inventoried the kitchen for simple hot meals and tried to answer everyone's questions about the weather forecast.

"Forty rooms have been canceled," Karen said softly at noontime, "and about half our current guests checked out earlier today. Trying to beat the storm home."

Amanda winced at the lost business, then sighed. "I'm not surprised about the cancellations, but I think our guests would have been better off with us than on the roads."

"Not your call."

"I know." She pushed her fingers through her hair. "So, how many people are still here?"

"The hotel has about fifty folks, adults and children, and the cottages and condos have about the same."

Amanda immediately turned to Karen. "Move those people to rooms here at the hotel. Let's all stay together." She tapped her head with her finger. "Did I forget anything, Karen? Oh, look!" She waved toward the window. "The snow's started to fall. You'd better call them now."

She walked toward the front door and saw Zach trotting down the hall straight to her.

"Tell Molly I want to see her, please."

She'd almost forgotten about Molly! "I don't think she's come in yet, Zach."

"The lifts stopped running ten minutes ago. The patrol's almost all in. When Molly arrives, please send her to me in the office. I'll be checking on the latest weather information."

Amanda nodded, grabbed her jacket and cell phone, and walked outside. She scanned the area for a group of youngsters, one in a bright-orange ski jacket. She greeted a few intrepid skiers as they returned to the lodge, smiling at their unfaltering enthusiasm and at their lingering glances at the sky. There were always a few diehards in the crowd.

But the snow started in earnest then. The wind picked up, and icy needles stung her face as she continued to search the near slopes for Molly and her friends. Not a soul came into view. The earlier knot in her stomach returned threefold, and she intuitively knew that her sister had once again left the established alpine trails for the nature trails in the woods.

What bad judgment! Those trails were narrow paths that would be obliterated by the quickly falling snow. And how would the girls get back? There were no lifts where the woods ended. Only roads, which would be buried in snow.

She jogged to the end of the building and looked around the back, hoping the girls would be there. No luck. Well, there was only one thing to do. She continued to the kitchen door, then went through the kitchen and down the hall to her bedroom, her thoughts focusing on the weather and the girls. Some guardian she made.

She dressed as warmly as she could. Hat and hood, goggles, wool socks, ski gloves. She knew the area well; she'd find the girls before Zach even knew she was gone.

Exiting the back door, Amanda braced herself

against the snow and wind. Once inside the large garage, she easily found the array of snowmobiles. Smiling when she saw the full tanks of gas, she inwardly saluted Zach. He did know how to prepare for emergencies. She mounted a machine and walked it to the garage door. The thickly falling snow propelled her into action. She sat down and pressed the throttle with her thumb, relieved when the engine caught at once. She leaned forward, peering through the windscreen, and slowly started her descent to the trees.

IN HIS OFFICE, Zach sat in front of the computer, getting the latest readings from the regional weather station. He shook his head at the forecast. Worse than he expected. Amanda would be a wreck at the loss of business, but it couldn't be helped. He'd take this information into the dining room and share it with the guests. He'd reassure them about the resort's preparations and insist that they not leave the lodge for any reason until the storm had passed. In this kind of emergency, there was room for only one leader and he was it. He had the experience to support his decisions.

He started to rise when, from the corner of his eye, he spotted movement outside. He would have missed it if the night-lights hadn't illuminated a bright-pink ski parka and hood.

He leaped to his feet and pressed his face against the picture window. Amanda? That was Amanda's ski suit. What the hell did she think she was doing? He raced to the lobby. Last week she couldn't drive a car, and today she was shooting the hills on a snowmobile in a storm!

"Did the kids come in, Karen?"

"Not yet."

"So that's why Amanda's out there." Zach reversed direction and jogged back to the family's quarters. "I'm going after her," he called over his shoulder. "If Molly and her friends show up, tie them down with a rope!"

Five minutes later, Zach skimmed along the open hills as quickly as he could. The falling snow had almost obliterated Amanda's tracks in the little time it took him to dress and retrieve a machine. But enough of an imprint remained for him to follow. The thick flakes and wind interfered with his visibility, but he dismissed that problem. He knew the mountains as well as he knew his own face, and he knew which trails Molly enjoyed.

He opened throttle and pushed the machine to its limits while he was still on clear slopes. He hoped Amanda wouldn't cover ground as quickly, and he'd gain on her. But who knew what she'd do? Her professional armor had worn thin since she'd arrived. He'd been having a harder time predicting her reactions in the past few days.

He peered ahead but couldn't see her. Couldn't see anything because of the thick barrage of flakes. Couldn't reach the speed he wanted because of the wind. He kept trying, however, and slowed only as he entered the forested area, still following the depression made by Amanda's machine. The wind whipped through the bare trees, and Zach tugged the neck of his ski mask more firmly inside his jacket.

Where was she? The trail would wind for another three miles before opening onto the county road. He'd kill Molly for this stunt! He really would.

Damn, it was cold!

SHE COULDN'T FEEL her face. The snow and wind brutalized her unprotected skin. Only her eyes and head were shielded from the elements, and she berated herself for her stupidity. The thought of frostbite made her shudder. Why hadn't she grabbed a mask before she'd rushed out to find Molly?

Amanda reduced her speed and peered ahead through her goggles, trying to identify the girls' tracks. Difficult when riding face to the wind, vision marred by an unrelenting snowstorm. But she'd been lucky so far. Eight skis on a narrow trail left a track she'd been able to follow.

Following them became harder. The snow had accumulated faster than she'd thought possible, effectively wiping out evidence of the youngsters' presence. She looked through her goggles at the terrain around her. Everything seemed different in the false dusk, but she recognized the defined natural trail and resumed her ride.

If only she had a scarf to wrap around her face. She tried to smile, to wrinkle her nose and force silly expressions, anything to encourage circulation, but couldn't tell if she succeeded.

She lifted her gaze toward the invisible horizon and

suddenly saw a ski. One ski. Sticking up out of the snow as though planted there. She accelerated, and although she didn't recognize it, eagerly continued down the trail. Until she saw the second one. Molly's ski. Planted exactly like the first. But where were the girls? Amanda resumed her ride, slowly now, swiveling her head to search both sides of the path. And spotted a third ski. Then a fourth. A trail of skis meaning what?

The girls had to be on foot, or at least two of them were. The trail widened to open country and suddenly the woods were left behind. She hunched over the handlebars, shivering in the renewed fury of the wind and ice. Her old ski jacket was no match for this storm. She stopped the machine and covered her face with her gloved hands. Surveying the area, she saw four more skis pointed to the sky as though supplicating the heavens.

The girls had to be walking. Could their feet be any colder than hers? Vehicle idling, both feet on the ground, Amanda sank back on the seat, tucked her chin into her chest and covered her face with both arms. Just for a minute. She needed to warm her face for just a minute. And then she'd continue to the road and home. Only three miles back to Diamond Ridge.

Maybe the plow had already cleared the road. Maybe one of the drivers had taken Molly and her friends in a truck. She should pull her hat off and cover her face with it. That was what she should do. Yes. She still had a hood for her head. A hood for her head. Sounded like a poem. *Get moving, Amanda.*

Time to get moving or she'd turn into a snowman. Or was she a snowwoman? Did it really matter? She closed her eyes, her thoughts drifting. The snowmobile lurched forward, hit a mogul and tipped over. Amanda lay in the snow.

Use the phone, Amanda. Use the phone. She pushed herself to her knees, slowly straightened, and reached into her pocket. *Concentrate!* She carefully pulled out the cellular, then stared in dismay at the shattered remains of her lifeline.

What now? First Molly. Then her. Poor Zach. And a hundred guests to worry about. She'd screwed up. Always screwed up with him and Molly and everyone here. She pictured him pacing his office, pacing the lodge, checking the family kitchen, wondering where she was. If he could see her now, he'd realize she belonged in the city. Instead of helping, she wound up causing him more trouble.

Her eyes filled. *I'm sorry, Zach. So sorry.* She'd apologize—profusely—when she saw him again. *When you love someone, you shouldn't cause them pain.* Startled, she almost fell again. Love? Amanda Shaw in love? What a concept! She tried to laugh, but the truth slammed her in the solar plexus.

She loved him, and that frightened her just as much as the storm did. Maybe more.

She looked toward the road hoping it had been cleared. She couldn't tell through the whirling snow. But she had to get back on the snowmobile, no matter how cold and tired, or numb. She flailed her arms to improve her blood flow, reached for the machine, and then heard the roar of an engine approaching from behind.

She twisted around and there he was. Zach. As though conjured up from a dream. Mask, goggles, hat, and bundled for the weather. The clothes didn't matter. She'd recognize him anywhere, how he moved, how he acted and how quickly he reacted.

He brought his machine to a stop and ran toward her with unbounded energy.

"Don't ever run off again, you crazy woman, without telling anyone!"

His strong voice carried over the wind, but she ignored his words and looked at him imploringly. "Please. I'm cold. My face."

"What have you done, Mandy-girl, what have you done?" he whispered as he pulled her toward him, unzipped his jacket and drew her in. "Lean on me. Put that beautiful face right under my arm and I'll hold you."

She snuggled against his sweater, cut off from the whirling elements by the safe haven he provided. Her arms crept around his back and she could have stayed in his embrace forever. He rocked her, rocked them both as they stood defying the storm.

"Stamp your feet, Mandy. Get the blood going."

Left foot. Right foot. Left. Right.

"Now walk with me to my machine. I've got some woolens under the seat for you. Keep close to me and I'll lead you."

She shook her head and pulled back. "The girls, Zach. We have to find the girls."

He pulled her beneath his jacket again and started to walk. "We will, Mandy. In fact," he said slowly, "I think they're just ahead of us. The tips of their skis are pointed toward the road. Where else could they go?"

She nodded and followed, stopping when he did. She leaned with him as he reached down, and suddenly she was erect, her goggles off, a woolen mask slipped over her head with a scarf, warm from lying next to the motor, wound around her. She could barely see.

"We're going home, sweetheart." Zach replaced her eye goggles as he spoke. "Together."

"Okay." She started to walk back to her snowmobile.

He grabbed her arm. "No, Mandy. You're riding double with me. These machines are made for two."

Good idea. She'd probably fall off again, anyway, if she was alone.

She needed his assistance to climb on, but when he actually roped them together, she knew she was in worse shape than she'd thought.

"Hold me around the waist as tight as you can and squeeze. Let me feel your strength."

She tried. She kept trying as Zach maneuvered his machine to the road, as they passed the four remaining skis Molly and her friends had left, as he gave thanks to the public-works crews who had already plowed and as he made his way around curves and up rises, following the road home.

The ride seemed to take forever, but suddenly she

was in the kitchen. The familiar, warm, homey country kitchen, standing in the middle of the floor watching Zach pull off his own headgear and jacket before undressing her.

He wasted no movements as he unwound the big woolen scarf, removed the ski mask and unzipped her jacket. With brows set in a straight line, he examined her intently. He placed his fingers on her cheeks. She barely felt their gentle pressure, but it was enough to engender relief.

"I'm not totally numb. I'll be okay," she whispered. "No major frostbite."

"But you'll be in for serious discomfort as you thaw. Let's get the boots off."

She waddled to a nearby chair and let Zach continue his work. Her eyes closed as his warm hands took her feet and massaged them gently. First her toes, then her arches, her heels. Her feet tingled painfully as full circulation slowly returned. Then Zach's talented thumbs pressed and released the padded bottoms of her toes. Pressed and released. It was heaven. Little by little her entire body relaxed. Sleep almost claimed her when she recalled her thoughts as she'd stood half-frozen in the woods.

She lifted her lashes with effort and watched Zach care for her. As though she was special. He could have wrapped her in blankets and left her alone to thaw out. But he didn't.

"Zachary." She whispered his name as though tasting its flavor for the first time. And savoring it.

He lifted his head immediately, a question in his eyes. And she held them with her own.

"I'm sorry." Her tears surprised her and she swiftly brushed them away.

"I know," he said, still stroking her feet. "I know, and you should be."

The twinkle in his eyes turned to warmth, then to heat. He continued to stare at her, and suddenly any chill remaining in her body was replaced by red-hot fire. Her hand lifted toward him, slowly, hesitatingly, as though needing to find its way. Just like her.

HE WATCHED HER HAND reach out to him, so delicate-looking with its narrow wrist and tapered fingers, almost a child's hand—smooth skin, sweet and vulnerable. He wanted to run. As fast and as far as he could, but his legs remained planted on the floor.

Fear held him fast. Fear of a woman half his size, and stubborn to boot. A woman who had her own ideas about everything and whose ideas did not match his. A half-frozen woman with the ability to make his heart stop.

When he'd spotted her through the blinding snow, falling to the ground, his imagination ran wild and rage almost spun him out of control. He'd hurled curses at the fates and, had he been a beast of the forest, would have howled until every creature heard his song. Not again. Not again. Not to someone he loved.

But now, in the warm kitchen, he reached for the hand she held out.

"Sweetheart," he whispered, "I think you're finally home."

AMANDA FELT A SMILE slowly emerge and evolve into a grin. Her hand fit perfectly in his, and felt wonderful there. He gently rubbed and massaged it as she returned the pressure.

And then reality checked in when the telephone rang.

In less than a minute, footsteps sounded in the hallway outside the kitchen. Amanda turned to the entrance.

"Tom?" she asked, confused, as the doctor entered the room and made a beeline for her.

"I warmed her up as well as I could, but you'd better take a professional look," Zach said.

"How did you get here? Why are you here?" Amanda asked.

"I picked up four young girls a while ago on my way back from the hospital. Molly and her friends, on the side of the road, walking in a snowstorm after skiing all morning in below-freezing temperatures. They're all in the bathroom, dangling their feet in a tub of warm water, and now you come in looking as bad as they did."

All Amanda heard was the word *girls*. "Molly's here? Her friends are here?" When Tom nodded, she burst into tears and started to shake.

"Why are you crying now? They're safe!" Zach said as he leaned over her once more.

"I know. I don't know. I was so scared for her and I'm so relieved now." She wiped her eyes.

"Go change your own clothes, Zach," Tom said as he approached Amanda. "Take a warm shower and let me look at this patient. Seems like I should set up a satellite center here."

"Not for me, Doc. I'm just fine." Zach whistled as he left the room.

Two hours later, in the hotel dining room, Amanda scanned the tired, but healthy-looking faces around the dinner table. Only Mrs. Gallagher, who befriended everyone she met, had enough energy to hold a decent conversation. Molly and company, attired in sweat suits, bulky socks and a layer of remorse, strove to stay awake.

"Daddy is going to be mad when you tell him about this."

Amanda glanced at her sister. Molly's voice sounded so young, her eyes looked so worried. Amanda wanted to wrap the girl in her arms and kiss away her troubles. But that wouldn't accomplish anything.

"I'm not going to tell him, Mol," Amanda said. "*You* are, when the time is right. Meanwhile, you'll have to deal with Zach and me, your coach and your friends."

Molly picked up her soup spoon. "Mmm. I think I'd rather deal with Daddy."

"It was all Molly's idea." A young brunette ratted on her.

"Yeah, it was," a green-eyed blonde confirmed.

"But we followed her without even thinking."

Amanda acknowledged Molly's loyal sidekick with a raised brow. Petite Stephanie was a daredevil athlete who'd trade her schoolbooks for skis, skates or a bicycle in a New York minute.

Molly put her spoon down and faced her friends. "No," she said. "It was me who didn't think. I'm the captain, but today I wasn't a good leader. I should have been smarter. I'm…I'm sorry."

Molly turned to Amanda then, misery clearly written on her face.

Amanda reached for her hand. "But you are a leader, Mol. Leaders take responsibility when they make mistakes, and you've just done that. And since almost half the ski team is involved, you'll own up to your coach, as well." She leaned toward Molly and whispered, "I'm proud of you, honey. You're doing the right thing."

Molly's unexpected sobs caught Amanda totally by surprise. And when her sister ran from the room, Amanda followed. She found her lying across her bed, weeping loudly.

Amanda knelt beside Molly and rubbed her back. "Talk to me, Mol. What's wrong?"

Molly's face remained in the pillow, her shoulders still shaking.

"Are you afraid of what your coach will say? Or do? He may bench you for a couple of weeks."

Her sister shook her head. "He may…" The rest was unintelligible to Amanda.

"Turn over, Molly, and look at me. I can't understand you."

Molly complied, tears pooling in her eyes and running down her face. "I bet Coach won't let me be captain anymore, but I don't care about that, either."

Amanda was totally bewildered. "Then what's wrong? Why are you still crying?"

Fresh tears spurted as Molly turned into her pillow again.

"It's y-you. You came after me in a big storm and almost got lost. You almost got bad frostbite. You could have died. Why? Why'd you come after me? You don't even like me very much."

Stunned, Amanda couldn't move. "Not like you?" She leaned over and wrapped her arms around Molly. "I came after you because I love you. You're my little sister and I love you."

Molly bolted upright. Amanda moved back just in time to avoid getting smacked in the mouth.

"You do?" Molly asked.

"Of course I do."

Molly stared at her as though she'd never seen her before. Finally, a wide grin crossed the youngster's face. "Cool."

Cool? After all that emotion, her sister resolved it with one little word?

Molly got up from the bed and walked to the mirror. "Ugh. This face needs help." She turned toward Amanda. "So if you followed me because you love me, and Zach followed you—" she grinned again "—then he must love you."

Amanda felt a blush rise from her chest to her face. More complications! "We're family, Mol. Family members look out for one another. That's all."

"Well, well. She finally got it." Molly looked at the ceiling. "That's what I've been trying to tell you all this time. You are not a very good student, Amanda."

Amanda watched her sister flounce from the room and started to laugh. Molly had hit on the exact truth. Despite her high grades in school, Amanda had flunked where it mattered most. But not anymore. No more hiding from "messy emotions." No more using work to shield her from a personal life.

She closed her eyes and thought of Zach. Electrical currents danced to her fingertips and toes. Was this love? Was Amanda Shaw actually falling in love?

CHAPTER SEVEN

AMANDA RETURNED to the dining room for a cup of coffee. All the guests were still seated, bodies slightly forward in their chairs, as they focused their collective gaze on one man. Zach.

He stood in front of the crowd, totally relaxed, as if public speaking was something he did every day. Amanda sighed in admiration. She always reviewed her prepared speeches repeatedly before presenting, even if only before one judge. But Zach stood there, long legs encased in well-worn jeans and scuffed boots, looking as carefree as a kid throwing his line into the local fishing hole during the high days of summer.

She sat back in her seat, anticipating the pleasure of watching him in action. His scruffy beard gave him a rakish touch, and his square-cut jaw was strong and masculine. Her eyes moved to his mouth. A firm mouth, well-defined, the corners usually lifted in a smile. How would that inviting, sexy mouth feel on hers? Her vision blurred as she sank into her dreams. Time flowed through her until she felt a tap on her shoulder and heard a familiar young voice speaking impatiently in her ear. Startled, she blinked rapidly at

Molly, and the room came back into focus. She heard Zach repeat her name as he beckoned her to join him.

"For those of you who haven't met her yet, this is my partner and a member of the Porter family, Amanda Shaw. Amanda was raised at the Diamond. Knows the hotel business inside out. And has weathered storms as bad as this one and worse."

Amanda slowly made her way to his side. He should have prepared her. She had no idea what he was going to say next.

"Now, it's a funny thing about snowstorms," he continued. "They can be exciting and they can be dangerous, but when they're all over, we have a heck of a lot of snow to ski on."

The guests cheered.

"So for all of you who can stay an extra day to ski when the hootin' and hollerin' are finished, your current lift ticket will be honored and the room is on the house."

The cheers were joined by whistles and applause.

He's crazy. We've had forty cancellations, we haven't gotten through the storm yet, and he's giving rooms away!

"Now, we've got plenty of food and a strong generator backup when the electricity goes out. Unfortunately, if the phone lines go down, we may be without service for a couple of days. Amanda's going to tell you about some adjustments in our activities due to the small staff that's here now."

"And what would they be?" she asked under her

breath. *She'd kill him before the storm was over, despite her lovely daydreams.*

"Buffet meals, do-it-yourself linen. You know the routine. Nothing much has changed in those departments."

Of course she knew the routine. It had just been a long time since she'd executed it. She smiled at the guests, started explaining and suddenly felt like a hostess, the way her mother must feel year round.

"Our chef is here, but we'll be keeping it simple. She has only one helper and there's still a hundred of us. So if any of you have ever been curious about what a professional kitchen is like, you're invited to find out...and help out."

She looked at the group, satisfied that she had their attention. "Remember, tomorrow's an indoor day. You'll want to be busy."

She glanced at Zach. If he could give away rooms, she could extract some free labor!

"I'll help out wherever you are, Amanda," called an eager twenty-something.

"Ignore him and take me. I work harder and I play harder," seconded a voice from the same table.

Amanda laughed. She could handle harmless comments from young males in high spirits. She'd always been good at thwarting advances.

"I'm sure you're all a great bunch—"

"—of poker players," Zach interjected. "Card room is set up for poker, bridge, canasta or any game you want to try. Pool tables, too. Help yourselves."

Amanda raised her eyebrow at the interjection.

She'd been standing on her own for a long time; she didn't need any help now.

Zach lifted his hand for silence and scanned the entire crowd again. "We will do everything possible to provide a safe and happy environment for the duration of this bad weather. In return, we expect you to abide by the rules. And the first one is, no one leaves the building for any reason until the storm is over.

"My staff and I will plow the hotel road and parking areas all through the night. We are the only ones allowed outdoors. Any questions?"

The overhead lights flickered just then, and the assembled guests emitted a collective gasp of surprise.

Amanda instinctively searched for Molly at their table. Her sister was huddled in conference with her troop, but looked up just in time to meet Amanda's gaze. Her eyes sparkled, and a smile lifted the corners of her mouth. She looked like the confident, secure girl she usually was.

A quick recovery from the day's adventure, Amanda thought, as she returned Molly's smile. Just as well.

Molly left her chair then and headed toward her guardians at the front of the room. She squeezed Amanda's hand, but tugged on Zach's arm until he bent down to listen to her. "Please, Zach, introduce me, too. I'm part of the family and I can help tomorrow. I have a great idea."

Zach spoke quietly. "You, young lady, are lucky you're not in the corner eating curds and whey for the great idea you had this morning. Don't you think that one Molly idea a day is enough?''

Amanda's heart twisted at the plea in Molly's eyes. Anyone could see that Zach meant the world to her. He was a brother, a cousin and now a father all rolled into one. She started to intervene when Zach placed Molly in front of him, his hands gently resting on her shoulders.

''Here's the youngest member of the Porter family, folks. She says she can help us. I haven't heard her idea yet, but knowing Molly, it's got to be interesting.'' He tousled her hair. ''Go for it.''

Molly stepped forward with all the aplomb of Dale Carnegie. ''My friends and I are going to run a day camp tomorrow for all the kids here. I did it last summer. Zach called it Camp Run-a-Muck, but he was only joking.''

Molly's attention remained on the guests during the laughter that followed. Amanda, chuckling herself, admired Molly as she waited for the crowd to fall silent.

She looked at Zach. ''Camp Run-a-Muck?''

''It's an old joke,'' he whispered. ''She kept those kids so busy, ran them so ragged, they slept all through the night every night. The mothers were grateful, and Molly earned a lot of money in tips.'' He paused and met Molly's gaze. ''Not this time,'' he said. ''No tips this time.''

Just as giving away rooms went against her grain, so did giving away services. But Amanda nodded. After what happened today, Molly couldn't be rewarded. Amanda tuned in once again to her sister.

"We'll start tomorrow at ten o'clock," Molly said. "And there will be no charge for the camp. And no gra-gra..." She turned to Zach. "What's that word that means tips?"

Oh, her sister was smart! "She told the guests before you could," Amanda whispered with delight after Zach answered Molly's question.

"Sure she did. Hair shirts are mighty uncomfortable." He reached for Molly and pulled her toward him. "I'm proud of you, Popcorn Girl."

Molly hugged him. As Amanda watched, two tears slowly trickled down her sister's face. The intrepid Molly needed the love and approval of the people she cared about. That was a feeling Amanda was getting used to herself.

IT WAS ALMOST MIDNIGHT, and Amanda should have been exhausted. She sat on her bed in purple sweats, leaning against the window frame, watching the snow continue to fall. This was the first moment all evening that she'd had time to sit down.

The cleanup after dinner had proved challenging. Molly and her friends were really too tired to be much help, and Amanda had sent them to bed shortly after the meal. Besides which, as Molly explained, "They had to plan their activities for camp."

When Amanda had checked on them a short time later, they lay sprawled across Molly's double bed, heads and feet in every direction, with blankets and sleeping bags piled high. Their deep breathing reflected their fatigue.

Some of the guests had helped, but Amanda shouldered the major responsibility. Stacking plates, loading dishwashers and organizing for the next meal. Karen had joined her in the kitchen later on, tired herself and worried about Tom, who had left after treating the adventurers.

"He was nuts to try to get to the hospital in this weather, even if they were short-staffed. He should have stayed right here where it's safe," she fumed.

Amanda looked at her sympathetically. "He's very dedicated to his patients, Karen, and to his profession. From what I can see, he's not the type to refuse a call for help."

Pride displaced the anger in Karen's face. "I know," she said softly. "It's part of what I love about him. But it shouldn't occlude his common sense!"

"Common sense seems to be a rare commodity around here," Amanda grumbled. "Zach virtually gave away thousands of dollars to our guests with his promise of an extra day's stay at no charge."

Karen's silence was more powerful than speech, and Amanda looked at her impatiently.

"Come on, Karen. We don't guarantee the weather when people plan vacations here. Sometimes you're lucky and sometimes you're not. But we don't have to feel guilty about the storm and give away rooms."

"It's not guilt, Amanda. It's marketing. It's people."

Amanda shook her head. "It's money out the door. And we can't afford it. We're already taking a beating with all the cancellations."

"You're wrong, my friend. It's return on investment." Karen started pacing. "Look, he's taking a negative situation and spinning a positive one. These people will think Diamond Ridge has heart, has great owners, that it's the best place in the mountains. Most of them probably won't be able to stay, anyway, but they'll tell their friends about how they were treated. Word-of-mouth advertising is incalculable."

Looking out her bedroom window that night, Amanda had to admit that Karen's take on the situation was probably right. Zach seemed to know all the angles, while all she seemed to do was panic. So maybe he was right about the loans, and about the huge expansion he'd encouraged.

She heard the thump of the kitchen door and felt her body relax instantly. Zach had finally come in from the cold.

HE HEARD THE *SWOOSH* of her slippers a second before he saw them—furry and pink—while he was removing his boots. He deliberately forced himself to raise his eyes slowly, to savor the woman he would find. Pink feet and purple long johns, not very sexy—on anyone else. But Amanda's never-ending legs made fleece something to reckon with.

The long shirt skimmed her hips, those hips that drove him to distraction every day as he watched her walk through the hotel. For a moment, he pictured her legs bare, with only the sweatshirt for cover. Instantly, he ached. He throbbed. He kept his jacket on.

"Why are you still up?" His voice sounded gruff, even to his own ears.

"Oh, Zach," she said. "Are you getting a sore throat?" Running to him, she reached for his forehead.

It was the sweetest gesture she'd made to him since she'd returned to the Diamond. Instinctively, he snagged her by the waist and hauled her onto his lap as he sat down. He didn't respond to her question, but nuzzled her neck, instead.

Amanda quivered, then froze. The stillness in the room was repeated in the stillness of her posture. The clock's ticking almost hurt her ears.

She turned on his lap then, and stared into the depths of those sooty-gray eyes. He sat motionless. She searched and found warmth, tenderness, a faint passion.

"Zach?"

"Yes?"

"What's going on?"

And now she felt herself being studied as though she were under a microscope. A wary expression flashed across his face, and she lowered her gaze to her lap.

"Hey, sweetheart." His hands caressed her cheeks. "Look at me again. Please."

She did. And saw his eyes darken with emotion, with eagerness.

"What's going on?" he asked rhetorically. "I'm not sure. But I'd like us to find out together."

She nodded.

"And you know what else, Amanda?"

She waited.

"I'm pretty damn scared."

Zach almost laughed out loud at her stunned expression. Wide-eyed amazement that was almost comical. He swallowed his chuckles and, instead, stroked her hair, silky and soft. Then his fingers explored the ridge of her straight nose, and finally outlined those lips that had always enticed him. Her tongue tasted his fingertip; he forgot to breathe.

Easy, boy, easy.

He leaned over and kissed her lightly on the forehead, then moved on to her smooth cheek and down to her tempting mouth. Gently at first, and then, when he felt her tentative response, he allowed his hunger to show. She answered him with a sweet demand of her own. He felt her tongue brush his lips.

His heart beat in triple time. Amanda felt wonderful in his arms. He inhaled her scent and kissed her again. Until he felt her pushing him away.

She jumped from his lap and looked toward the hall. "No more, Zach, no more." Her voice quivered only slightly as she turned back toward him. "Good night." And then she was gone.

He watched her leave—long strides, body erect—seeming totally in control. He closed his eyes and slumped in his chair. It had been a long day, an emotional day, a life-and-death kind of day. He'd handled it. But he couldn't make sense of what just happened.

AMANDA PUT ONE FOOT in front of the other until she reached her room. The distance seemed like miles.

Once inside, she leaned against the closed door as her legs turned to rubber. She wanted to slide to the floor, but forced herself to walk to her bed and get in.

The wind continued to howl in the cold, moonless night, and not even a shadow at the window kept Amanda company. She would have welcomed the distraction, because all her thoughts and feelings at the moment centered on Zach. She closed her eyes and was visited by a collage of memories, each scene tumbling over the last.

She remembered her girlhood crush. Almost fifteen, she'd lived under the same roof with him for about a year before she began to trust him. Big, strong men like Zach and Ben were not high on her list of people to trust in those days.

But eventually, her fear of Zach had turned to admiration. And then to teenage fantasies. What would it be like to kiss him?

She hadn't thought about those dreams in years. Her life had moved on. But now she knew the answer to the question. His kisses were wonderful, so wonderful she wanted more. She loved the solid feel of him against her and of being held in his arms. But she'd spent ten years preparing herself for the life she wanted, the life she was meant to lead. She and Zach had chosen different paths, and she could only travel one of them.

She'd never questioned herself, had always believed she was right in her choices. Until now. Until she'd felt his arms encircling her, embracing her the way a man holds a woman he cares about. A special woman.

She'd felt both excited and secure in his embrace. The reality was better than her fantasies. And that made her pause.

Was she revisiting comfortable old memories, or was she simply grateful for his rescue that afternoon? Or could it be the beginning of love?

She just didn't know.

AMANDA DID KNOW, however, that life at the Diamond had to go on as usual. With two cups of early-morning coffee in her hand, she made her way to the office. Zach stood up from his desk, the corners of his mouth lifting in a smile, his eyes studying her, as he reached for his caffeine fix.

She glanced at him, then quickly looked away, memories of the night before still too vivid in her mind. Memories of the day, as well. Finally, she raised her head and met his gaze.

"I never did thank you properly for rescuing me yesterday," she said softly. "Freezing alone on a mountainside is not my idea of winter fun."

"Don't think about it anymore," Zach replied, as he stepped closer to her and looked into her eyes. "It's over, Mandy, and you're okay."

"Thanks to you," she whispered. "So, I'd like to treat you to the best dinner in town."

"It's not necessary," he replied.

"I know," she answered, "but I want to. No arguing. We'll go as soon as things get back to normal around here."

A grin crossed his face. "So," he said, "are we going on a date?"

She felt heat rise from her neck to the top of her head. "A…a date?" she stammered. "Dinner, Zach, just dinner."

"Whatever you say, boss. Now, let's get to work. We've got another long day ahead."

She nodded as he outlined the plans for keeping everyone safe and sound. She watched his lips move, and pictured them against her mouth. She heard the sounds he spoke, but focused only on the words *are we going on a date?*

Is that what he really wanted? Is that what *she* wanted?

Her attention returned to his to-do list. Meals to be prepared, rooms to be cleaned, roads to be plowed, phone lines to be checked. It was endless. Where were the law briefs? The meetings? The strategy sessions? The cases? That's what she'd gone to school for. That's why she'd chosen New York.

She looked around the office and then through the window. Living in Vermont had never been part of her long-term plan. It had been a good place for her mother's second chance at love, but to Amanda, it was a temporary period away from the big city.

She knew that loving someone came at a price. But she was certainly not ready to pay that price. A quiet dinner with Zach would be just a dinner. A chance to strengthen family ties. Nothing more.

LATER THAT MORNING, Amanda gazed out the window of Molly's bedroom. Snow blanketed the world and was still falling. The phone lines were down, and only the generator provided some vestiges of modern convenience. The picture-postcard beauty of the moment belied the true situation. Impassable roads, no emergency service, unskiable trails, broken lift cables, plenty of work, short staff, no new business and mountains of bills.

Amanda glanced at her sister, tossing in bed, cheeks flushed. Molly was sick, the only youngster who was. Her little foray into the woods yesterday had taken its toll in the middle of the night. Her high fever and croupy cough had Amanda worried. Dr. Hunter wasn't on the premises, and he certainly couldn't get through.

Amanda walked to Molly's bed, placed her hand on her sister's forehead and winced. The child burned. Poor kid would be laid up for several days at least.

Mr. Garroway was expecting Amanda back at work in two days. Hopefully, he'd learn about the storm from national weather reports. Maybe he'd tried to reach her on the cell phone, and hadn't realized it was broken. It hardly mattered. Molly was so sick Amanda couldn't think of leaving.

Three hours later, still worried, she tracked down Zach in the office.

"How many aspirin can I give her? She's still hot. And do we have anything else for cough other than this baby stuff I found?"

"There's a medicine cabinet in the corner closet," he said. "But stick with the recommended dosage until we can ask Tom."

She walked across the room to do what he suggested. "I've got to stay with her, Zach. I can't leave her alone."

"Okay," he replied. "I'll handle everything else. Look outside. The snow's stopping. Conditions should improve by tomorrow. Maybe life will be back to normal then."

"Don't hold your breath. Molly's going to take a while to recover. She's really sick."

Zach approached her and put his hands on her shoulders. "Between the two of us, we'll get through this. We're a powerful team. In the morning, we'll have a full staff meeting and see where we stand."

At ten the next morning, Amanda dragged herself to the office. Her eyes felt gritty, her muscles stiff. Karen's mom was with Molly now, but Amanda had been up most of the night with the girl.

Zach was speaking. "Power came back on an hour ago. The Highway Department is plowing the main county roads. We should be able to get out to groom slopes and check and repair the lifts. New guests should be arriving in a day or so. The fresh snowfall should bring them in droves."

He looked at the audience and at Amanda. "Any questions?"

The phone rang on cue.

They all laughed, Amanda included. "Guess we know the phones are back." Zach picked up the receiver and motioned to Amanda. "It's your boss." He looked at the rest of the crew. "If there are no questions, meeting's over."

Amanda almost hobbled to her desk. She'd never felt this exhausted working late in the city. Right now, she felt like anything but an up-and-coming lawyer, and she knew she'd be lucky to string two sentences together.

"Good morning, Mr. Garroway," she said.

"I've been concerned about you, Amanda. Haven't heard from you lately, and then this storm cut you off. Couldn't reach you by cellular, either. What happened?"

"Sorry," she replied. "My phone broke just before the storm blew in."

"By the looks of the weather, you'll need a couple of days to get back. So shall we say Wednesday or Thursday?"

Amanda took a deep breath and crossed her fingers for luck. "Actually, Mr. Garroway, I need a couple of weeks. My sister's ill with possible pneumonia. The hotel needs to get back to normal, as well."

"I see," her boss replied slowly. "That's too bad. But not all is lost. I've been researching schools for your sister. Will she be ready in two weeks?"

"We're working on it."

"Good. Sarah can continue handling your cases. She's doing a good job. Keep in touch."

Amanda hung up, confused and dismayed.

"What's going on, Mandy?" Zach asked.

"Nothing much. Just reality hitting me full force. My vacation's over, but I just bought two more weeks because of Molly."

"And then what?"

"I go back to the city. With Molly." She forced a smile. "It'll all work out."

CHAPTER EIGHT

ONE WEEK LATER, Molly was almost back to her energetic self. The snowstorm was history, but the slopes remained in perfect condition for downhill skiing. Amanda glanced at the reservations, pleased to note the hotel was booked to capacity for the upcoming weekend. Yes! This was what they needed. With a bounce in her step, she waved to the evening reception clerk and retired to the family quarters.

She'd check on Molly first and then find Zach. She was looking forward to her dinner date with him. She needed a change of scene, a change of routine. That was all. Her excitement had nothing to do with an opportunity to be with Zach alone.

The week since her rescue had been…interesting. She and Zach had tackled the responsibilities as if they'd worked together for years. Which, in a way, they had. But now there was a difference. At the end of the day, they often relaxed together in front of the hotel's big fireplace, sometimes alone, sometimes with their guests. His hand seemed to find hers as they sat together on the sofa. She swore his lips brushed the top of her head a dozen times during the week. And his eyes seemed to laugh, then study her feature by

feature as if memorizing her face. Their relationship
had gotten stronger. Now they were more than friends.
They were good friends. Her mom and Ben would be
pleased.

She walked into the kitchen to find Molly on the
phone, eyes glowing with excitement, instead of fever.

"Really? Really, Mom? Oh, Amanda's here. Can I
tell her?" Her sister twirled around, wrapping the telephone cord around her. "Guess what, Amanda?
Daddy wants to see me. Mom said I could go to New
York for a visit. Maybe I'll have to miss school and
everything."

"Then Pops must be feeling better, Mol." Amanda
smiled as she reached for the phone.

"Hi, Mom. Is there some good news?" With Molly
at her side, Amanda listened to Lily's explanation and
forced her grin to remain in place. Nothing was ever
simple. Ben's efforts in therapy showed slow results.
To be expected, they said, but the use of a walker was
in his long-term future. Skiing was out of the question
indefinitely. And Lily had taken a nursing job at the
rehab center.

"A job, Mom?" Amanda asked as she ruffled
Molly's hair. "Isn't Pops keeping you busy enough?"
What was going on in New York? Her mother hadn't
had an outside job since she'd married Ben. "Well,
you sure fooled me. I didn't know you still had your
license."

Lily's voice came in clearly over the phone line. "I
worked very hard to become an RN, Amanda. I'd

never let my license expire. One never knows when the ability to earn a living might come in handy.''

Amanda kept her grin pasted on her face, but her stomach clenched, not only at the words, but at the forced gaiety in her mother's voice. Why was Lily so concerned about money? It hadn't been that long since Ben's stroke, and Lily wasn't one to borrow trouble. Amanda needed to speak to Zach. She hung up the phone without telling Lily about the efforts to find a school for Molly.

An hour later, with Molly finally asleep, she found Zach still in the office, feet propped on the desk and eyes closed. Her heart softened as she looked at him in repose, the picture of a hardworking man at the end of a long day. After their weeks together, Amanda now appreciated how committed he was to Diamond Ridge. He gave a 110 percent of himself every day, always with a smile and a friendly greeting to everyone he encountered.

She approached quietly and set the mugs of hot tea she'd brought on the desk.

One eye opened. Then the other. Two twinkles appeared, followed by a smile. ''An angel with Earl Grey.'' His feet hit the floor as he sat up and reached for the tea.

She allowed him a minute to enjoy the beverage before speaking.

''I just talked to my mother. Something's going on in New York.''

She got his full attention and continued, ''Not only

did she take a nursing job in the hospital Pops is in, but she's talking about how beautiful the city is. How everything is so convenient. How easy it is to get around. The synergy, the people, the museums.''

She stopped to gather her thoughts and then turned toward him. ''Molly's going there for what she thinks is a visit, but Mom told me she's·going to watch her reactions, see how she likes it. Zach, what do you think?''

His brow raised. ''I think Lily sounds like a tourist. Only considering the pluses.''

''Is that all it is?''

He held her gaze. ''I'm not sure, Mandy. But I do know that there's an important voice missing here.''

She inclined her head.

''Ben's. What has he got to say?''

She shrugged. ''Mom didn't actually mention him, except to say that recovery is slow.''

''Well, I've been around them for the last five years. They make family decisions together. Sounds to me like Lily's putting the best face on things.''

''And she's making sense.'' Pacing again, Amanda ticked her reasons off on her fingers. ''Pops needs to use a walker, and he's better off in a city. He can't ski anymore. His doctors are there. She's got a job— I never knew she worried about money, but with the Diamond in debt, who knows—and Molly'll have so many opportunities. Gee, Zach, the list goes on.''

''And I can counter that list with one sentence. Ben has a business to run...with me.''

HE DIDN'T WANT to face reality, Amanda thought as she brushed her teeth before going to bed that evening. When she crawled under the covers in her room, random thoughts and images kept popping into her mind. Zach's face when he'd spoken about Ben. His voice, hard and frustrated, countering her comments. Well, he'd have to get over it. If Ben wasn't able or didn't want to pick up his life at Diamond Ridge, then some major decisions affecting all their futures would have to be made. And soon.

"I HAVE GOOD NEWS and I have bad news."

Karen's morning greeting sent a shiver down Amanda's back. Overly sensitive since the night before, she dreaded hearing the bad-news part of her friend's announcement.

"The good news," Karen began, as she slowly waved her left hand in front of Amanda, "is that Tom and I are engaged to be married."

Amanda felt herself begin to smile, a warm, genuine, happy smile. She caught Karen's hand to take a closer look at the sparkling solitaire she wore on her finger.

"It's lovely, Karen. Perfect for you." The round setting, flanked with two baguettes, showed off the diamond to perfection. "And I wish you every happiness." She paused and looked at her friend. "A whole lifetime full."

"Thanks, Amanda. I'm so happy right now I feel like I'm flying without a plane."

"Around here, that's called skiing a perfect run. Come on. Let's do it."

"Wait a minute. You haven't heard the bad news. You might want to forgo the celebration."

Oops, she'd almost forgotten about it in the excitement of the engagement. With all this joy, how bad could it be? "Okay, spill it."

Karen's eyes met hers briefly and then looked away. "After working here for so long, it's kind of hard to say, but I'll be leaving Diamond Ridge. I'm going to manage Tom's private practice."

The glow faded from Amanda's spirit as quickly as the sun faded over the mountains. "You're leaving? But you're so much a part of the place. You know the business as well as we do."

Silly to feel abandoned, Amanda thought, as she tried to maintain her smile. Karen had every right to move on. But it was a wrench. Another change at the Diamond in the middle of such a critical season. She'd have to search for qualified candidates. More work to do.

"I'll stay until you replace me, Amanda. And I'll train whoever you hire. But I'm hoping it won't take more than a month."

"You'll be a tough act for anyone to follow. We'll miss you, Karen." Despite her best efforts, Amanda's voice started to crack, and suddenly tears rolled down her face.

"My goodness. Here's a tissue, you nut. It's a wedding, not a funeral."

Amanda sniffed. "I'm happy. I really am. And I

don't have the slightest idea what's wrong with me.
You know I never cry!''

"Then this really is a special occasion. Amanda is
crying. Seems to me that I'm not the only one on a
merry-go-round of ups and downs.''

"You can say that again. I'm supposed to be back
in New York in five days, and now you're leaving.
The storm's over, Molly's well, and I have five days
to find your replacement. Somehow, Diamond Ridge
is not letting me go.''

AMANDA CHECKED her reflection in the mirror that
evening, pleased with the result of her efforts. She'd
worn very little makeup during her workdays and
hadn't had an occasion to dress up since she'd arrived at the Diamond. Her hair had grown, her natural wave lending it a tousled look. She leaned forward to adjust her silver hoop earrings. The matching
necklace gleamed richly against the midnight-blue
cashmere sweater she'd chosen to wear with a long
straight skirt. High boots with a medium heel completed the outfit.

She felt very feminine, very powerful. She laughed.
Sure, she did. She'd always felt secure in her female
armor! She snatched her purse from her bed and left
her room to meet Zach.

*MY GOD, SHE'S BEAUTIFUL! New York men must be
blind!* Zach stood on the landing to his second-floor
suite, about to walk down the stairs, when he saw
Amanda leave her room. He stood, rooted to the spot

for a moment, before softly calling her name and descending to the first floor.

She turned instantly, and a slow, sexy smile crossed her face. The kind of smile that a man would kill for…or die for.

"Looking good, Zach," she said as she approached. She placed a hand on his sweater-clad shoulder. "Shirt, tie and a black V-neck in fine wool. Dress attire for a Vermont winter."

That was what he'd thought when he'd thrown on his clothes after his shower. It was standard wardrobe, but…Amanda was admiring it.

He roused himself. "Turn around, Mandy-girl. Let's see all 360 degrees."

She obliged him with a laugh. "Do I pass?"

"Mmm. Let's just say, you clean up good," he drawled.

THAT WAS THE BIGGEST compliment she'd gotten so far that evening, Amanda thought as she sipped a glass of wine with her dinner. She smiled to herself. His actions revealed the truth. He hadn't taken his eyes off her at all other than to attend to his driving. He'd helped her from the car, held her arm as they walked the slippery pavement to the well-reputed steak house, assisted with removing her coat, pulled out her chair before taking his own.

As she looked at him across the table, his eyes still devoured her, but his expression gave nothing away.

"What are you thinking?" she asked.

"I was remembering," he replied. "Remembering

when you first came to the mountain, and how I called you Baby-girl."

She chuckled. "Only because I was afraid to ski. And wouldn't leave the baby hill. Excuse me—now it's called the bunny hill." She looked at him in mock exasperation. "Well, what did you expect from a city kid who'd never seen a mountain up close and personal in her entire life?"

"I thought," he said, "that either you were afraid to ski or that you didn't like us."

Surprised, she stared at him. "You were seventeen. I was a stranger in your home. Did you even care what I thought?"

"I wasn't all that happy, either. But, boy, my uncle sure was."

"So was my mom."

She returned his smile. Ben and Lily provided a sweet memory.

"I was afraid of everything," she finally admitted. "But after two weeks of watching the rest of you have a great time out there, I decided to ski, also!"

"And I was stuck on the baby hill," he groaned.

"You loved it!"

"Did not."

They laughed, and to Amanda, the sound was just right. She sipped her wine.

"So tell me about New York," Zach encouraged. "Why not practice in Boston? Or Los Angeles?"

Her fingers clenched, her wine almost spilled, and she placed the glass down carefully. One offhand question could still grab her when she least expected it. But she was feeling a bit mellow.

She glanced at Zach. There was nothing in his expression to suggest anything but genuine interest. No hidden agenda. But he'd asked about a piece of her that she shared with no one. She reached for her wine. One glass was all she allowed herself. She sipped, and still he waited.

"Boston and L.A. were not far enough," she finally said.

His brow furrowed. She saw his expression change. "You're speaking cryptically. I don't understand."

She inhaled deeply. "Do you know how far it is from Hell's Kitchen to midtown Manhattan?"

His eyes never left her face, but she sensed his hand reaching for hers, and then felt his touch as he squeezed her fingers gently. "Not exactly," he replied in a quiet tone. "Maybe twenty blocks or more."

He was so wrong. "No, Zach. That's what most people would say, but they'd be wrong, too." She paused. "The distance between Hell's Kitchen, where I grew up, and midtown cannot be measured in city blocks or miles," she said slowly, choosing her words carefully. "They are *worlds* apart. Light-years farther than the distance to Boston or L.A. So coming to Vermont when I was fourteen was simply a detour I was forced to take."

She placed her wineglass on the table and caught both his hands in hers. "Don't you see, Zach? I had to prove him wrong."

The lines on his brow disappeared. "Charlie?"

"Yes." Charlie, her poor excuse for a father. "He said I'd never amount to anything, that if it weren't for him, we'd have nothing. And I almost believed him." Her throat became tight, her delicious prime-rib dinner now felt like a meal of stones inside her.

"What happened?"

She took another deep breath. "A couple of teachers in junior high. They told me I was smart. My grades were good. They improved after Charlie was gone. And…and you know the rest."

He nodded. "I guess I do," he said. "And I also know that Charlie is still calling the tune."

She leaned forward and shot him a lethal glance. "What? How can you say that?"

"Because you haven't moved beyond Manhattan, beyond midtown. You haven't allowed yourself other options because you're still trying to prove something to him."

She knew her mouth was open because he leaned over to tap her chin. But damn, if he wasn't right. "Old habits? Old needs?"

He nodded.

"Then tell me, Zach, why are you still married to the mountain?"

She hadn't expected an answer, and wasn't upset when Zach remained silent. As she walked arm in arm with him in the parking lot, her mind raced, but her heart felt light. At least lighter than it had in a long time.

"Thanks for dinner," Zach said. "I owe you one."

"You owe me nothing," she said, "unless I return the favor and rescue you."

"I hope it never comes to that," he laughed, "but tonight was a real pleasure."

His words sat nicely in her mind. It had been a pleasure, more than a pleasure. His arm came around and held her firmly. "Watch your step here," he said. He continued to hold her as they walked to the car, and Amanda didn't mind at all.

Once seated, she leaned back and relaxed. She tipped her head and smiled at him. His gray eyes startled, then warmed, then turned hot enough to burn her.

Her heart began to pound, not with fear, but with excitement, when he leaned over and kissed her. A kiss of hunger, of desire. She wrapped her arms around his neck and returned the favor for all she was worth, surprised by her eager response. But not worried about it. Kissing Zach felt right. So right.

"I've got to get us home," she heard him mumble.

"Then step on it," she said. Desire laced her voice. She saw the longing in his eyes as he bent to kiss her again.

"I'll drive like a New York cabbie," he said gruffly.

THEY REACHED HER BEDROOM DOOR. Zach turned her in his arms, and leaned down to kiss her as he had every five feet along the hallway. Kissing her was as natural as breathing…as skiing. How had she managed to creep into his soul in just a few weeks? Or had it been a process over the years? All he knew was that his soft spot for Amanda grew larger every day until there was no room for anyone but her.

Zach lifted her in his arms and heard not a murmur of protest. Down the hall and up the stairs, her arms stayed firmly around his neck as he carried her to his suite. His heart pounded erratically, like a drum corps before perfecting its cadence, and he mentally said goodbye to any last bit of reason he possessed. Just a few nights ago, he'd admitted to himself that she was dangerous to him. That didn't matter anymore. If the future held more pain for him, he'd just have to handle it, but for now, the present seemed too wonderful to ignore.

He halted when he reached his suite and looked down at the woman in his arms, who leaned against him so trustingly. "Sweet Amanda?"

Her eyes fluttered open.

"Is this what you want?"

"I'm with you, aren't I?" she replied.

He kissed her soundly and without hesitation crossed the threshold into his suite. With one hand he turned on the wall switch and set the dimmer to low. Soft, diffused light illuminated the interior of the living room. He crossed to his bedroom door and walked in. Amanda shifted in his arms, and he set her down gently.

He thought she'd look around, make comments about the room. But her eyes remained fastened on him, the normally blue irises now a dark violet bordering on black.

With infinite care, he caressed the sides of her face and thrilled when she stepped closer.

"You are so lovely, Amanda," he whispered. "And you are turning me on so much with that look."

"I'm glad," she whispered.

"Tell me what you want," he urged. "Let me love you in any way that will make you happy."

"And you, too," she said, her voice quivering. "I want so much for you to be happy, too."

That did it. If there was any thread of resistance left in him, it was gone. Completely. He was lost.

Suddenly, he couldn't wait another moment. He pulled the comforter from the bed while pulling her toward him. Her eyes lit up. Excitement? Fear?

"Come here, Mandy." He kissed her then, tasting her, loving her. The enticing fragrance of her perfume added another dimension, and he prolonged the kiss as he led her to the bed.

Instantly, he felt Amanda resist.

"Zach?" A husky plea colored her voice.

He gathered his strength and self-control, took a deep breath and gazed into her eyes. Was she telegraphing simple confusion or distress? He hadn't a clue.

"It's okay, sweetheart. It's not too late to change your mind."

She shook her head. "I'm not changing my mind. I want to love you, Zachary. But—" she turned away from him, and he had to lean closer to hear her "—I'm not very experienced."

As if he cared! "Guess you fought the wolves off pretty well."

He felt her relax again as she laughed.

"Most of them, but one got through. When I was in law school. I let my guard down. I wanted to be like everyone else, get to know people better, but—"

she turned back to him then, palms open, her secret exposed "—it was awful. I was awful. He was probably no better or worse than any other guy. But not for me. So…I don't know what to do."

She was irresistible in her distress, and he had to act.

"You know more than you think. And I know a little something myself." He extended his hand to her. "Trust me. Come here and we'll figure it out together."

She wanted to believe him. He could tell by the hope now shining in her eyes. She walked straight into his arms, and followed his lead onto the bed.

AMANDA KNELT on the bed next to Zach, her hands exploring his body, fingers impatiently working on shirt buttons. "Help me get this off," she pleaded. "I need to feel the real you."

The shirt disappeared in one quick motion. He didn't seem to care about the buttons scattering on the floor. She leaned over him, hands busy roving his chest, weaving her fingers through the dark mat of hair. His pectorals flinched at her touch, and her confidence grew. She heard the sharp intake of his breath as she continued her explorations lower to the waistband on his jeans.

"Baby, you're killing me already, and we've barely started."

His words came out breathlessly and they excited her. She, Amanda Shaw, was going to make love to a man she loved. To a man who cared about the real woman inside. Not just about a pretty face. For her whole adult life, she'd been so afraid to feel, to share another person's life, that she'd put herself in a box marked Untouchable. But in only a few weeks, a stressful, yet fabulous few weeks, Zach had managed to change everything.

And was still doing it.

"It's your turn, Mandy. I need to see you, to touch you, to hold you."

His eyes clung to hers as he spoke, desire shining in them.

"I thought you'd never ask," she whispered.

"Is that right?" Quick as lightning, he pulled her down on top of him and gripped the hem of her shirt. "Off we go," he whispered.

Goose bumps rose as soon as the cool air hit her skin. Her breasts tingled, but she had no time to think about it, because somehow, almost instantly, every bit of clothing was on the floor—hers and his.

"I liked that black silk thing," he said, "but not as much as I like the real thing."

She felt herself blush.

"You *are* beautiful, Amanda," he continued, as he stroked her gently.

She shivered every time his hand touched sensitive spots, which seemed to be everywhere. His fingers made magic as they skimmed her thighs, her breasts, her lips. She took them into her mouth and bit gently.

"Going wild, are we?" Zach growled softly. "Want a little more?"

Her pulse kicked up another notch at the promise

in his voice, and suddenly his lips were on hers, his fingers fondling her breasts. She started to burn way down deep inside herself. Her stomach tightened; she almost stopped breathing. It was crazy; it was wonderful.

Zach was right. All she wanted was more.

His fingers explored lower, somehow slipping into the place where a banked fire waited to explode. Her legs thrashed, flexed and straightened. She turned toward Zach. Hot colors filled her mind. Red and yellow and orange. Burning. She rolled toward Zach again, needing him, needing something.

"Zach… Zach…"

"I know, Mandy. Hang on. I need to protect you."

She felt him leave her, heard a crackling sound, and then he was there. Warm and close, and over her.

"Wrap your legs around me, sweetheart, and we'll take it nice and slow." His voice sounded husky. "I promise."

She didn't want slow. Her knees tightened around his sides and she pulled. And watched his eyes widen.

"I don't want to hurt you, Manda."

She pulled harder. And suddenly they were one.

"MY, MY, MY!" Amanda exclaimed a while later. "Why didn't anyone tell me I was missing so much?" She lay cuddled next to Zach, her head nestled on his shoulder, his arm around her back. Her body felt as relaxed as a house cat napping in the sun.

He chuckled at her remark, and she felt a playful tap on her bottom. "And what should we have said to the daughter of the house? Go out and have some flings?''

She giggled. "Now that you mention it, I think my mother did tell me I needed to get out more.''

"Lily must have been worried."

"Yeah. Well, she won't be worried anymore.''

His silence shouted louder than church bells on Easter morning. She raised herself on her elbow and gazed at him. "Something the matter, Zach?''

He met her gaze squarely. "So, where are we heading, Amanda? How far are we taking this?''

She knew what he meant. His mind had already jumped ahead to the realities. Her job, his job; her needs, his needs. The family. She didn't want to think about any of that.

"Let's fly with the Eagles, Zach, and 'Take It to the Limit' one day at a time. Would you please kiss me again?''

"With pleasure, my love.''

Joy filled her. Such special words. He pulled her head down and proceeded to demonstrate just what his kisses could do to her. "You're delicious, Manda.'' He turned his head and yawned, a big jaw-cracking yawn. "Sorry about that. Come lie down with me.''

"We're both exhausted," she said. "But it's nice.''

She felt his arm wrap snugly around her and knew she wouldn't be returning to her own room that night.

She heard his breathing deepen, long regular breaths leading into sleep. Her own eyelids drooped then, and she cuddled closer. Naked and warm. Normally an oxymoronic condition during a New England winter. But not tonight. Not when she had Zach as a bed partner. She shifted position and felt his arm automatically tighten around her. A revealing gesture. She smiled, though tears stung her eyes.

Yes, they were bed partners. They were also business partners and guardianship partners. Life kept getting more complicated. And more exciting. All because of one man who managed to turn her well-ordered world topsy-turvy.

CHAPTER NINE

"BUT WHY CAN'T WE GO to New York *this* weekend?" Molly wailed. "The competition doesn't matter. It's not that the team really cares if I'm there or not. Not since Coach made stupid Melinda captain."

Amanda sighed as she leaned against the kitchen table where Molly's schoolwork covered the entire surface. Dinner in the big dining room was long since over, and Amanda had gone to the family residence for a quick check on her sister. She'd been hearing the same refrain about the coach and Melinda since Molly had returned to school. This preview of parenthood made her wonder why folks ever had more than one child.

"Stop feeling sorry for yourself, Mol. They need you for moral support. You'll still be the strongest skier the team has. Your friends will come around."

The story of the four girls' escapade during the storm had become larger than life at school. And Molly did seem to be shouldering the brunt of criticism about using poor judgment, especially when the team captaincy was stripped from her.

"I don't care about them. Or the team. I just want to go to New York this weekend."

A month ago, Amanda would have jumped at the chance to take Molly to New York. *So what am I doing? Using Molly's ski team as an excuse not to go to the Big Apple? Why am I not taking advantage of it?*

"So you can run away, Molly?" Zach stepped into the kitchen in time to hear the latest complaint. "Cowards run away. Captains hold their ground. The choice is yours."

Amanda watched as Molly riveted her whole attention on Zach. "But I'm not the captain anymore."

"Titles don't matter, kiddo. You matter. The person you are matters."

Amanda glanced quickly at Zach, instinctively realizing that his last sentence encapsulated his philosophy of life and reflected the way he chose to live. It explained why he had so many friends. And why he looked like the Pied Piper when the hotel was full of kids. People really mattered to him.

She then focused on her sister. Could the twelve-year-old possibly understand Zach's meaning?

"I'm not a coward!" Molly's eyes brightened with anger, and her words emerged through clenched teeth.

As Amanda continued to watch her, Molly's nose crinkled, her brows came together and her jaw relaxed. Tension seemed to ooze from her body as she looked at the big brother in her life.

"Okay, bro. You win. What am I supposed to do? Give all my ideas to Melinda?"

"Only the good ones."

Molly groaned in mock defeat. "I guess I still want

the team to do well. But they shouldn't treat me like I have the chicken pox or something!''

Amanda put her arm around Molly's shoulders. ''In another week or so, you'll be old news. Hang in there. Right now, doing what's best for the team is also what's best for you.''

She looked up and winked at Zach. Her words applied to both her and Molly.

''And there's one more thing, Mol,'' Zach said. ''We have a full house this weekend. So we really need you here.''

''Okay, okay. You win. I'll stay and tough it out. But if any of those kids makes wisecracks...'' She left her threat unfinished as she gathered her books and stood up.

''You'll handle it,'' Zach said.

''Yeah, yeah, yeah.''

''Come here, Popcorn Girl,'' Amanda said as she extended an arm toward her sister. She hugged her tightly. ''Thanks, Mol. I love you.''

She felt Molly squirm. ''Yeah, I know. Me, too. Good night.'' Molly broke away and ran from the room. Amanda grinned widely at Zach.

''So do you think we're doing okay in the Molly partnership?''

''Sweetheart, I think we're doing okay in every type of partnership.''

She watched Zach walk toward her and felt his gentle embrace. His eyes darkened as he held her, as his head descended, as his lips touched hers. Her lids closed then, and all she could do was feel. Feel the gentle strength of his arms holding her, the rapid beat of his heart against her breast, and the light pressure of his lips taking little sips of hers.

"I forgot my math—yuck! What's with the two of you lately?"

Amanda broke away and spun around at the exact moment Zach did to look at the young intruder.

"What do you mean?" Amanda asked.

"You guys are always holding hands or something," Molly replied. "It's gross and I've already told Mom. So there."

Amanda choked on her sister's words, but Zach didn't seem to have the same trouble.

"And what did your mom say to that?" he asked.

"She said to stay out of your way."

"Good advice, kiddo. Now take it."

"I'm history." With those words, Molly loped out of the room.

Amanda looked away, her mind racing. She and Zach had been thrown together because of work. They enjoyed each other's company and she loved many things about him, but where was it going to lead? How would it end?

"Molly's got a great imagination, doesn't she," Amanda said.

"Either that, or she's very observant," Zach replied with a twinkle. "It's tough keeping a secret around here when all I want to do is kiss you every time I see you."

He started toward her, his intention clear. She rose to meet him, leaving her doubts behind for the moment. For as long as possible, she wanted to enjoy every kiss.

ZACH SKIED SLOWLY down the trails set aside for the middle-school competition. The weather promised to cooperate. Even now, the morning sun glistened off the snow-covered slopes. No frosty breaths blew from the north, and the temperature was due to hit thirty-five degrees. A beautiful day to enjoy the outdoors.

The snowmaking equipment had produced fresh powder for the kids, perfect in consistency. He checked the distance between flags for the giant slalom. The Diamond would see plenty of action today with nine schools competing, and youngsters—many with parents—coming from all parts of the region up to a hundred miles away. The hotel was booked solid, including the cottages and condos.

This was how he envisioned the business. A combination of community activity, reasonable profit and sharing the joy of his guests' accomplishments as their skills improved and they conquered the slopes. Just like Amanda had, when she changed from a wary young girl to a confident teen after he taught her to ski.

Satisfied that all was as it should be, he skied to the base lodge, which housed the rental shop. He stored his skis in the office and changed into work boots. He wouldn't be skiing any more that morning. The buses would be pulling in soon, and a full day awaited him.

Three hours later, he couldn't decide whether he'd spent his time talking snow or talking gambling. Several parents with ski-related businesses converged on him as soon as the kids were settled, and the local newspaper covering the school competition had also asked his opinion about the likelihood of casinos coming into the mountains.

"They can try, but they won't succeed," he'd said. His answer ignited a further flurry of questions, until he raised his hands to signal no more questions and returned to watch the races.

"How's Molly doing?"

Zach turned at the sound of Amanda's voice. She offered him a captivating smile, full of warmth and delight, and he forgot about everything but her. He reached out, captured her around the waist and gave her a quick hug.

He laughed as he answered Amanda's question. "Our girl is skiing her personal best, as a matter of fact. Seems she has something to prove to her team."

"And to herself."

"That, too," he admitted.

She leaned against him so naturally his heart kicked into gear.

"It's a good day," he said, "and you can't complain about the bookings this weekend."

"We need more days like today. We need more of the corporate types who just checked in. They're on a five-day executive retreat with their whole tab being reimbursed by their company." She flashed him a grin. "Let's make sure they have a great time so they'll send their friends."

He squeezed her close. "Good strategy, but don't get too friendly, sweetheart. I don't like to share."

She felt the blush rise to her cheeks. "Hey, it's not me they asked about. One of them, as a matter of fact, asked for you. Said the two of you cut up on some old stomping grounds."

Zach thought for a moment and shook his head. "Someone from college?"

"He didn't say, but I'm sure he'll find you later."

Zach shrugged and returned his attention to the hill. The morning session was winding down. "I hope the dining room is ready for these kids. They're going to be ravenous."

"We're ready. Meatballs and spaghetti by the tub-fuls. Send in the ski patrol working the meet, too."

"That was my plan."

"Good." A smile slowly spread across Amanda's face. "You know something, Zach? Sometimes I think we really are in sync with each other." She blushed, turned and ran back to the hotel.

Zach stared after her, enchanted by the ingenuous side of Amanda. Maybe there would be a future. A real happily-ever-after future where both of them could be winners. But she was right. He was married to his mountain. And he couldn't move it to New York.

"ZACH? ZACH PORTER. Wait up."

Zach gave a start at the familiarity of the voice. He turned quickly and watched a tall, lanky fellow about his own age approach him outside the base lodge. Everything about the guy seemed familiar—the tilt of his head, the long, easy strides, the crooked half smile— and then it clicked. Zach grinned and extended his hand.

"Jerry Fontaine! Welcome to ski country. It's been a long time."

"Five years too long, Zach. How the hell are you?"

"Couldn't be better."

Jerry slapped him on the back. "Zachary, my boy, life can always be better. But I admit—" he laughed "—that we're riding high in the Windy City right now. And you could have been flying along with us all the way."

Zach shook his head and smiled. "Paradise Hotels and I weren't a match. But you, Jerry, you were made for corporate suits." He stepped back to study his old Paradise teammate. Beneath the bluff heartiness and relaxed visage was a piercing gaze. "So where on the ladder are you, Jerry? VP of Sales? Marketing? What?"

"Nothing as grand as a vice presidency. I do a little of this and a little of that. Research, development." He glanced sharply at Zach. "A little real estate."

Bingo! Jerry was showing his cards early. Zach halted his steps and stood toe-to-toe with his visitor. "Real estate is a dirty word when hotel chains come visiting. Diamond Ridge is not for sale, Jerry. Not today, not tomorrow, not next year. Not as long as there's breath in my body."

"Whoa! You're going too fast, my friend." Jerry

raised his hand like a traffic cop stopping a string of cars. "Who said anything about buying your place?"

Zach raised an eyebrow, then nodded his head at the surroundings. A busy hill full of active, happy people enjoying a good time, and in the background, majestic mountains bringing peace and beauty to the eye and to the soul.

"You've got a dream operation here, Zach, I admit it. But we're not interested. My team and I are using Diamond Ridge strictly as a home base while we're in the area. After all, why should we stay anywhere else when you're right here?"

Bullshit. No serious hotelier would overlook a "dream operation," but Zach didn't question the remark. The number-one rule of negotiation flashed in the back of his mind like a neon sign on a Las Vegas strip: the first one to blink loses. He had no intention of blinking. Ever.

"So you're scouting around?" Zach asked. He'd play the game for a while. Hang out with Jerry until he learned what he needed to know.

"Why not?" Jerry replied. "Paradise is looking to expand, and this seems to be the year for Vermont."

"The pending legislation?"

"Roulette's a big lure, but not the only one. Paradise wants to grow its image from a big-city metropolitan hotel chain to include mountain resorts, dude ranches, waterfront locations and anything else that's appropriate. So we'll be hanging out for a time, getting the feel of New England in the winter."

"I hope you brought your snowshoes."

"We'll buy what we need here. We believe in the greening of the local economy, so...we brought money."

Because you want to play hardball. It would be an interesting reunion.

"We've already developed an itinerary of properties to see, but I was hoping that you'd share some of your insights, as only a native can." Jerry stared at him intently. "We always prefer working with local talent. And you, Zach, were the best and the brightest back then. Hell, we were all full of piss and vinegar."

"We sure were...and it seems we still are."

He meant what he said. The hungry young cubs out of the university had roared to adulthood, each stalking personal goals and gains. Each one a player, with no apologies offered and none needed. Including Zach. But Zach had left that corporate game. And his former cohorts were not welcome to play on his turf.

ZACH DRUMMED HIS FINGERS on the bar in the chalet that evening while he waited for his usual soft drink. He watched the animated faces of the group at the opposite end. A group that included Amanda. The Paradise people had been quick to pinpoint the other decision-maker on the Diamond's team. Either their sonar was tremendously acute, or they had an eye for a beautiful woman. Probably both. He sighed as he rose to join them. Every darn man in the place had an eye on Amanda, even with their wives beside them.

Amanda glanced up and waved him over with eager gestures. Her eyes shone in the soft, dim light, the

usual cornflower shade now a cobalt blue. The cling-
ing black sweater and matching stretch pants she wore
hugged every curve.

His spirit lightened in response to her invitation, but
his hands itched to hold her, and the front of his jeans
seemed instantly snug. How could he possibly blame
other men for looking when he, himself, reacted like
a randy teenager?

His stride lengthened as he approached the group.
A path seemed to open, and like a heat-seeking mis-
sile, he came to a stop at Amanda's side.

"Hi, Baby-girl," he whispered in her ear. It was
her old nickname. She shivered slightly in response,
and he almost laughed aloud. His pants remained
snug. He'd live with it.

"Your friends are telling me all your secrets,
Zach."

"Is that right?" He put his arm around Amanda's
shoulders and gently pulled her toward him. "You
must be pretty bored listening to nothing."

Her body felt so exactly right, so relaxed and trusting as she leaned against him. He raised his eyes to
Jerry and crew, and waited a significant heartbeat before speaking. Long enough for the visitors to take a
mental snapshot of Amanda in his arms. In the body
language of the dominant male, his message was loud
and clear.

And received. Zach replied to Jerry's raised brow
with a minuscule nod. When his old friend smiled
with understanding, Zach felt himself relax. For a man
who until recently was hell-bent on leading a single

life, he was now as vulnerable as any other man in love. Love? Was he thinking *love?*

"I'm not bored," Amanda said. "I could listen to their stories of your years in Chicago all night. I hardly know anything about them."

"I was a kid, Mandy. There's not much to tell."

A chorus of opposition greeted that statement, and for twenty minutes his old comrades regaled Amanda with inflated stories of their escapades, always labeling Zach as the ringleader.

"If I had done everything they said, I'd be in jail today." He laughingly turned to everyone. "Enough is enough. We all tore that city apart."

"We sure did," Jerry said. "But you instigated. You led the pack at work, too. I still don't know where you got the energy. We could barely keep up. You were the one who spoke for our management-trainee class. You got that internship policy changed. God, we thought nothing would stop you."

"You were right," Zach said quietly. "Nothing did."

"But you wound up where you started."

Instant silence as the group waited for Zach's reply. *These guys would never get it, but he'd try.* "I missed the mountains, Jerry. I'm a country boy at heart. Tearing up the city was the best I could do to it because I couldn't live in it."

"I don't believe you. You were as hungry and eager as any one of us at that age. You wanted the career as much as we did—and do."

"You're wrong."

"You came home because of your uncle."

"I came home because I wanted to breathe fresh mountain air."

But Jerry continued as if Zach hadn't spoken. "It's not too late, Zach. You can still have it all. We can do it. Right here. In your mountains. With you in charge of the location."

He knew it! He knew it the minute Jerry had mentioned their lack of interest in the Diamond's "dream operation" that afternoon. Everything would be okay now, because the issue was out in the open. Nothing personal. Just business.

"I already do have it all. So if the Diamond was your objective in coming here, boys, you've wasted your time. We can book you a flight out by tomorrow night so you won't have wasted as much of it."

"Same old Zach," Jerry roared. "Always fast on his feet. But we're staying around, pal. You'll have plenty of time to change your mind. And besides, we haven't heard from your beautiful partner yet."

They sure hadn't. Zach looked down at Amanda and realized she'd been silent during the entire debate. He recognized that intense expression and knew she had filed away everything she'd heard. She'd analyze her data and ask him a zillion questions when they were alone.

"His 'beautiful partner,'" said Amanda with a yawn, "is exhausted. An interesting evening, gentlemen. If you insist on staying the week, then go skiing, walk in the woods, enjoy yourself. And go see the other properties on your list. Don't count on this one. It's not for sale.''

"Everything's for sale at the right price, Ms. Shaw.''

"Zachary Porter isn't.''

AMANDA BIT the inside of her lip as she watched Zach pace the bedroom. "Sorry you didn't stay in Chicago?''

He pivoted to face her. "Not for a minute.''

"Then why are you so restless?''

"Just trying to figure out their next move.'' He ran his hands through his hair.

"They've already shown their hand, Zach. They're looking to buy. They're interested in the Diamond. What could be plainer?''

"I don't know. But it was too fast. Too easy.''

She walked over and reached for his hand. "No one can make us sell, but…I've been thinking.''

"I was counting on that.'' His eyes focused on her. "And what grand conclusions have you come to?''

She winced at his eagerness. She knew he wasn't going to like her idea, but she was trained to explore all possibilities. "It's too soon for conclusions, but maybe we should at least hear them out. They may offer something you could live with and something that would relieve the financial worries around here.''

She expected him to yell or pace or curse or do something! She didn't expect the silence.

So she spoke again, quickly. "They're just the first investors that will come here. Others will follow.

Every privately owned hotel is vulnerable, and knowledge is power. So think, Zach. Let's find out as much as we can. And don't forget Ben. We'd have to tell him about everything we learn, because—and I don't want to rub this in your face—he's still the majority owner. You don't really have the final say."

She should have kept her mouth shut. Zach's eyes widened; she heard him exhale. He walked over to the window and gazed at the darkened landscape.

"I'd almost forgotten," he whispered. "And with Ben so vulnerable…" He crossed to the night table and reached for the phone. He studied her carefully. "You're in full charge tomorrow, Mandy. I'm going to New York. Thanks for reminding me."

She could have cut her tongue out. What craziness was he going to do in New York?

"If my uncle and Lily are willing, I'll own fifty-one percent of the business by the time I return. And we'll all be happy."

She sat down heavily on the edge of the bed. "Do you want to explain happiness to me? The Diamond is Ben's dream, too. Why would he want to sell a majority holding? And where are you getting the money to buy twenty-six percent more stock?"

He replaced the receiver and knelt on the floor in front of her. He clasped her hand. "Look at me, honey."

She looked into eyes filled with hope and excitement.

"Ben doesn't want to sell the business to a chain any more than I do. But who can guarantee the future?

If I give him a lump sum now, he'll be secure. All the risk will be mine. That should make Lily happy. And I'll be able to make decisions without any legal hassles. And that will make me happy.''

Which should make me happy. But it wasn't enough. ''And the money?'' she whispered.

''I've got some left from my college trust fund because I had a lot of scholarships. Never had to use all the money in the fund, and it's still growing. It still might not be enough, but I'll work out something with my uncle.''

''But it's your safety net. Your nest egg. You can't use that money.''

''Why not? The Diamond is my future. My investment.''

Like trying to ignore an elephant in the kitchen, Amanda attempted to push her fears aside. But her palms felt sweaty, and her stomach started to lurch. She took a deep breath, then another in her search for tranquillity. She had to make him see reason, and she needed to remain calm.

''If you're determined to invest every penny you have, Zach, shouldn't you research what Paradise and the others have in mind so you'll know what you're up against? Knowledge is always power.''

''Of course. I intend to. In fact I'm going to contact every owner in the mountains and share information.'' He kissed her quickly. ''Thanks, Baby-girl, for reminding me about Ben. We've worked together for so long that I tend to forget we're not really equal partners.''

What had she done? In an effort to pull in the reins, she'd unleashed them. Once again, she learned that Zach was his own man. No wonder he couldn't stay in Chicago. His old friends really didn't understand. He'd been telling the truth all along. He needed his freedom.

She loved him, but his independence scared her. That was the truth, too.

"WHO'S HE TALKING TO in New York, Amanda?"

Amanda looked at the Chicago crew, who made a habit of finding her each evening. She shook her head in mock reprimand.

"He went to see family, that's all," she said.

"Try again. We fly in from the Midwest and he runs to New York. No way."

"It must be Trump. There's no one bigger than the Donald in New York. He's gonna cut a deal with him."

If only it was true! "Sorry, fellas. He's just visiting his uncle, but now that we're alone like this, why don't you tell me what Paradise has in mind?"

She didn't miss the significant looks exchanged between Jerry and his closest lieutenant. She raised her alertness level a notch and took note of the expressions on all their faces. With gleeful anticipation, the predators turned toward their prey—her.

She lowered her lids for a moment, then raised them and met their gazes one by one. "Well, boys," she said in a cool, clear voice, "are you going to lay down your cards?"

"Maybe a hand or two," Jerry replied slowly. "While I figure you out."

She nodded.

JERRY HADN'T HAD a snowball's chance. Amanda congratulated herself as she prepared for bed that evening. She'd kept the five of them with her for two hours. They never folded, never left the game. She lay on her back under the quilt, hands behind her head, staring at the ceiling. A grin spread across her face. A good night's work.

Basically, the parameters of a buyout offer were on the table. And she now had information to pass on to other owners. To prepare them, to help them make well-considered decisions.

The phone rang. It could only be one person, and Amanda reached for it eagerly.

"Hi, sweetheart. How're you holding up?"

"Better than you think. But first tell me, are you a mountain mogul yet?"

She heard him laugh at her unintentional double entendre. Skiing the moguls, or planned bumps, required the greatest of skill.

"Hopefully, I'm overcoming any moguls that get in my way. But yes, we've signed a letter of intent. I'll be the majority owner. Ben seems happier than I would have thought. He's doing a lot better, too. Wants to come home already."

So she was right! Lily and Ben were worried about their futures or they'd never accept Zach's money all at once. "Come home? What about Molly's visit and all that other stuff?"

"Well, the docs aren't letting him out so fast. So the visit's still on. Uncle Ben just wants to be where the action is, as usual."

"Are you sure you want to do this, Zach?"

"Of course I do. In fact, I feel like a weight's been lifted from my shoulders."

"And I feel like a weight's been dropped on them. You now have total responsibility for the success or failure of Diamond Ridge."

"I welcome it."

"You can call the shots about selling it, too."

His hesitation vibrated over the line. "Do you think I bought it in order to sell, Mandy? Or is that what you want?"

"What I want is for you to be happy." *And not lose money.*

"I know. And I am," he said gently. "Thank you."

She melted. A tear ran down her face and she wiped it away impatiently. Let him enjoy his moment. Why did she have to keep pinching a sore spot? Because she was Amanda, the insecure. Because she was used to examining all the angles. That was the way she lived. That was the way she survived.

"I trust you, Zach. And I know you're too smart to ignore the information I've gathered. You'll see why selling out to the big hotel chains will be tempting to folks. In fact, it might be in their best interest. Like the Davises from Holly Hill. They're getting on in years. They might want to retire to Florida now. Who knows?''

''I know everyone in the mountains. I'll start calling them as soon as I get home and we talk. I want to know what you've learned so I can educate our neighbors. I'll be back once everything is finalized.''

She hung up the phone with a lighter heart. At least he agreed to a discussion. It would give her a chance to prepare different scenarios and help him see which was best for them. She rearranged the covers and lay back on the pillow. Of course, Zach's definition of best could be different from hers. She chuckled. Not could. *Would.* He played offense; she played defense. It didn't matter as long as they were on the same team.

She reached for the phone again and dialed Mr. Garroway's home number.

''Sorry to disturb you so late in the evening, but I didn't want you to find my office still empty on Monday.''

''Oh?''

''Yes. I *am* making some progress. My sister's feeling better, but now seems reluctant to go to New York. I've got to get my mother more involved. The bigger issues relate to the business. A key member of the staff has resigned and we're seeking new financing, which will tie up some of Zach's time.''

She paused for a breath. ''I know it's a bit unusual, Mr. Garroway, but I really need a little while longer here before my life returns to normal. I'll gladly forfeit my next vacation to make up for missing time now.'' Her hand tightened on the receiver in a deathlike grip.

"I'd really hoped to find you here on Monday, Amanda. We also have a business to run, and we had every expectation of giving you a larger role in it."

Amanda heard his pause, and held her breath.

"It seems," Mr. Garroway continued, "that you still have too many loose ends up there to resolve in a few extra days. Why don't you take an official leave of absence, Amanda? Another two months, for a total of three. But the offer of the partnership is withdrawn. And on your first day back, I want to see you in my office to discuss your career."

She couldn't really blame him. She wouldn't have accepted her scenario from someone else, either. Her situation didn't qualify for time off under the Family Leave Act, and she doubted they'd be any happier with her absence even if it did.

So, in the end, there was no freedom. She earned her income at a price. True security didn't exist. Although there were always choices, they weren't necessarily good ones. And no one was totally in charge of his or her own life.

Not even Amanda Shaw.

CHAPTER TEN

"THE BEST PART about going away is coming home again." Zach laughed as he kissed Amanda and danced her around the kitchen floor. "Thanks for waiting up."

The flight had been late. It was now after midnight, and tomorrow would be another busy day at the hotel, his last one with Amanda, before she returned to the city. He wouldn't have blamed her for falling asleep, but was thrilled to see her.

"My pleasure," she murmured against his neck. She leaned back to look at his face. "You're smiling from ear to ear. And don't say it's because of me."

"I'm a contented man, sweetheart. My feet are barely hitting the floor. And you're definitely part of it." He loved her. He would have loved the whole world right now, if it weren't for Amanda's imminent departure.

"And the rest is Diamond Ridge, isn't it," Amanda said.

"You bet it is. I don't know if I can explain it exactly, but I'm excited, happy, challenged. I feel I could run a marathon right now."

Her sweet smile made his gut tighten. He bent down

to kiss her, and her response made him forget the hotel, the marathon, everything but her.

"My room or yours?" he growled as he continued to kiss her cheek, her neck, any part of her soft skin he could reach.

"Slow down, cowboy. I want to clue you in on what I learned today from your old friends. If we go upstairs now, we'll fall asleep afterward and never talk at all."

"It can wait. I can't. I've missed you incredibly in just the two days I've been away." He straightened and cupped her cheek in his palm. "Tomorrow's soon enough to catch up, and I've only got one more day with you before you're gone." Didn't she realize that her smile could turn him on his head? And that her concern for him squeezed his heart? "What do you say, Mandy-girl?"

"I say," she replied slowly, "that we can talk every day for two more months."

His grin never completed its journey across his face. Not when he studied her expression. "But?"

"But I lost my promotion."

"Promotion? Was that what was going to be announced at the party?"

She nodded. "Junior partner."

"And well deserved."

"I thought so, but..."

"I still think so."

Her eyes riveted to his face.

"You haven't lost your talent, Amanda. That brain

of yours is sharper than a set of honed kitchen knives. You can do anything you want to. Anything."

He saw her tears gather. "Don't cry, sweetheart," he said as he drew her toward him.

"Your vote of confidence is nice." She snuggled against his shoulder.

"I meant every word." He held her in his arms, never wanting to let go. But if her happiness depended on a partnership in New York, what then? Could he ever leave the mountain again? Could he watch her walk away?

He held her closely as he led her upstairs.

THERE WAS NO TIME to speak privately about anything important in the morning. Karen called in sick. Amanda was at the front desk waiting for Molly to relieve her so she could confer with the housekeeping staff and the ski-school coordinator.

Zach was on the phone with Sam Johnson, the family lawyer. She could imagine what they were discussing. The saving grace was that as long as Zach was on the phone, the Paradise group couldn't grab him, either. In his buoyant mood about his majority ownership of Diamond Ridge, Zach could easily tell them to get lost. She had to get to him first.

Amanda kept one eye on the corridor for Zach, one ear to the phones, and the rest of her poised for anything. She sighed with relief when Molly came to the desk.

"I'm taking a semiprivate lesson with Carol in half

an hour. So come back quick. I don't want to miss it.''

"Lucky you! She must have had a cancellation. Thanks, Mol. I'll be in the office with Zach. Call me if you have to, but it better be an emergency!''

Amanda glanced at her watch as she strode to the office. In reality, she had twenty minutes. She organized her thoughts, marshaling arguments that Zach would think reasonable. She opened the door and stopped in her tracks.

She was too late. The room was full of men. Paradise Hotel men. They turned as one when she walked into the room.

"There she is," said Jerry Fontaine. "You are one lucky devil, Zach. She's not only beautiful, but bright. Sharp as a whip.''

"And rare," another piped in. "A woman who knows how to be quiet and listen!''

She caught Zach's surprised expression, caught the grin and wink that was just for her, before she focused on the last speaker. She walked directly toward him without saying a word. She stared at him until she saw a flush stain his neck.

"If we were outside," she began, "I'd take your sexist head and bury it in a snowbank." Her eyes swept over the rest of the men, dismissing them like so many specks of dirt.

She glanced at Zach before moving to her desk. His damn grin was still in place as he gave her a thumbs-up. From behind her, she heard Jerry Fontaine's voice.

"Hollander, apologize and get out of here.''

Zach interrupted. "You'd all better make a graceful exit while you still can, Jerry," he said with a chuckle. "I don't think Amanda's feeling too sympathetic to your cause right now."

Zach was on the money. The macho jerks had pushed one of her hot buttons, but in addition to that, they'd been foolish. They'd given her no time to speak quietly with Zach. In their anxiety, they'd ruined a good opportunity.

Amanda held out her hand. "No hard feelings, Mr. Fontaine. I never allow emotions to get in the way of business decisions, so we've lost nothing. Your timing, however, could have been better."

The man winced. She knew he was kicking himself, but a moment later, she had to give him credit for his composure.

"When can we speak again, Zach...Ms. Shaw?"

"Frankly, we have nothing to discuss," Zach said, "relative to business."

"Have dinner with us tomorrow night," Amanda said simultaneously. She looked meaningfully at Zach. "You have to eat, anyway."

Zach stood up and positioned himself in front of his desk. "The lady has a point." He looked at each man in the room. "We'll see you in the dining room around seven tomorrow evening." He opened the office door and waited while they all left.

Then he faced Amanda. "You've just had a taste of it. Do you still want me to listen to what they have to offer?"

"I don't understand," she said.

"The politics, the bureaucracy."

"With any large organization, including ours, there's always a chain of command. Responsibilities are divided up. We have to abide by a variety of laws. And on and on."

"I'll gladly enforce the laws, Amanda, but I won't have to operate by committee and go through a hierarchy to do it."

He was talking freedom again, and he had a point. With her hands on the desk behind her, Amanda hoisted herself up so she'd be closer to eye level with him. "I hear you, Zach. But for every minus, there's a plus with a large corporation like Paradise."

"I know all about corporations. For Pete's sake, I worked at Paradise for five years. I know how they operate."

She closed her eyes and prayed for patience. He was so stubborn! When she lifted her gaze again, she reached for his hands. She had to make him listen, to believe her, and they always communicated better when they touched.

She took a deep breath. "You haven't asked, but I'm going to give you some advice. Keep your options open, Zach. Don't shut any doors. It's early in the game yet, and the rules might change. And I'm not talking only about casinos and expansions by large chains. I'm also talking about you. You've now got the ultimate responsibility for the entire success or failure of Diamond Ridge. And it's a brand-new responsibility. A huge risk.

"A single Paradise location has substantial corporate backing if it has a lousy year or two,'' she continued. ''Independents like us have only our own resources. It's hard to compete.''

She flinched at her own words, knowing he'd receive them like a knife in the heart put there by his best friend. She searched his face and saw only a blank mask. ''I'm not trying to hurt you, Zach. Never that!'' she cried. ''But you need to consider the options and the odds.''

''We've been independent all these years, Amanda. What makes it so different now? The fact that Ben's not here?''

Lord, he was taking it so personally! He thought she didn't believe in him. ''Of course not. I know you can run the business,'' she replied quickly. ''But times are changing. If casinos come in, if other owners sell to the big boys, if we don't take advantage of the opportunity, we'll get eaten alive and you'll have nothing!''

She beseeched him. ''Please think about it. Timing is everything in life, Zach. After all the effort, the years, the money, you don't want to wind up with a small hotel that can barely survive.''

She felt his withdrawal then. She'd gone too far. He stepped back as though she was unclean. Her heart ached, and tears welled up in her eyes. Impatiently, she wiped them away. A woman's defense. She never used it.

Sure enough, Zach reacted. He grasped her shoulders gently and rested his forehead on hers. ''What happened when I was gone, Mandy? What did they say to you?''

She shook her head. "Nothing that I didn't want to hear. I spent time with them on purpose to get information, and I did. I thought I was so smart, playing it cool and getting them to reveal their plans. But maybe they were playing me, giving me enough to scare myself, but also enough to see a way out—with them.''

He straightened and caressed her smooth cheek. "Don't worry about it, Mandy. It's their first foray with us, and they're planting seeds to make us nervous. They'd like to buy us cheaply. But we'll plant our own seeds. I've got a lot of calls to make today. Cheer up.''

But she couldn't. Her spirit lay heavy inside her. She looked at the man she loved, the only man she'd ever love, and knew, deep down, that love wasn't enough. Not for them.

The irony! In the beginning, she'd thought they were too different but in the end, they were too much alike. Their needs, their outlooks, the way they approached life and work were too similar. But it was their work—her need for security and his need for independence—that would keep them apart. For the moment, those two differences seemed to outweigh everything else.

Zach was right. There were no mountains in New York City. And there were no powerful law firms in the Green Mountains to provide the security she needed. How could their relationship ever work?

Tears filled her eyes again, and all she could think

about was escape. She looked longingly at the closed door.

She had to get out of there, away from Zach, before she destroyed him. Before she destroyed them both. She began to push herself off the desk when Zach's hands shot out and circled her waist, effectively stopping her. "If you think I'll allow your fears to destroy us, you're wrong."

How did he know? Amanda raised her head and looked into Zach's smoky-gray eyes, now dark and intense. He was such a good man, such a strong man. A fighter. But this time he'd lose.

She shook her head and tried to smile. The trembling in her lips told her she failed. "See why I never liked messy emotions? This is what happens when you think with your heart, instead of your head."

"Oh, sweetheart, you're just feeling human. Like the rest of us mortals."

Before she could reply, he lifted her and sat down with her on his lap. His arms cradled her. His hand stroked her hair and gently massaged her shoulder. Tears threatened to fall again. How could he be so loving when she'd insulted him only a minute ago? Questioning his decisions, his choices, his lifelong dream?

"Twelve hours ago, you were so happy, and now I've ruined it!" she cried, trying to wriggle off him. But he held her firmly, continued to touch her and rain kisses on her.

"No running, Mandy," he whispered. "It's all right."

"God, I hate myself for hurting you. I should have stayed in my apartment, living my uncomplicated life. Handling my own legal cases, all by myself."

"I'm thankful every day that you came home to Vermont," he replied.

The man was either a saint or a masochist. "But why?" she asked, totally confused. "All I am is trouble!"

His eyes twinkled before he replied, "You're a whole lot of things, but trouble is at the bottom of the list. At the top, the most important attribute, is that you've been yourself. You've been totally honest, sometimes brutally honest, because you love me. You care."

"But, but—"

"And don't try to deny it," he continued, ignoring her interruption. "We've made love, Amanda. And we both know it wasn't a game. I've never liked playing games. And you've never done that. And I don't like yes-men...or -women. With you, I will always get an honest opinion. And of course, I know it's always for my own good."

She laughed ruefully. "I guess that's true."

"And we're both stronger for it."

"Don't go overboard, Zach! I can't buy into that."

"Why not? You're the cautious one, and maybe I'm too optimistic. Together, we balance. We're a perfect match!"

She had to chuckle again. His logic was incredible. On the surface, it was sound, but like any good lawyer, she knew she'd find the flaws. So she'd postpone the search. Maybe she didn't want to find any more flaws today.

A loud knock at the door startled her, then Molly's impatient voice called her name. The door opened before she could jump off Zach's lap.

"Are you two at it again?" Molly stood with her hands on her hips, her expressive face, her posture, reflecting the image of an outraged parent.

Amanda tried not to smile, but it was no use. Her sister's unconscious parody tickled her sense of humor, and her giggles escaped, quietly at first, but then grew to full-bodied laughter, bordering on convulsions. Zach's deep chuckles joined in. Poor Molly stared at them, looking totally bewildered.

"What's so funny? If we're supposed to be a team, how come I'm doing all the work? It's not fair!"

"You're right. It's not." Amanda held her sides, and tried to speak. "But you're so funny." She started laughing again.

"We're right behind you, Captain Molly," Zach said. "We have a magnificent team at Diamond Ridge. The best."

"I think you're both nuts. If this is what happens when you fall in love, I'm never doing it! Goodbye." The slammed door punctuated her statement.

The sudden quiet hurt Amanda's ears. She looked at Zach. "I think I was a bit overcome there, the laughing and all."

"I'd rather you were overcome here, with me." Zach approached, a familiar gleam in his eye.

She knew what to expect and raised her face in

eager anticipation. She reached for him, twined her arms around his neck, and when his mouth met hers, it took no more than three seconds for her blood to sizzle.

It doesn't get any better than this. The thought twirled repeatedly through her haze of desire. Zach had to be right. They were a perfect match.

AMANDA STUDIED the paneled dining room of the hotel as the staff set up for lunch. She smiled at the memory of dinner the night before with the crew from Paradise.

Zach had been the perfect gentleman, as had Jerry Fontaine and his team. Everyone was on their best behavior, but no one forgot the underlying purpose of the visit. The guests had been busy visiting properties on their list and speaking with owners. And Zach had tipped off every single one. Now the Chicago crew was in the process of checking out, and Amanda breathed a sigh of relief.

She needed a break, even from the hotel itself. The division of labor had put her in charge of all lodging, as well as the ski school, while Zach oversaw the lodge with its restaurants and ski-rental shop, the chalet, and hill operations. A lot of work, a lot of responsibility. She missed her mother and Ben. They always made it look like fun.

And she missed the skiing! Darn it, she never had the time. Here she was at one of the prettiest ski resorts in the country, and she spent most of her time indoors! She needed some fresh air. Glancing at her

watch as she quickly left the dining room, she wondered where Zach was. It would be fun to tackle a
black diamond with him. Or maybe even a double-
black, the steepest type of slope. She hadn't been on
the new trail, Diamond in the Rough.

"Zach's in the office," Karen said thirty seconds
later. "Making a lot of phone calls. I think you'll be
going to a meeting this week. Regional ski association."

"That's fine, but right now I want to ski—"
Amanda laughed "—and I hope he'll postpone those
calls."

"YOU WANT TO SKI the Rough?" Zach asked, keeping
his voice neutral while he gave thanks she hadn't gone
off on her own.

"Think I can't do it?"

Her eyes shone with challenge and now he struggled not to grin. This was the Amanda he remembered. The Amanda he had admired years ago. "The
teenage Amanda could, but I haven't seen you ski in
a mighty long time."

"Can you get away from the office, Zach? Look,
the sun's shining, the wind's down. It's gorgeous out
there, and I'm itching to schuss right down the fall
line."

"On the shortest straightaway to the bottom?
You're in a wild mood, my girl. Let's go."

Fifteen minutes later, legs and skis dangling from
the chairlift carrying them up an intermediate slope,
Zach pointed out the acreage he and Ben had acquired.

"We're not as big as Stowe, and we'll never be as big as Killington, but we sure are a solid, medium-size facility with challenges for everyone."

Could he make her see the mountains through his eyes? "Sometimes, after a heavy snowfall, when the runs are still virgin powder, I'm the first one up the highest face. I look down, and the slope is clear and smooth and untouched. Pristine. Inside, I'm excited. It builds up, and I want to fly. But I make myself wait. I wait quietly until I feel the mountain within me. All the facets. And then I float down. I float with the mountain. On a good day, it's unbelievable. A wonderful addiction."

He turned to her then. "Do you know what I'm saying?"

"Of course I do," she replied, before a wide grin crossed her face. "You've just described our sex life. I like being a wonderful addiction."

He laughed as they disembarked from the lift. "Okay, enough talk. Let's see what you can do." He watched her survey the intermediate trail and the surroundings. Then she nodded.

"You win. It's beautiful. Let's go."

He skied beside her, letting her set the pace, take the lead. Her natural ability was still there, technique was good, and with a little practice could become excellent again. But he didn't correct her flaws. She was having too much fun, and he wanted nothing to prevent that.

On their second run down the same slope, he saw

immediate improvement and was very glad he'd kept his mouth shut.

"Are you satisfied, boss?" she asked with a twinkle in her eye. "I want to try the Rough."

She wasn't ready. Not yet. "How about Foxfire?" he asked, naming a single-diamond trail used by upper-intermediate and expert skiers. Amanda had skied it many times before—years ago.

"Oh, Zach. Don't tell me *you're* turning into a worrywart."

Keep it light. She's really having a great time. "That's me. Old worrywart Zachary."

The twinkle in her eye disappeared, but she didn't argue. "Foxfire it is," she said quietly.

"Good choice," he said.

"I figured arguing wouldn't have done any good, would it?"

He shook his head.

"You're the expert here, so I'd be a fool not to listen. And besides, my ego isn't *that* fragile."

If he hadn't been wearing skis and carrying poles, he would have swung her around and kissed her. "Thanks, sweetheart."

Zach stood with Amanda at the top of Foxfire, reminding her of features she may have forgotten. "It's damn steep, so slalom or traverse, don't schuss. And you can't see ahead where it veers off to the left. How about you follow me this time?" In his mind, it was a statement, not a question.

"I'll be fine, Zach. I've been on this trail. And you taught me, remember?"

"Yeah, yeah. I know. But for now, I'll still lead. Follow my tracks."

"Maybe next time, I'll come alone," she grumbled.

"Fine. But *this* time, we're together."

He hoped she'd copy his every move, because now he did want to take her to the Rough. In fact, he had to. Or she'd try it by herself.

"Ready?" He smiled at her.

She nodded.

He led off to the right, going into his first turn. He took it wide so he'd have time to glance back at her.

She went to the left. Deliberately. And avoided his gaze.

If she'd been a regular paying student, he would have ended the lesson immediately. Now all he could do was watch her and hope she made it to the bottom in one piece.

She traversed past him and continued into a turn. Good form, good pole placement. He started his own run after her, keeping his distance while she worked her way down. She stopped in the middle of the mountain.

"What's wrong?" he asked as soon as he was close enough.

Now she met his gaze. "I'm sorry, Zach. I'm acting like an idiot. I guess my ego was insulted when we didn't go to the new hill right away. If I were the instructor, I'd end the lesson now."

"Great minds think alike, Mandy," he said. His voice sounded harsh to his own ears. "You know the ropes."

"So, are we turning in after this run?" she asked in a small voice.

Her sweet honesty saved both their egos. "I thought you wanted a crack at the double-black?"

She turned to him eagerly. "Oh, I do."

"Then let's go."

She turned quickly and promptly fell. And started to laugh. "I guess that's really a bruised ego," she said as she brushed the snow from her derriere.

"You'll survive."

"You bet."

BUT WILL I SURVIVE this? Amanda looked down the slope of the Rough and wondered why she'd insisted on coming up. A twenty-five-hundred-foot vertical drop starting with a very steep descent at the apex. The signs around the trail had the traditional two black diamonds and the words For Experts Only on the adjacent signs. No wonder Zach had been reluctant.

Hell, she could do this. She'd skied steep runs before. She'd been on double-blacks before. She just needed to learn this hill.

This time she listened closely to Zach's instructions. And followed him through two turns, looked at the horizon and promptly fell. She waved away his offer of help and got up. Followed him again. Hit a mogul and fell. Came to a steeper incline and fell again.

"This is embarrassing," she said as Zach stood over her for the third time. "I don't know what's wrong."

"Let go of the mountain."

"What?"

"In your mind. The fear is in your mind. Every time you come to a steeper part you're holding on to the mountain in your mind and you fall. It's a mental thing. Let go. And ski."

"Let go?"

"Have faith in your feet. They know what to do. You've been skiing for years. You've got good form. You've got good balance. Now balance your body and your mind. Let go of the mountain. And ski."

Let go? She understood fear. She felt it. How did a person let go? She looked down. A long way down. She had no choice now but to ski. Unless Zach sent a patrol to get her. She'd never get over that embarrassment.

"Ready?" he asked. "Be at one with the snow. With the mountain. I promise you'll be fine."

She followed him. She watched him. Zach was at one with the mountain. With the snow. Graceful. He carved his way swiftly and skillfully through the bumps and made it look easy.

She started after him and repeated like a mantra, "Let go. Let go. Let go." She felt herself relax. Her muscles loosened their static grip. She followed Zach's lead. Her feet felt light, her body perfectly balanced. She could do anything!

Suddenly, they were on the flats outside the lodge.

"My God, Zach! That was wonderful. You are incredible. The best. How can you ever stop skiing? Let's do it again."

When he didn't answer immediately, she removed her goggles. Then reached for his. His eyes devoured her.

"I'm incredible, huh? I should have taken you up there sooner." He kissed her swiftly on the mouth. "Sweetheart, we are going to do lots of things again. Skiing is just one of them."

She blushed.

He kissed her one more time.

She knew what the evening held and welcomed it.

"I HATE LEAVING YOU in the middle of the night," Zach grumbled as he got out of bed.

Amanda lay under the covers, watching him get dressed until the only bare part of him was his feet. He was almost as sexy putting his clothes on as he was taking them off. His broad shoulders and well-muscled body moved with powerful grace as he donned his shirt. She almost asked him to stay, but she bit her tongue. Although remaining discreet was becoming harder, they couldn't forget Molly for a minute. He carried his shoes and walked to the door.

"I don't like it, either, darling," she replied. "It gets mighty cold in this bed without you."

He pivoted and walked back to her. "Say that again, please."

"What? That it gets cold in the bed?"

"Before that. What did you call me?"

"What did I call you?" she repeated slowly as her memory kicked in. "Darling?" She gulped.

He crouched beside her bed and held her hand. "You did. And that's the first time."

She couldn't say a word.

He kissed her tenderly and whispered in her ear, "I like it, sweetheart. Good night."

He left then, closing the door quietly behind him.

Amanda couldn't sleep. A kaleidoscope of scenes from the busy day filled her mind, but the most vivid of all was the picture of Zach skiing down the slopes. She'd remember him always, reflecting the joy he took from the sport. He'd shared it with her, just as he shared it with all his students and guests.

Now she understood. Zach was born to ski and he belonged here, truly a part of the mountain he was raised on. He had explained it to her with words during the past weeks, words like freedom, fresh air and elbow room. But until she saw him tame those hills, she didn't really appreciate what he meant. Finally she did.

So he'd never fit into the New York scene. Not even part-time. And he'd never sell out to Chicago. She sat up and punched her pillow. And she'd never get to sleep tonight.

And where had that "darling" come from? Amanda wasn't one for pet names, and obviously, Zach knew it. That was why he'd pounced on this one. It just slipped out after some fantastic lovemaking when she was feeling amorous. Which would make sense.

Her thoughts went back to the slopes. Zach and the slopes. Zach and Diamond Ridge. She understood it all. But the question was, could *she* live the life? Did she want to?

CHAPTER ELEVEN

THE HIGH-SCHOOL auditorium was only a quarter full when Amanda and Zach arrived at the ski-association meeting. Zach seemed to know everyone there, and took his time speaking with each person. To Amanda's surprise, everyone knew her. Knew why she was at the Diamond, asked about Ben and Lily, and enfolded her into their midst as one of their own.

She remembered several of the closer neighbors easily, and searched her memory to recall others. She shook hands with them all. Working a crowd and meeting new people were part of her training, both as a model and as a litigator. And as a member of a reputable high-profile law firm.

"The room is filling up fast," said Zach ten minutes after they arrived.

Amanda's glance around confirmed Zach's words. "Seems like the meeting has drawn from all over the state. Hey, Zach, isn't that State Representative David Webster from this district? And he's got a couple of buddies with him."

She watched Zach check out the newcomers. Saw his eyes gleam with satisfaction. "Sure is, and he has.

I know David, and we're going to talk with all of them. Right now.''

Deeper and deeper. Up to her neck was how she was beginning to feel. But she wanted to hear everything the politicians had to say. Knowledge was power. She could work an offense or a defense, but she needed information. If the Diamond was to survive on Zach's terms, they'd need all the information they could glean. And two sets of ears were better than one.

"We're only here to gauge the sentiment of the crowd," David Webster said after Zach greeted him. "The question of legalized gambling in the state will be on the floor of the legislature in April or May."

"Can you tell which way the wind is blowing in the statehouse?" asked Zach.

The politician paused, as though weighing his next words. "We're all listening to our constituents, of course. But I will remind you, Zach, that not everyone has as strong an opinion as you do. Some folks think we can have both. People can still ski, and more jobs will be created in the casinos. Sorry, nothing's ever as cut and dried as we would like."

"But this is a no-brainer for us. Come on, David. You know the ski industry will be hurt. The nonskiers will take up lodging space needed for our guests. The regular skiers will run to New Hampshire or Maine, and we'll have fewer people on the slopes. Business will be cut by half."

Amanda sighed. Of course, if he sold to Paradise, it wouldn't matter which industry prevailed. They'd be in a win-win situation. The hotel would cater to everyone. And the Porters would have a hefty bank account.

"I hear you, Zach," David Webster replied. "And you can voice your opinion at public hearings that are being scheduled all over the state."

"You can bet I'll be there." Zach extended his hand. "Keep in touch, David. I'd appreciate any new information that comes your way."

When they finally took their seats, the auditorium was almost full. Amanda looked around at the intent faces, wondering how many felt as Zach did, and how many welcomed the thought of more jobs with casinos. Not everyone in the crowd owned a mountain!

But three hours later, she understood the ramifications of a depressed ski industry. The industry supported myriad other businesses in the area. Lots of bed-and-breakfasts, motels and other lodging places, restaurants, apparel shops, ski shops, ski rentals, even antique shops.

Most folks in the room felt threatened, and the association had no problem organizing committees to attend all public hearings, to lobby representatives in the statehouse and, perhaps most important, to disseminate information. Zach chaired the public-hearing committee.

"I'm sorry I'll be away a couple of evenings a week, but I really have to do this."

Amanda nodded.

"I'm fighting for my life here, sweetheart. For all

our lives. I could probably influence people at the hearings.''

"I know. I know you need to attend them, but I wish someone else could do it. We barely have enough time to handle all the work as it is.''

"We'll get some extra help. Maybe Pete from the ski school.''

She shook her head. "Maybe he can help. But…it's just that we won't have time to steal away up the mountain anymore. And I really loved doing that.''

He laced his fingers with hers. "And I really love you.''

AT NOON THE NEXT DAY, Amanda hung up the phone in the office and looked at Zach. "That's the third call I've had this morning from people at the meeting last night. This one was from the two widowed sisters who run the B and B a mile up the road from us.''

Zach turned to her, a frown of concern on his forehead. "What's up with the ladies? Did they have an accident going home?''

"No,'' she answered. "Nothing like that. They're scared.''

"Scared? Why?''

She stood up and started to pace the floor. "They want to retain me. They know I'm a lawyer. They know I'm part of Diamond Ridge and that I was with you last night. They said they trust me. They want to retain me just in case they need help in holding on to their home.''

A long, low whistle was Zach's first reply. Then he asked, "What about the other two calls?"

"Well, one asked me questions about eminent-domain issues, and the other one wanted an appointment with me."

"When are you seeing them?"

She started to pace again, then glared at him. "Don't sound so enthusiastic. I don't have a license to practice in this state, so I referred them to Sam Johnson."

"Good choice. So why don't you sit for the Vermont Bar exam?"

Instantly, her heart thudded and her palms became moist. Commitment loomed. "What?"

When the phone rang again, she lurched for it like a lifeline.

"Hello, Sam. We were just— Yes, I did…" She held the phone away from her ear as Sam Johnson boomed questions at her. "I know you want to retire, but what could I do? They need a good lawyer."

"I thought *you* were a good lawyer," Sam yelled.

Zach's face split into a wide grin. She wanted to throw the phone at him.

"I am a good lawyer. But not in Vermont."

"So practice with me until you pass the bar, and then let me retire!" *Crash.* The receiver slammed into the cradle.

She looked at Zach, unable to say a word. Amusement lurked in his eyes.

"Always liked that man," he said. "Couldn't have said it better myself."

"Was that really Sam? He was debonair and sophisticated in Ben's hospital room. What happened?"

"The man wants to retire, and he wants his clients in good hands. You're not cooperating fast enough."

"I feel a noose tightening here, Zach. And it's making me nervous." She stepped back, putting distance between them. "I'm on a leave of absence," she continued slowly. "And then I go back to the city. Nothing's really changed."

How can she think nothing's changed? Zach stood outside the hotel preparing to take his nightly walk around the grounds. From the chalet, he could hear the faint tinkle of music as the guests enjoyed après-ski social activity. Recent midweek bookings had been good, unusual for a nonholiday period.

Doesn't she understand that I love her? That I want to marry her? Surely she knows that's where we're headed. His boots crunched in the hard-packed snow, and he kicked a chunk of ice out of the way. Then he looked for another chunk to kick.

Women! He'd already admitted he didn't understand them. But he thought he understood Amanda. He'd had years to observe her. Didn't that count for anything? He'd have to back off. Maybe he was rushing her. The comment about the bar exam hadn't gone over well.

He stood in the middle of the road and slowly turned in a full circle. The shadowy outline of the mountains that surrounded him formed a cradle, with the resort in its center. His home. His world. Was he expecting too much of Amanda? They'd both left this home once, but he'd returned. She hadn't. If she left again, the Diamond would never be the same for him.

He had a lot of thinking to do. In the meantime, he'd follow her lead once more and take life one day at a time.

AMANDA SHUT OFF the radio with a hard click to the button. Damn the weather, anyway! Who needed a thaw at the end of February right before school-vacation week? They were booked solid and now this. Either there was too much weather or not enough. Their extensive snowmaking equipment would be useless if the outdoor temperature was sixty degrees, and if it rained as predicted, they'd have only mush.

She buried her face in her hands. It was crazy to run a business that was so dependent on the weather. So how had Ben done it all these years? She grimaced. Ben didn't have the enormous debts they had now. Even Molly felt the difference.

Just last night before going to sleep, Molly had offered all her savings to go toward the month's loan payment.

"Wow, Mol! You've got quite a bundle." Amanda, sitting at the side of the bed when Molly brought out her old flowered tin cookie jar, had been truly impressed by the wad of bills inside. "I didn't know you'd done so much baby-sitting."

"And at the ski-school nursery, too," Molly explained. "I want to be just like you, Amanda. I want to have a lot of money so we don't have to worry."

Amanda, startled by the innocent remark, winced. Molly had been raised with two wonderful parents and a good home. She shouldn't have that attitude. Zach's brows rose significantly. Then a thoughtful look came into his eyes before they began to twinkle.

"Mol, you know your sister's the biggest worrywart in all of New England. She's going to get old-lady lines on her pretty forehead if she keeps it up."

Molly started to giggle. And Amanda played along, grabbing a handheld mirror and pretending to search for lines.

Molly laughed harder and hugged her sister.

"There are no problems here, Popcorn Girl," said Zach. "But I'll tell you what you can do. Save all that dough. Let it grow. And if we ever do need it, we'll know who to ask. Is that a deal?" He extended his hand.

"Deal," she replied, before reaching up to hug him. "I love you, bro."

Zach kissed her on the forehead. "I love you, too, Molly. Sleep tight."

Now, Amanda sat at her desk, reminded once more of how complicated relationships can be. Her responsibilities to Molly, to Zach, to her mother and Ben, to her firm, to the hotel, to the folks who called for advice, all of these added up to much more than she wanted. That was why she lived alone. That was why she handled cases by herself as much as possible.

But how could she give up Zach? How could she turn her back on the sister she'd rediscovered? How could she ignore her mother and Ben when they needed her?

"Why the long face?" Zach asked as he walked into the office.

She shrugged. "The usual. The weather forecast, for one."

"So we'll have spring-skiing conditions for a couple of days and then the cold front will sweep in."

"What cold front?"

"The one that's going to hit midweek. The one I got on the radar computer reports."

Suddenly her heart was light. "Really? We're going to get some cold weather? Yes!" Her pencil flew into the air.

"Mandy, you can't keep this up." Zach walked behind the desk and gave her a quick kiss. "You're going to wear yourself out."

Even quick kisses made her sizzle. Amanda watched him as he straightened to his full height. All the philosophizing in the world couldn't stop her heart from quickening every time he walked into a room.

"You can't think one day at a time with the weather, Amanda. Think by the season. It'll all average out."

His words flew by her. She heard sounds, not meaning. But her gaze never left him. She loved him. The weather be damned!

"Do you want to get married?" It was her own voice she heard. Squeaky, but hers. And when Zach turned around quickly enough to create a breeze, she knew she'd really said it aloud.

She met his probing look, noted his tentative smile.

"If I thought for a minute you were serious, I'd tell you to name the date and time. But once you do," he added slowly, "there'll be no backing out."

She focused on breathing. In, out. In, out. Where was her courage? She stared at him and blinked.

"Tell you what, sweetheart—" Zach gave her a quick kiss "—ask me again after the season, and you'll get the answer you really want."

"August first, this year, 2:00 p.m.," she replied to his earlier statement. She pulled the date out of the air, but her whisper was barely audible.

Zach heard it. And stared. "Just hold that thought, Amanda. Until late spring. When everything else is settled. Then you'll really know."

He didn't say yes. Warm, loving, kind. But he'd turned her down. She'd never find the courage to ask again. Not when she was so frightened the first time.

She needed to get away. She jumped out of her chair, but wound up in Zach's arms, cradled, protected and loved. She felt it in his hands as he caressed her, in his mouth as he kissed her, in the strong beat of his heart as it thumped against her chest.

His love surrounded her, but commitment was absent. Maybe he wasn't ready. Maybe he was right and she wasn't ready. But nothing was better than being in his arms.

He waltzed her around the office, humming Billy Joel's "Always a Woman." Not bad. His voice held when he changed to "Wind Beneath My Wings." But that was when her tears came. He wanted to fly...with her. Despite their differences. Despite his tabling of the hardest question she'd ever asked in her life.

They swayed together, his fingers gently tracing the outline of her mouth. She was drowning in the warmth of his eyes.

"How did I ever get so lucky?" he whispered.

Her lids closed, another tear escaping. She prayed he'd always feel this way.

"A JERRY FONTAINE is on the line for you, Amanda," announced Nancy, the new front-desk manager. It was the first week of March. They had survived vacation week, which Molly had spent in New York. As promised, Karen had spent almost the entire month working with Nancy before she left, and Nancy was proving her mettle.

Amanda reached for the phone reluctantly. Jerry would be calling for only one reason: to convince them to sell. This was his fifth call since he'd left in January, and he always asked for her.

"Amanda? Good. I'm glad you're in. I wanted to talk to the more rational partner, so I'm calling you."

Her ears perked up. "I'm listening."

"Look, we know you guys are in a financial bind. We know about your stepfather's stroke. We both know what it costs to get extensive rehab like that. Despite health insurance. And you'll be wanting to make adjustments at the hotel for him and all.

"Talk to that man of yours, Amanda. He's a stubborn one, Zach is. But we want him, too. Think of it. No relocation for anyone. You all stay. You run the show. Zach is manager, with almost a free hand. Paradise assumes all debts with a bundle left over. What could be better?''

''Why us, Jerry? And don't give me any 'auld lang syne' about knowing Zach years ago.''

''Thought you'd ask. Well, we looked at a lot of locations up there. And there are a bunch of fine properties to be had. Yes, there are.''

''Uh-huh.''

''It's simple, really. Access road. You've got the best access road and you're close to the interstate.''

''I see.''

''Not, of course, that we couldn't work around that with someone else. Road-building projects are mighty attractive to folks who need work.''

''How hard are you lobbying for casinos, Jerry?''

''As hard as I have to. We've got somebody working the boys in Montpelier. I won't hide it. But Paradise is coming to Vermont with or without casinos.''

And she was a monkey's uncle. Gambling would make even a mediocre ski area a valuable property. But once it arrived, most of the local townsfolk wouldn't own anything.

Diamond Ridge would be a winner either with or without casinos. Of course, without gambling, Paradise might pay less for the Diamond, but they'd have to give Zach more freedom. ''So what exactly are you saying, Jerry? You'd better give me some numbers if you want me to speak to Zach.''

He started to talk numbers. And more numbers. Bigger numbers.

She gripped the phone more tightly. "Want to repeat that?"

She wrote it down. "Impressive. But Zach's his own man, and he likes the Diamond just the way it is. Do you have a set of numbers in case gambling doesn't get voted in? I can't promise anything."

"No point in doing all that work," Jerry replied. "With the amount of wining and dining we're doing around the state and at the capital, legalized gambling is a done deal."

"You can buy a done deal at the statehouse, but you can't buy Zach."

"Then maybe I'll visit his uncle."

Her spine went rigid. "Don't even think about it," she said in a slow, deadly voice. "I'll nail you to the outhouse wall until you sing soprano if you even go *near* the hospital."

"Threats, Counselor?"

"A promise. A promise that a restraining order will be first on the list."

"Mandy, Mandy, Mandy. A restraining order? Among friends? Come on. We're talking straight business here."

"The name's Ms. Shaw to you. And, by the way, Zach holds majority shares in this resort. So his uncle is of no use to you whatsoever. It all boils down to Zach."

Of course, Jerry didn't have to know about the love and respect uncle and nephew had for each other. Each one's opinion would have weight with the other.

That wasn't his business. She hoped she focused him only on Zach.

She'd barely hung up from Jerry's call, mentally making plans to alert Lily to the possibility of a surprise visit from the hotel chain, when the phone rang again.

"This is the principal of Green Mountain Middle School, looking for Amanda Shaw or Zachary Porter."

Molly's school. "This-is-Amanda-Shaw-what's-wrong-with-Molly?"

"Nothing, physically."

"Thank goodness." Amanda's relief was short-lived.

"But you'd better come down here."

"I'm at work right now. In the middle of a million things—"

"Molly has $323 stashed in her locker. Do you know how it got there?"

Would her sister be so dumb as to take her baby-sitting money to school? "Just a minute while I check her hiding place."

Amanda ran down the hall to the family apartment. Down another corridor to her sister's room, reached under the bed and grabbed the hideaway tin. It was filled to the top. So the money in school came from somewhere else.

Shoot! Now what had Molly gotten herself into?

"POKER? YOU'VE BEEN playing poker with your girlfriends? And taking their money?"

"Not my girlfriends, Mandy. They don't even know how to play. It was the stupid boys. They're always showing off and talking about how we're going to be like Las Vegas. And how they're going to get rich and win millions of dollars. So, I shut them up. Fair and square. I didn't cheat or anything!"

"Gambling of any kind is not allowed in school, Molly," the principal said.

"We didn't play in school," Molly protested. "We played on the bus."

"On the bus?" Amanda echoed. She sounded like a parrot. The day was going from bad to worse, and her thought process was nonexistent.

"Yeah. In the back. But I didn't cheat."

"Molly, you have to return the money," Amanda said quickly. "Even if you didn't cheat. That's not the point. Gambling is not allowed on the bus or in the school. Am I right?" She turned toward the principal.

He nodded. "Your sister hustled them, Ms. Shaw. I've gotten calls from three parents so far. We are very disappointed in Molly."

She looked at Molly, and Molly looked at the floor. "Hustling, Molly? Explain it to me."

"All I did was start at a penny and two, then when they won a little, we played five and ten. And then I won. I don't see why you're so mad. We need the money." Molly folded her arms in front of her, defensive and belligerent.

The whole day was a nightmare that wouldn't end. "We do not, I repeat, do not, need your money."

"Yes, we do. And besides, I don't want the Diamond to become a casino. I want everybody to be happy and stay like we are.'' She started to cry. ''And the boys said all the hotels will become casinos and nobody will go skiing anymore. And what will we do?''

She's just like me. Borrowing problems before they exist.

''I can tell you one thing for sure, Popcorn Girl. We're always going to be a family, no matter what. You don't have to solve the problems all by yourself. Didn't Zach tell you not to worry a couple of weeks ago?''

''Yeah. But you're still worried,'' she accused.

''Only a little. Mostly, I'm working hard to fight back.'' She looked up at the principal. ''If Molly returns all the money, can we consider this incident closed?''

He nodded, and looked rather relieved. But did add that he expected Molly never to gamble again on school property.

''I suppose it wasn't really fair,'' Molly said as they kicked snow in the parking lot. ''They're such a bunch of babies.'' She giggled. ''They couldn't even hide their excitement when they got one little pair.'' She shook her head and tsk-tsked. ''Amateurs. Mere amateurs.''

Astonished, but choking on her laughter, Amanda could barely speak. ''And where did you learn all these wonderful skills?''

Molly looked at her totally surprised. ''From Daddy. We play all the time. He's the best poker player around. Didn't you know that? Mommy calls him the King of Hearts.''

"THE KING OF HEARTS, Zach? Your uncle, who is also my stepfather, the man we both love, has taught his daughter to hustle twelve-year-old boys!"

If he didn't stop laughing soon, he knew she would kill him. "It's not as bad as you think," he gasped. "It's a little friendly game he and his cronies play once in a while."

"How often is once in a while? Every week? Every month?" She drummed her fingers on his desk. "Okay. It doesn't matter. He's an adult. He can do what he wants. But how much is it costing us?"

"Costing us?"

"I mean, has he lost the price of a monthly loan payment?"

He tried to catch his breath and phrase his answer diplomatically. "Actually, Amanda, quite the opposite. Let's just say that by the end of the year, he's usually ahead."

"If he's all that gung-ho about card games, then maybe he'll want to run a damn casino. After all, he won't be able to ski. Did you ever think of that?"

Zach rose from his chair and walked to the picture window. He couldn't see much in the reflected moonlight, but in his mind's eye, the landscape appeared as clearly as it did on a sunny day. It was a view that always brought him peace. "He's in no condition to run anything right now, Mandy. But he recently invested megabucks to expand what we have. That's where his heart is.''

"I know,'' she said, regaining her composure. ''And I know it's where your heart is, too. And you belong here doing what you're doing. I'm just not sure where I belong in this picture.''

Not sure? He wasn't sure that the heart she'd referred to still beat in his body. He watched her wander restlessly around the room, touching a book, touching the back of her chair. Not able to sit. ''What are you saying, sweetheart?''

"I don't know where I fit, Zach. In fact, I'm thinking of going to New York for a couple of days. Get some perspective.''

"I thought we belonged together,'' he said quietly. How could she think otherwise? He loved her as much as a man possibly could. She had to know that!

"How do you feel about a future with me commuting from the city? If we need the income, that's what it may boil down to.''

"What about practicing here? Wouldn't that be logical? I'd help you get started in any way I could.''

She smiled sadly. ''I couldn't make the same money, Zach. Not compared to New York.''

"And it all boils down to money?''

"Money buys freedom. It can buy you the freedom to hang on to the Diamond. Or it can give you the freedom to let it go. So don't get on a high horse and give me any speeches about it being the root of all evil, et cetera, et cetera. Money can make things happen.''

Logical Amanda. Not avaricious. Not a Uriah Heep. Just following her own common sense. "Point taken. Now, think about this. Have we missed one payment to the bank? No. Have we had to ask for any extensions? No. Has the bank called us with any concerns at all? No. It seems to me, sweetheart, we're hanging on to the Diamond all by ourselves."

She nodded, a thoughtful expression on her face. "Okay, point to you."

"And we'll continue to do so. The success of Diamond Ridge does not—do you hear me?—does not rest on your shoulders. Don't you think mine are broad enough?"

"Are they broad enough to handle a phone call I got today?"

He raised his brow in question.

"Jerry Fontaine called earlier to make us a deal, an offer he thinks we can't refuse."

"That's interesting." Zach laughed. "I can refuse any offer."

Amanda nodded. "Jerry's people are certain that the state legislature will approve gambling. His offer to buy the Diamond is impressive. So is the salary he wants to pay you."

"I'm not for sale." Zach's reply was curt and emphatic.

"If gambling passes, plenty of folks will get in line to sell. Idealism is always for sale at the right price. And Paradise knows it. They've got all those numbers worked out, but didn't bother costing out a deal if gambling fails to come in."

An alarming thought crossed his mind. His eyes locked with hers. "Tell me, Amanda," he asked, "are you trying to negotiate selling the Diamond to Jerry?" He paused when she didn't answer. "You don't own the major share of the mountain, and I didn't authorize you to be my lawyer. Next time, tell Jerry to call me."

"I was just trying to help," she replied. "Fact-gathering is my specialty. Now you have more ammunition to use."

"Do me a favor," he said as he held out his hand. "Help me in every other way you can, but don't get involved with Jerry and his bunch. I'm not selling the mountain."

She walked toward him and wrapped her arms around him. "Being lovers is more fun than being business partners, anyway."

He took her in his arms, enjoying the feel of her as she wrapped herself around him, bestowing kisses all over his face. And then homed in for the sizzle.

She tasted like honey and felt like silk. Instantly aroused, he felt every muscle tighten as he tried to remain in control. But when she said, "I love you, Zach. You are such a good man," and when her tongue invaded his mouth again, he swept a pile of papers from the desk and lifted her onto the surface.

Her eyes brightened, and without a word, she leaned back on her elbows and raised her bottom so he could ease off her pants. Her eagerness touched him more than she'd ever know. Only in his arms did she let go of her mind and lead with her heart. Only in his arms.

Then she leaned forward and unbuckled his belt. She lowered his zipper and with one fast tug on his waistband, shoved his pants to the floor. She reached for him.

"Wait, Amanda. I need to get—"

"Not a problem," she whispered. "I started on the pill last week."

It took a moment for the significance to register. Joy filled his heart.

"I love you, Amanda. You'll never be sorry."

"I know that," she whispered. "Deep down. Now don't waste time. Kiss me again."

He gladly obliged—after he locked the office door.

Kisses and more. One arm held her while his other hand roamed under her sweater. He heard her gasp as he stroked her, and again when her nipples grew taut.

"Oh…oh…"

He reveled in her moan, his fingers pausing, stroking, pressing, before traveling lower to touch her most sensitive spot.

"Yes, yes…Zach…" Her whole body trembled, and she raised her hips. "More…"

"Anything you want."

Oh, she was ready for him. Hot, moist and very ready. Her legs tightened, her whole body stiffened, and her arms twined around his neck, pulling him down.

"Kiss me again. Closer… I want…I want…all of you."

"Yes, my love….easy, easy." He positioned himself above her at the edge of the desk and joined with her easily. She was made for him. He held her still for a moment, just absorbing the sensation of being surrounded by Amanda. Allowing her to absorb the sensation of being filled by him.

And then there was no waiting. One thrust of her hips and he answered in kind. They flew, then soared. He reveled in their flight, in her moans of joy. He'd never tire of her. He'd need a lifetime to discover everything she was.

But now he knew one truth. She was the other half of himself. Regardless of her outward fears for the future.

In his arms, she had no fear. In his arms was where she belonged. And where she would stay. He caressed her in the afterglow, holding her on his lap in his big swivel chair, and rejoicing in the lingering tremors of her fulfillment.

She rested against him so trustingly, her head on his chest, one arm around his waist, her eyes closed. And finally her body felt totally relaxed.

He looked at the face he loved. The face of a complex, intriguing woman who would make his life complete.

THE CALL FROM HER BOSS came the next morning just as Amanda was on her way to cover a beginner's class for the ski school.

"Spending time on the slopes sounds like a tough assignment," Mr. Garroway said.

"You don't know the half of it," Amanda replied, ignoring the hint of sarcasm in his voice.

"I don't have much time, Amanda, but I wanted to touch base with you. Your leave is over in two weeks. Will you be ready for a caseload?"

Another reality check. "As a matter of fact, I'm planning a quick visit to my folks in a few days. I'll call you for an appointment."

"Excellent, Amanda. We want to see you back with us."

As Amanda replaced the receiver, she glanced at her desk, the surface of which was covered with neat piles of color-coded folders. In one corner were four blue files, cases she was referring to Sam Johnson. Next to them was a red folder labeled Paradise Hotel. She'd kept the notes and the figures from Jerry's conversation. The Paradise group wasn't giving up.

Three additional folders containing notes of discussions she and Zach had had with other hotels and real estate developers lay beside a stack of information on pending legislation related to gambling, including the schedule of public hearings Zach would attend. She glanced at the new large calendar on the wall. All the meetings, times and locations were listed there, also.

She also had a file for the local Chamber of Commerce, as well as for the regional ones. And most importantly, there was a special folder listing every state representative in Vermont. Their local reps had individual folders.

The place looked like a war room, Amanda thought. And perhaps it was. Zach had already held two meetings there with other resort owners. Auxiliary-business owners came, too, concerned that their livelihoods were in danger. As the widow ladies next door said, "We don't want to sell to anyone. This is our home. We want to live here."

So everyone had their own needs. She knew that some people wouldn't mind selling out and walking away with a bundle of cash. Where was the right and the wrong in this issue?

And what did she want? She shook her head impatiently. She was still working on it.

She glanced at her watch and dashed for the door. Her class was waiting, and she looked forward to being outside with them. Beginner classes were the most fun to teach. Naturally, most students were a little nervous at first, but after only two hours, they would be loving it. They'd know how to stop, to turn, they would have enjoyed going down a slight straight run, and they would have ridden the lift. They'd feel like they conquered the world.

She really had to get recertified with the Professional Ski Instructors of America. Diamond Ridge maintained high standards for their staff. She would be no exception.

ZACH STOOD AT A DISTANCE, watching Amanda laugh with her students. She wore a new turquoise ski outfit that made her eyes rival the bluebonnets of Texas. Her animated face, her gestures became photographs in his mind. He wanted her happy like this. Enjoying life, instead of worrying about it. And he wanted a full-time wife.

He knew how to guarantee both. Taking a deep breath, he walked into the hotel and into the office. He looked at the red file on Amanda's desk. Jerry's figures were in it.

CHAPTER TWELVE

"I'LL ONLY BE GONE a few days, Molly. I'll be back before you know it. Do you think you can stay out of trouble for that long?" Amanda stood in the middle of the kitchen facing her sister, her arms resting loosely on Molly's shoulders. Her small valise sat near the back door.

"I don't get into trouble on purpose, you know," Molly protested. "It just happens."

Amanda grinned at her sister's logic. "I know. Next time, try using the J-word—judgment." She ruffled the girl's hair and gave her a hug.

"You weren't so perfect, either, when you were my age," Molly grumbled. "Zach's told me lots of stories about you."

"Zach didn't know me when I was twelve. Back then we lived… Oh, never mind." She preferred not thinking about those years anymore.

"So what kind of stories has Zach been telling about me?" Amanda asked as she pulled herself back to the present. She looked over Molly's head at the culprit, who stepped back in protest.

"Would I tell stories about you, Amanda-mine? Must have been Uncle Ben."

"Liar," said Molly.

"Okay, you two. Behave." Amanda searched Zach's face. "Is everything under control in the office? Is there anything you need before I go?"

"Only this." He approached her with deliberate steps, his gaze riveted on hers.

Her pulse leaped with anticipation at the promise in his eyes, and then she was in his arms, being thoroughly kissed. In ten seconds, her limbs felt like Jell-O. Her knees wobbled and her arms weighed a hundred pounds each. She leaned into him and licked her lips, savoring his flavor. "Wow," she whispered.

"Want more?" he asked.

"No!" Molly shouted before Amanda could catch her breath. "That's enough yuck."

Amanda laughed. With the spell broken, she pushed herself away from Zach and walked to the door. "See you Thursday." She blew them a kiss, grabbed her valise and stepped outside.

She slid behind the wheel of the Jeep, still grinning. Her answer would have been different from Molly's. Yes, she wanted more. She'd always want more. But at what cost to herself?

Suddenly sober, she kept her eyes on the road as she made her way south to the Big Apple. But her brain continued to hum.

She noticed the silence about ten minutes after leaving the hotel. It surrounded her. And jarred her. This was the first time she'd been totally alone since she'd arrived at the Diamond. From the moment she'd stepped into her mother's kitchen, she'd been constantly surrounded by people, noise and responsibility.

How ironic to have no privacy at all, when she was so used to years of total privacy. It was a miracle she'd survived these three months.

The five-hour drive seemed interminable. By the time she pulled into a garage near her apartment, she felt stiff and tired. She took her overnighter and walked to her building as quickly as possible.

"Your mom's not back from the hospital yet," the friendly doorman greeted her. "She usually gets in around nine."

"Every night? Isn't that kind of late?"

Tony was silent for a moment, then smiled. "Like daughter, like mother? It's those twelve-hour shifts she works. Gets off at seven, then visits with your father. But I keep an eye out for her, Ms. Shaw. That I do."

"Thanks so much, Tony. I appreciate it."

Amanda unlocked her apartment door. She stood on the threshold letting her eyes absorb what she hadn't seen in weeks. The white carpet. It did remind her of snow. The pristine furniture in fabric suitable only for a fashionable city dwelling, not for a busy hotel filled with athletes of all levels and ages.

Everything looked so precise. In place. So cool and sophisticated. She'd been a good little girl, coloring within the lines. White on white. With not a trace of passion. Or love.

She walked into the foyer and slowly turned in a

full circle. The walls seemed close, the apartment small. Even in white.

"What's the matter with me?" she whispered. "I chose this apartment. I created this home. I was happy here." A headache started to build. Her palms became damp. Nerves jittered throughout her body as she faced a painful truth.

She didn't belong here anymore.

The headache demanded release. She raised her hands to her temples and started to massage.

But could she make the Diamond her home? Despite Zach's best efforts, there was no security there. Bank loans had to be paid, and worrying about the damn weather for the rest of her life would kill her.

A single tear rolled down her cheek. She wiped it away, walked into the kitchen and swallowed two aspirin. Where did she belong? Where did she fit?

She whirled from the kitchen and ran to her bedroom. She needed shelter. She needed peace. She needed comfort. Her country-style room provided them all.

Especially with her mom's personality flavoring the place. Unbelievably, she'd almost forgotten about Lily, but her sweater rested on the back of the rocker, her slippers on the floor near the bed. Pictures of the family were propped everywhere. Even on the fridge in the kitchen. Some favorites Lily had brought with her, but some were new ones of Molly taken last month during her visit to New York.

Amanda shook her head and changed into clean sweats. She couldn't remember the last time she needed her mother's comfort. What a day! She crawled into bed. Right now, her brain was fried.

"ARE YOU EVER GETTING UP?" asked a familiar voice.

Sunlight streamed in the window, hitting Amanda right in the eyes. She groaned and rolled over, then felt a kiss on her forehead.

"No fever. Just fatigue. Has Molly worn you out?"

Amanda grinned and rolled onto her back. "Hi, Mom!" Her eyes scrolled her mother's face, so familiar and dear, yet so far away in recent years. Unexpectedly, tears welled. She sat up quickly, hugged Lily and ran to the bathroom. She washed vigorously, dallying behind the locked door until she felt in control again. Waterworks had never been her style. Recent developments seemed to have changed that, and she'd be a liar not to admit it.

She patted her face dry, brushed her hair and walked out, almost knocking Lily over.

"What's going on, Amanda? Did Zach do something I should kill him for?"

She should have known her mother wouldn't ignore her tears. "No, no. Nothing. Everything's great."

"Then why are you crying?"

"Can't I just be happy to see you?"

"Sure you can," Lily said, giving her a hug, "but you would have run toward me, not away from me, if that's all it was. So what's wrong, honey?"

Despite her thoughts of the previous night, she found she wasn't ready to talk. For the past ten years, she'd handled everything by herself. Some habits were hard to change. Besides, her relationship with Zach was private. The best strategy right now was to change topics.

"So tell me about Pops. How's he doing?" Amanda sat against the pillows on the big bed and looked up at her mother.

Lily's piercing glance changed to resignation as she lowered herself into the maple rocking chair and set it in gentle motion. "Okay, Amanda. We'll play it your way. For now. And Pops actually is doing very well."

Her mother's blue eyes, so like her own, lit with happiness as she spoke of her husband. "In fact, and don't mention this to Molly yet, we may be coming home by April."

Gladness filled Amanda's heart. "Home? You've decided to come home? That's fantastic. I can't wait to see him. And all of this will be over sooner than expected."

"Slow down a minute," Lily said as she suited action to word, leaning forward in the rocker, stopping its motion. "What do you mean by saying I *decided* to go home? Where else would I go if not home?"

"Well, how about your job? And all the talk about living in New York now that Zach bought out a chunk of the business from Pops?"

Her mother looked puzzled at first, then a bit guilty. "I'm working because I needed something to do here. I'm used to being busy all day. I can't sit with Ben every minute."

"Oh." Confusion reigned in Amanda's mind, dashing her preconceived concepts.

"Pops doesn't want to stay here. He wants to go home," Lily reiterated.

"But the sidewalks are flat, and getting around is easier. And Molly said you were going to see if she liked it here. I thought Florida might be better where the weather is always good. No snow for him to fall on."

Lily shook her head repeatedly, her expression more baffled than before. "I feel like I fell down the rabbit hole with Alice. Where are you getting these crazy ideas?"

"Well, it makes sense," Amanda replied as she started to justify herself. "You've got a good nest egg now. You're safe. Why should you want to live with the concerns of the business anymore? Zach's got the fifty-one percent share. It's his problem, and he wants to run the place."

"You should have penned fiction, my girl, instead of legal briefs. Listen to me. We are going to the Diamond because that's where home is. That's where our children are."

"But once on the phone you said—"

"On the phone? What do you…? Oh, now I remember. But I was very worried then. I wasn't sure what was happening with Ben. How much he would recover. And staying in the city seemed logical at the time. I must have been a little nutsy."

"Mmm, that's kinda what Zach said."

Lily laughed. "Zach called me nutsy?"

"Worse." Amanda winked before she loudly whispered, "He called you a tourist."

Amanda enjoyed watching Lily laugh at herself. Her mother laughed for a long time. Probably the first big laugh she'd had since bringing Ben to the rehab center. "I bet he called me a few more things besides a tourist."

Amanda grinned. She'd pull out the jokes to keep her mother laughing as long as she could. "Well, he said you were just getting ahead of yourself, but you'd straighten up in no time. And that Molly would drive you crazy being indoors more than she's used to."

"He's right about that. Oh, Mandy, it's so good to have you here."

In an instant, Amanda found herself clasped in a bear hug as Lily joined her on the bed. Her mother's strong grip told its own story, and Amanda felt a tear roll down her cheek again as she returned the embrace.

What had she been thinking all these years, separating herself so much from the family? Hardly visiting them. Here she was, crying with her mom, feeling all those sloppy, messy emotions she'd always avoided, and it was okay.

"So you and Pops want to go back to Diamond Ridge when he's released?"

"Pops can't wait."

"But…but…are you aware of what's going on with big hotel chains coming in and the casinos and the politics of the gaming industry? Are you aware of the debt on our place?"

"Of course I am. So what? We've had debt before, which we paid off. It's just operating expenses."

Now her mother was really nutsy. Totally unrealistic. But Amanda wouldn't be the one to argue finances with her.

"I need to take a shower, Mom. Clear my head." Was she the only one in the family who saw the risks? Or was there something wrong with her?

TWO HOURS LATER, Amanda watched her stepfather walk down the hospital corridor, using only a cane. With fire in his eyes, he waved her back and continued to make his way toward her.

"Wants to show off for you," Lily whispered.

"He has a right to." The difference between the Ben in the Vermont hospital and the Ben walking now was so great Amanda had to remind herself that he was recovering from a serious stroke. She glimpsed her mother's expression. Money couldn't buy the joy in Lily's eyes. *Oh, yes, it could,* the practical side of Amanda argued. But his recovery was worth every penny.

The strength of his hug as he handed Lily the cane and wrapped his arms around Amanda said it all.

"And you're tall again, too," Amanda joked.

His laughter almost drowned his answer. "Tall enough to tower over you, squirt." His speech was still slower than normal, but clearer than before.

"Molly never explained how terrific you are."

"Molly wants her old dad back."

For the first time, she saw a flash of pain in his eyes.

"She's a child, Pops. She sees things in black or white. Wants everything to be perfect."

"Seems to me," Lily said softly, "she's not the only daughter who wants perfection."

Amanda glanced sharply at her mother. And didn't touch the comment. She stayed at Ben's side, providing support, as he continued to stroll down the hall.

"Tell me about Molly," he said.

She latched on to her sister as a topic, and could have spoken for hours to avoid the personal questions she knew would follow.

"That weak-kneed principal should have let her keep the money. Taught those boys a lesson, she did."

"Pops! She hustled them."

"She's too young for boys to be sniffing around, so she got 'em good. My daughters can take care of themselves."

Amanda nodded, not trusting herself to speak as the pride in his voice struck a chord. Waterworks threatened again when she realized his pride was misplaced. Sure she'd proved she could take care of herself. But only financially. She wanted more than that.

And now she loved a man who might lose everything. Everything he'd worked for and loved. The only way to protect him was to live apart in order to earn a lot of money. And that might not be enough. So the only safe way out of all risk was to sell the Diamond. Or…walk away. Totally. Go back to New York, to her old life. No involvements, no messy emotions.

And Zach would be free to find someone else. She wouldn't be a chain around his neck with her pessimism.

What a great rationalization for copping out of a relationship! But the tape played over and over in her mind until she felt another headache coming on.

SHE ATE LUNCH with Ben and her mom in the patients' dining room, where she felt like a six-year-old on display as Ben introduced her to everyone who walked in. But finally, they were alone at their table, and she saw that the love Lily and Ben had for each other was stronger than ever. The gentle pats, the touches, the smiles. She could have that with Zach.

"So now tell me about you and Zach," Ben said, eagerly leaning toward her.

She was trained to talk and persuade, or introduce red herrings if needed. Fifteen minutes later, Ben had a complete picture of Zach's activities, vignettes of guests, the story of the nor'easter and anything else she could remember.

"My daughter," Lily said to her husband, "is 'full of sound and fury signifying nothing.'"

Shakespeare had it right, Amanda admitted to herself as she stood up. "I've got to make a phone call."

As she left the table, she heard Lily say to Ben, "Her father really left his mark on her...and I...I couldn't erase it. She's never going to let love in, Ben, not the for-better-or-for-worse kind." Amanda turned around and saw her mother's face in her hands. She hurried to the phone and called Chicago.

"Just want to get my ducks in a row here, Jerry," she said, "before I argue a buyout with Zach."

"No problem. Zach'll love it. He'll manage the place. Free hand to hire anyone he likes, including his uncle. We know a good thing when we see it."

"You sure do," Amanda said as she rubbed her forehead.

"In fact, we've already got blueprints for the improvements we have in mind. Everything's already in writing. I'm under a lot of pressure to get this done quickly. It's unbelievable. By the time we finish, you won't recognize the place." He paused for a beat. "So when can you speak with our boy?"

Her headache exploded.

ZACH WALKED THE LOBBY of Diamond Ridge, nodding and smiling at the guests as he always did, but for the first time he could remember, he felt like a robot. The hotel had a fair-size crowd for the middle of the week. He should have been very satisfied. He barely cared.

All he felt was lonely. The place seemed empty without Amanda. And she'd only been gone since morning!

He rounded up Molly and brought her into the family kitchen for dinner.

"So if you marry Amanda, will you be my real brother?"

Zach smiled. "When I marry Amanda, I will continue to be your brother, just like always."

"Are you going to let her work in the city all week?

She wants to, you know. Because she went to school for a lot of years so she could make a lot of money."

"Don't remind me."

"Maybe she could be a model again. They make scads of money. And she's prettier than a whole lot of them, and she's not too old, I don't think."

"Popcorn Girl, you think too much. That's how you get into trouble."

She grinned at him, totally unrepentant. "Want to play some gin rummy? I'll spot you twenty-five points. If I win, I get to stay up an extra hour."

He glared at her.

"Okay," she added. "Just a half hour."

"I want to see your homework, pal. All of it."

Later, after Molly was asleep, he walked the familiar roads. When he looked around, he saw only buildings, impersonal hardwood, brick, mortar, glass. They could have belonged to anyone. The snow was dirty at the edge of the road. No fresh flakes had fallen in a couple of weeks. In the distance, he heard the engines of the big cats as they groomed the slopes. The night crew was working. But they could have been anyone's crew. Any good manager could make the business work. It didn't have to be him.

He grimaced at his belated honesty. Amanda was suffering because of him. In his heart, he'd always known it, but he loved her and hoped against hope that love would be enough. But the truth was, she'd be happier with someone else. Someone who wasn't fighting an uphill battle for survival. Someone with whom she'd feel secure.

Sadness filled his being. If he missed her so much after only one day, how would he survive a lifetime without her?

It wouldn't come to that, he vowed. He still held an ace up his sleeve. Paradise wasn't such a bad deal. No worse than any other hotel operation. He knew their ways. He knew the people. All he had to do was call them and discuss their offer.

"WANT THE NEWSPAPER before I throw it in the recycling bin?" asked Lily the next morning.

Amanda reached for the paper, but let it lie unopened on her lap. She sat in the rocking chair in her bedroom, thinking about Zach, but no closer to finding perfect answers for them than she'd been before she came to New York. She was also dealing with another new emotion, and she didn't like it.

Loneliness.

She missed Zach dreadfully, and she'd only been gone two nights. How would she survive seeing him only on weekends? And even weekends were optimistic once she was involved with her cases. Work came first at her firm. If she wanted to make full partner one day, it had to. The money would be fabulous. But did she want it badly enough? Three months ago, she had, but now the cost seemed too high.

Selling the resort was not an option yet. At least not selling it to Paradise. The money would be great, but after speaking with Jerry Fontaine again, she knew *the cost was too high.* Under Paradise rules, the Diamond would never be the same. The corporate policies and procedures would be enforced. New logos, building facades and standard facilities. All the unique charm of Diamond Ridge would vanish. Zach would lose more than the security Paradise's money could provide. But she hadn't told Jerry that. The final decision had to be Zach's.

The cost was too high. The phrase rang over and over in her mind. Wouldn't the cost be too high for Zach to pay, no matter who the buyer was?

She had to face the truth. Zach had always been his own man. She fell in love with him for who he was, including that spirit of independence and confidence.

Slowly sanity returned and, with it, peace. She wanted a life with Zach. He was the right person for her, and *loving the right person contained no risk at all.* The risk lay in running away. Everything else in their lives, they'd handle together.

She closed her eyes and lay her head on the back of the chair. She pictured Zach skiing with her down the Rough.

"Let go of the mountain," he'd said. "Let go of your fear."

"Okay, my love," she whispered. "I'm flying right beside you."

She didn't notice the now ever-present tears on her cheek until Lily handed her a tissue and said, "Want to talk, darling?"

She looked at her mother. "Everything's going to be just fine, Mom. I promise."

"I know it will be. You're *my* daughter, too!"

Amanda laughed, squeezed Lily's hand and idly

picked up the newspaper on her lap. She browsed through the pages, stopping at the business section. Usually it was the first section she read after the front page. She noted a small article on the impending legislation in Vermont, about how major hotel chains were poised to step in. She sighed, then turned to the stock exchange and Nasdaq listings. She automatically picked out her investments, her mind clicking like a calculator. A minute later, she sat bolt upright in her chair.

"My God, why didn't I think of this before!"

She had all the answers now. She could move her relationship with Zach forward. She'd have no worries, and Zach would be happy. And a wedding on August first could happen.

Tomorrow promised to be a busy day.

THE FOLLOWING EVENING, a weary Amanda placed a call to Zach. "I'll be home tomorrow night," she said by way of a greeting. "I need a little more time."

Zach sat straighter in his chair. "What's going on, honey? Did Molly call you or something?"

"No." She laughed.

"Want to clue me in?"

"Well…I need the morning to clean out my office."

He almost dropped the phone.

"Are you there, Zach? Say something."

"There must be static on the line. Could you repeat what you said?"

"I resigned today, Zach. From Stanhope Jones."

He could barely find his voice. "I love you, sweetheart. More than you know. I guess you weren't so wild about the commute, either."

"You got that right."

"Everything's going to work out, Mandy. I promise. You won't have to worry at all. Life is going to be absolutely sweet."

"You're right again. We'll be together and handle everything as a team."

"You bet we will. Good night, baby."

He replaced the phone gently into its cradle. All thoughts about Amanda being better off with someone else flew away. He'd been blessed with a wonderful woman. What she sacrificed for him, he could certainly do for her. He was probably being unreasonable all this time, anyway. Working for Paradise wouldn't be so bad. The family would still be at the Diamond.

In fact, he'd buy a round-trip ticket to Chicago right now. He reached for the receiver just as the phone rang again.

"Want to say good-night one more time, baby?" He almost purred into the phone.

"I didn't know you cared, you old son of a gun," boomed Jerry Fontaine's familiar voice. "But now that we have a buyout arrangement, maybe you do."

Zach laughed. "Do you have ESP? I was just thinking about visiting."

"Well, come on over. We've got papers to sign."

Zach shook his head to clear it. "Papers? I'm a little confused, Jerry. *We* haven't discussed anything yet, so how could *we* have an agreement?"

Silence greeted his comment.

"Hello?" Zach spoke directly into the phone.

"You obviously haven't spoken with Amanda yet."

"Amanda? What's she got to do with this?"

A stream of mild, then heavy obscenities crossed through the wire into Zach's ear, before Jerry replied coherently, "Amanda's got just about everything to do with this, except screwing it up. I've done that part all by myself."

AMANDA DROVE SLOWLY along the state highway leading to Diamond Ridge. Although she couldn't wait to see Zach, she needed a few minutes to rendezvous with her future.

Most people would probably view it as coming home. Going full circle. But they'd be wrong. To her, returning to the mountain was a brand-new adventure. With Zach, everything was new.

Snow was still piled high on the side of the road where the plows had pushed it a couple of weeks ago. She glanced at the sky. They'd be getting a fresh cover by tomorrow if she wasn't mistaken. And if they didn't, the snowmaking equipment would assure good skiing conditions.

Zach was right about the snow. Think by the season, not by the day. In the end, they hadn't really lost any business. She sighed deeply. As usual, she worried for nothing.

Her thoughts flew to the seasons ahead. Spring and summer brought hikers, mountain bikers, canoeists and folks who wanted a hotel vacation. And in the autumn, nothing could compare with the foliage of Mother Nature. The hotel would be booked all of September and October. She felt confident about that.

She glanced at the cartons of law books lying on the seat next to her and on the floor. More were piled in the back, along with personal items from her apartment. Have books, will travel. She giggled. She had no idea where to unpack them yet. She'd figure it out later.

The familiar landscape beckoned now. She viewed the scenery with a possessiveness and pride that surprised her. The trees didn't belong to her, yet they were hers. Just like the town and the road. And the mountains. Always the mountains.

She signaled her turnoff to the Diamond's private road. The closer she got to home, the more rapid her heartbeat. She leaned forward over the wheel. Had it only been four days since she'd seen Zach?

She drove to the family entrance and hopped out of the car. Eagerly opening the kitchen door, she tossed her jacket aside and shook off the twinge of disappointment as she viewed the empty room. Silly to feel let down. It was late afternoon, and Zach could be anywhere on the property. She automatically headed for the office.

He was there. Sitting at his desk, eyes on his work. She looked her fill—the strong profile, broad shoulders, hardworking man—and her heart overflowed with the love she felt for him, stronger with each day that passed.

She could have stood there forever, but she wanted

to feel his arms around her, wanted her arms around him. She stepped forward.

"Hi, Zach." She smiled and crossed to his desk, eager for reunion.

He looked up, plainly startled by the interruption, and stared at her.

No smile, no twinkle, no hug. Nothing, except perhaps desolation.

Amanda's heart lurched. "My God, Zach. What's happened? You look like you lost your best friend."

One corner of his mouth slanted upward. "Aptly put, Amanda. That's just the way I feel."

She stared unblinkingly. Her eyes started to burn. He had to be referring to her. She was his best friend.

"What?" she whispered. "What did I do?" But in her heart she knew.

"Do the words *Jerry, telephone, Paradise, agreement,* mean anything to you? How about the fact that you called Jerry after I asked you not to? How about that you gave him the impression that you'd keep working on me until I agreed to sell?"

She collapsed into her chair, her fears confirmed. Zach had obviously found out about her recent call to Jerry and was out for bear. Steel-gray eyes met hers. Any degree of warmth was absent.

She reached toward him, her hand extended. "I can explain. I was scared, and Paradise seemed like an answer. But I changed my mind. And they were going to change everything, including adding neon lights. The Diamond would be just like all the other Paradise

Hotels.'' She sounded like a runaway locomotive, but she couldn't slow down.

"Since when does all that matter to you? You've been pushing me to sell since you got here. So don't complain about the reality.''

Zach rose from his chair then and shook his head. "Your words don't matter, Amanda. Your actions do. There's no excuse for going behind my back, especially after I asked you not to. If you're scared, you talk to me. Did you think you could manipulate this Green Mountain boy like I was a country bumpkin? Did you think I could be so easily led? After all this time, don't you know me at all?''

Tears fell. Hers. Her clever tongue was tied in knots. Despite her own angst, she knew he was hurting. She'd never seen him like this before. Never.

He walked to her chair and leaned over her. "In a relationship, betrayal can take many forms. And then the relationship dies.''

He straightened and turned his back toward her. "Consider yourself a free woman, Amanda.''

She had no words, no breath. Twenty minutes ago, she was humming a happy tune in the car on her way to her new life. And now, nothing.

"No! I won't.'' Where had that courage come from? "I'm sorry, Zach.'' She gulped. "I didn't mean to hurt you like this. You didn't give me a chance to tell you about the phone call, but I was going to.'' Did he hear her thready voice? "You'll just have to believe me.''

She heard him sigh deeply. "I believe you'd have

told me sooner or later. But the real message is still clear. You don't think I can run the mountain, and instead of talking it over, you acted against me. But what the hell? I'll get over it." He walked to the door. "Right now, I need some fresh air."

CHAPTER THIRTEEN

SHE STARED AT his retreating back as tears blinded her. Tremors shook her body. Cold. She felt so cold. She needed a cup of tea, but her shaking hands would surely spill it even if she found the strength to fill the kettle.

Her eyes remained glued to the door as though Zach would reappear in a moment. Foolish thought. He'd left her. He'd get over her. That's what he'd meant by, "I'll get over it." He meant her.

She sat quietly. Had no choice really. She couldn't move. The afternoon faded to evening before the enormity of the day finally hit.

She'd gambled everything and lost.

No job, her apartment for rent, and now no aggressive investments. She patted her pants pocket and felt the envelope she'd hidden there hours ago. A gift. For Zach and Diamond Ridge. She'd converted all her mutuals to a cash money-market account, and she never had a chance to give it to him.

Tears welled up again. She'd planned to tease him into taking it, joke about giving him a dowry. But that was before. He'd never accept it now. Not with a million explanations. It was too late. Too late. Too late.

Pain made her whimper. No Zach. No future. No fun. No playful loving, or tender loving, or hot, sensuous, sexy loving.

She laid her head in her hands and visualized an endless string of gray days ahead, working somewhere, living alone again. But this time, she'd hate it. Now she knew the difference between existing and living.

She wished she'd never learned.

ZACH WALKED OUTSIDE and welcomed the cold March wind in his face. He inhaled deeply, and automatically checked the sky. They'd have new snow by morning. He nodded matter-of-factly. Weather he understood. Women he didn't.

What a jackass he was to have loved her. All during his twenties, and still at thirty and thirty-one, up until the day Amanda had come home, he'd played the field. Sowing those wild oats could have lasted a lifetime. He would have been content. He would have been safe.

And now he hurt. Hurt like hell. Why'd he let her get so close? Hadn't he lost enough in his life? His parents, of course, hadn't chosen to die. His aunt Rose hadn't, either. But Amanda's actions were deliberate. She'd consciously betrayed his trust. And without trust, they had nothing. A relationship built on sand.

He pounded his fist into his opposite palm. Damn! They'd been so close to the real thing.

Restless, he walked to the base lodge, put on his

ski boots and grabbed his skis and poles. What was the point of owning a mountain if he couldn't ski when he wanted to? He left word at the front desk and walked out into the night. Few people were around at the dinner hour. Being alone suited his mood just fine.

His staff was closing down operations when he arrived at the lifts.

"Hit the lights and leave them on."

"But we're not scheduled for night skiing tonight."

"I've scheduled a private session. Just for me."

He saw the crew exchange glances. His request was out of character, but so what?

"Give me ten minutes to get to the Rough and then shut down the lifts. I'll get rides back up on the cats."

Two minutes later, he looked down from his seat on the chairlift. The mountain seemed strange, with no chattering skiers to bring it to life. He lifted his gaze to the mountaintop, but it was hidden under the clouded sky. As the chairlift brought him higher, he felt the silence surround him. Silence. Darkness. Isolation.

He extracted himself expertly from the lift, then skied around the guardhouse and across a short stretch to the second lift. Recently installed, this lift allowed skiers to maximize the full vertical drop of the mountain.

He rode up until, finally, he stood at the top of the world. Alone. He looked to the right, then to the left. Not even a bird of prey to share the windswept slope.

His mind's eye suddenly captured a recent visit. In sunshine. With Amanda. God, it had been a wonderful day! After she'd relaxed and conquered her fear, they'd flown down the slopes together. He'd loved watching her, her animated expression with that beautiful smile, her graceful body as she traveled the trails. If ever there was poetry in motion, Mandy was it.

His jaw clenched at the memory, and he looked around again. He was alone at the top of a mountain. Alone. Everything and everyone he cared about was down below. But he wasn't ready to go back. The betrayal was too raw. He leaned forward and pushed off with his poles. The hell with the cats. He'd ski the whole damn mountain, and by the time he got home, he'd be tired and ready to sleep.

"WHY ARE YOU SO LATE? It's way dark outside, and I've been waiting to eat dinner with you, and I'm hungry."

He watched Molly slam the refrigerator door as she spoke and turn to him.

"I suppose I could make some scrambled eggs," she muttered. "For both of us."

"What's wrong with the hotel food?"

"The dining room's closed, Zach. Don't you know what time it is?"

He hadn't noticed. "The staff would have given you something."

"But we always have dinner together. I was waiting for you," she repeated.

She was right. The three of them had formed the

pattern of meeting for dinner each evening. He and Amanda wanted Molly to know she could have their undivided attention every night, no matter how busy their respective days.

"You could have eaten with your sister."

"She's sick or something. Didn't want to eat."

He felt his heart speed up. "Where is she?"

"In bed. She was freezing cold. I had to get the extra quilts from the closet."

He walked across the room to the hallway.

"She said not to disturb her. But maybe she's got the flu or something. Maybe we should call the doctor."

He kept on walking. He'd just peep in. Make sure she was okay. And then leave quietly. She couldn't really be sick. Upset? Yes. Ill? No.

He turned back to Molly. "I'll let you know. In the meantime, scrambled eggs and toast sound really good. Make plenty." He winked at her thumbs-up sign and continued toward Amanda's bedroom.

The family quarters were connected, but totally separate from the hotel. Even his bedroom suite on the second floor was connected only to the house. Amanda's room remained as part of the first-floor bedroom wing, part of the home Lily had created years ago. Zach didn't pause until he arrived at the corridor outside her room. It was dark. He flipped the light switch, turned her doorknob and peered into the room.

He blinked and waited until his eyes adjusted to the dimness. Molly had been right. Across the room, the bed was piled high with quilts. From where he stood, he couldn't see if Amanda, or anyone, lay in the bed. He opened the door wider to let in more light, and took a step forward.

He heard a mewing sound. A kitten? His eyes darted to every corner and then to the bed. He laughed at himself. They didn't have a kitten or a cat. He stepped closer to the bed.

Curled on her side under the covers, with her arm over her head, Amanda seemed asleep. Zach bent forward to touch her forehead and heard the soft sound again. It came from Amanda.

He looked harder. Her eyes were closed, but tears had stained her cheeks. He saw the path they'd taken down her face. Her lashes were dark and clumped together. She turned then. Turned and moaned in her sleep.

He stood still, waiting for her to settle. But she turned again, kicked at the covers. On her back now, her face was easily visible in the dim light. He saw a fresh tear take the path of its predecessors.

She didn't have the flu. She was suffering from another illness, one he couldn't do anything about. Wouldn't do anything about, although he ached, watching her.

She turned again, shoving her pillow away.

"Shh." He laid his hand on her forehead just in case. A little damp, but no temperature. "Shh," he whispered again as relief eased his tension. "Go back to sleep."

She stilled instantly. A smile crossed her face. "Zach?" she murmured. Her breathing deepened, and as he watched, she continued to breathe evenly and fell into a relaxed, normal sleep.

He closed the door behind him and leaned against the wall. She was hurting. He was hurting. He understood that. But he also understood that without trust, any relationship would fail.

AMANDA THREW OFF the last vestiges of sleep and sat up in bed. She smiled at the snow blanketing her window. Good. Spring skiing attracted lots of devoted athletes who didn't want to let the season go. Zach would be happy.

Zach. In a split second, yesterday's fiasco came crashing in on her. She fell against the pillows, now loath to get up and face the day.

Absently plucking at her blanket, she viewed her room. Chaos. Her bed looked like the aftermath of a land-mine explosion. The clothes she'd worn yesterday were strewn everywhere. When had she ever allowed her emotions to control her behavior? Never.

But, of course, she'd never loved anyone in her life the way she loved Zach. And that was the difference.

Love was messy, just like her room. She smiled at the ludicrous thought, but then pursed her lips. Their impasse wasn't funny at all. The truth was, she'd dropped the ball. Big time. Conspiring with Jerry had cost her Zach's trust. She should have dealt with him directly. Should have been in his face with her concerns. And everything would have been out in the open.

She had two choices now. Either patch up her life

in New York somehow and revive the safety of her solitary existence, or fight like hell for what she really wanted. Right here.

It was a no-brainer. She had nothing to lose and everything to gain. A thoughtful smile crossed her face. She was used to fights, used to defending herself, proving herself in school, proving herself on the fashion runway, proving herself in the office and in court.

And no one said she had to fight fair. Although she'd always depended on hard research and intellect to win her cases, this time she'd use whatever she could, whatever worked. She had more at stake now than an ordinary case, and knew it wouldn't be easy.

She folded the blankets and searched for her shoes. They'd go back to where they started. She and Zach. They'd be business partners, guardianship partners. She'd set the tone. Business as usual.

She rifled through the clothes in her closet. Now, where was that red sweater with the matching stretch pants? Zach loved her in red.

AN HOUR LATER, Amanda walked into the office with the usual two cups of coffee. Zach sat behind his desk, sipping from a different mug.

Surprised for a moment, she pasted a smile on her face. "You must have been a real early bird this morning if you couldn't wait."

"Didn't know whether you'd be here today, Amanda. Molly said you were sick and not to disturb you." He appraised her from head to toes as he spoke.

"Well, I'm feeling fine now," she snapped. "What are you looking at? Do I have dirt on my face?"

"Whoa, girl. Maybe you are sick. Did you sleep all right?"

This first meeting was not going the way it was supposed to.

She took a deep breath. "Good morning, Zach. I slept just fine after a while. Thanks very much."

"You're welcome," he said with a little smile. "Any time."

Now, what did he mean?

Fifteen minutes later, they were discussing maintenance plans, personnel changes and, as Amanda had hoped, business as usual. Except the fire was out. No loving glances, no innuendos, no teasing promises about the evening to come. So it wasn't really business as usual. It was business and only business.

And he hadn't even noticed her red outfit.

AFTER A WEEK, he knew he had to get away. Away from the Diamond, away from Amanda. That red sweater was a beacon flashing in his brain. She must have worn it every day since that awful night. Or so it seemed. Then there was the black, tight thing with the open zipper down the front. He wanted to zip it all the way down her head and take her to bed.

And that was the truth.

So he needed to put distance between them. Sex alone did not make a relationship. And keeping his mind strictly on business was getting harder every day. He sucked in his breath and looked across the kitchen table at the woman who lived in the back of his mind.

"I'm visiting the Gibson brothers tonight. Don't wait up."

"The Gibsons?" Amanda replied. "They were with the group I spoke to last night. I answered every question they had."

He shrugged. He'd visit Mickey Mouse just to get away. Tonight she was in pink. Hot. Almost red. Jeez, he didn't even know his colors anymore. Her body didn't quit. He knew that much. But what was she saying about last night?

"Were you out again last night?"

She nodded. "Mrs. Stein hosted a few neighbors and asked me to visit."

She'd been gone a number of evenings. He examined her carefully, ignoring the pink sweater but looking at the woman who wore it. Shadows under her eyes, her collarbone sharp beneath the wool, thinner than when she'd arrived. Damn! Why hadn't he noticed earlier? He would have insisted she stay home.

"Why?" he finally answered. "Why are you knocking yourself out like this?"

"Why? Because I no longer think turning these mountains into a Las Vegas strip is a good idea, and neither does Mrs. Stein."

"So you don't think selling is a good idea anymore?" He tried to keep his voice neutral. "Weren't you the one who wanted me to give up the Diamond?"

She lowered her eyes and started biting her lip. "Yes."

"Weren't you the one who spoke with Jerry after I asked you not to?"

"I did."

"Weren't you the one who told Jerry you could bring me around?"

"Sort of."

"So let's not play games, sweetheart," Zach said. "You know darn well you really don't want us to own this spread anymore. You've told me so in a million ways. So what's changed?"

"I'd like to talk to you, Zach, but I won't if you've made up your mind to be angry."

"I'm listening."

She nodded. "I was scared, Zach, plain old scared. I wanted you to sell the Diamond." She paused, obviously expecting him to respond. When he didn't, she continued, "I was frightened about everything. About the money, the weather, about the life up here, my career and the debts we have. I've called myself a million names since then, so you can't say anything to me that I haven't already said to myself."

She looked so appealing. Sad, concerned, apprehensive. He longed to put his arms around her. But that wouldn't solve anything.

She took a breath. "I'm not scared anymore, Zach. I don't want these mountains turned into a glitzy gambling mecca. I also happen to know that gambling is not a done deal yet in Montpelier. So it's very important that we continue the fight, keep it alive so the legislators know where their constituents stand, what they want.''

"Who's leaking information to you from the state capital?" he asked. "And why didn't you let me know?"

She looked at him directly. "Let you know? When? You haven't exactly spent a lot of time with me lately." She turned away from him. "Anyway, I have connections. In this case, Mr. Garroway. When I resigned, he was kind enough or interested enough to make some calls to his political friends."

"Have I really been that bad?" Zach asked, ignoring his first question.

"Worse," she replied. "But it doesn't matter. What matters is that I'm trying as hard as I can, as hard as you are, to protect the Diamond. For Pops, Mom, Molly, and for you, too, you big jerk! And I'm going to keep on doing it until we win. Until…I'm finished. Until I've done everything I can…"

Her voice cracked, and her chest inflated with a labored breath. "Zach?" she whispered. Her big blue eyes, wide open now, traveled over every inch of his face as though memorizing him for later viewing. "Do you believe me?"

He looked at her closely. Her eyes implored. Her entire expression was tense. Whatever happened in their future, he knew that his answer now meant everything to her. "That you've changed your mind completely about the mountains? Well, I think you believe it. And that's good enough for me."

Her chin dropped. Her eyes squeezed shut as she

shook her head. "You don't really believe me," she said, still in a whisper, as she opened her eyes again and slowly straightened her spine. "Well, don't worry. Pops and Mom are coming home soon. I'll be out of your hair before you know it."

It was impossible to think straight with her standing next to him. Her familiar fragrance, her expressive face so beautiful and haunted now, and her natural sensuality, tied him in knots. Yet he couldn't look away.

"Lily left you a message," he finally said. "I'm truly sorry about the timing." He handed her the note. "Your apartment's been rented. You have until the end of next month."

HER BREATH CAUGHT, and she forgot to inhale. How many punches could she take before she became totally numb? She reached for the note and donned her lawyer's demeanor. "Mom won't need it that long. So everything worked out."

"You know you'll always have a home here, Amanda. No one's kicking you out."

She whirled on him. "Don't patronize me, Zach. I'll figure out my life like I always do. Alone. But I'll give you fair warning. You *will* be seeing me. I've got a mother, and a sister, and Pops. And if you want me out of here, that's just too damn bad!"

She turned and started swiftly for the door. Suddenly she was spun back around.

"I can't continue the way we are," Zach growled. She stared into his eyes, and her heart started to sing. Just a little song. Because the look was there again. The molten, gray-eyed I'm-going-to-kiss-you-till-you-can't-think-straight look. Slightly cautious, but it was real.

Joy filled her, and she flashed him her most brilliant smile. He didn't stand a chance.

He leaned toward her, eagerness in every movement, and she wrapped her arms around his neck. His kiss was as powerful as dynamite and as gentle as a caress. His unique scent—pine and spice—teased her memory, and she inhaled deeply, while reveling in his strong embrace as he welcomed her home.

She gave as good as she got. Her tongue danced with his, and she nibbled his lips, kissing his face and neck everywhere she could reach.

"Lock the door," she murmured between kisses.

"No locks in the kitchen," he replied. "Come with me." Ten seconds later, in their locked office, he hastily removed her sweater. "I've missed you, Mandy."

"Thank goodness."

She unsnapped his waistband and tugged at his jeans. The proof of his longing stood at attention, and she stared at it hungrily.

He bestowed a crooked grin as he pulled her closer, bent his head and began kissing her breasts.

Waves of delicious tension caused her legs to tremble. She grabbed his shoulders. His talented tongue continued to tease, until he drew a nipple into his mouth. Her breath came faster. Her body swayed. She felt his arm around her, supporting her. "Oh, Zach…"

Suddenly, she was straddling him in his big desk

chair. She was hot, she was wet, and every time Zach stroked her breasts, she quivered with greater excitement. "Hurry!" she gasped.

In a heartbeat, they were joined. She quickly matched his tempo, noting that Zach's ardor for her hadn't diminished one iota. It didn't take long to reach her moment of ecstasy, and when she did, he exploded, too.

"Oh, yes, yes!" She squeezed him tightly one last time and collapsed onto his chest. With his arms around her, she could have lain there forever. But there were still issues between them.

Slowly, she climbed off his lap and gathered their clothing.

"Now, come here," he said, waving her back to the chair after they were dressed. "My lap is lonely for you."

She smiled and walked toward him, but pulled over another chair. "We need to talk, Zach, and we don't need any distraction."

His mouth turned up in a smile, and he nodded. "Fair enough. So look at me now." She complied and watched him take a deep breath. "Here's the truth, Amanda, and why I was so hurt."

He squeezed her hands gently. "I had already decided to call Jerry myself and negotiate a buyout. My hand was on the phone when he called me."

"But why were you going to do that?" Her voice rose with shock. "The Diamond is your home."

"I wanted you to be happy, Mandy. And not to worry."

The sincerity in his voice twisted her heart. Tears rolled down her face at his confession, but she forced herself to meet his gaze. "Zach, I wish to God I could undo my phone call, that I could undo my association with Paradise. But I can't. I was wrapped up in my own fears, and I'm sorry."

"And how do you feel now?"

"I feel...free. I guess that's why I cashed out my investments. I wanted to offer you my money because...because... Oh, my God! Because I didn't need it anymore!"

She jumped from the chair. "Do you hear me, Zach? I don't need it anymore." She paced in front of him. "I don't need that money the way I need you. I love you. I'd rather have a partnership with you, messy emotions and all, than any amount of money." She sat down again, leaned forward and took his hands. "Am I making any sense?"

"I have no idea what you're talking about, sweetheart. What money?"

Of course he didn't know what she was talking about. Her world had crashed before she'd had the opportunity to tell him. "I consolidated my accounts into one money-market account to give you for the Diamond. You can have it as...as my dowry! Will you take it? Am I making any sense now?"

She gazed into his face, waiting for his reaction. He blinked, his eyes unnaturally bright.

He shook his head. "You're making perfect sense, sweetheart. Just perfect. Except the part about me taking the money. I don't want your money. All I want is someone to share my life with. The ups and downs. The Diamond has to hold its own. We make decisions based on sound business practices. So go reinvest that dowry of yours before you lose it." He chuckled. "Thoroughly modern Amanda Shaw with a dowry! You are one funny lady."

She smiled but lowered her eyes. He was talking future. Lifetime partnership. And the future had to be based on truth. "I love you, Zach," she said, meeting his gaze. "I always will. But everything's not perfect yet. You don't quite trust me. And I can't force it. So it's going to take time."

He nodded slowly. "That's about as honest as it gets. And that's all I ask, not only of you, but of myself." He paused a moment. "Let's face it, Mandy. I'm not blameless here, either. This last week has been hell for both of us. I should never have reacted like that. We should have cleared the air and talked about everything, including whether I should have spoken to Jerry way back in the beginning. So I guess I was as scared as you were and stubborn, as well. I didn't want to hear an offer I couldn't refuse." He laughed ruefully. "Paradise could sure provide temptation. So I guess I'm going to have to earn your trust, too."

She kissed him then. Long and hard.

"I like your brand of kisses, Ms. Shaw."

"Then get ready for more." She raised her lips to his.

CHAPTER FOURTEEN

IN THE WEEKS that followed, Zach couldn't have been more attentive and loving. They hadn't actually spoken about the T-word again, and she almost felt that the trust issue didn't exist. Almost. A kernel of doubt still remained. In her head? In his head? In both their heads?

"Are they here yet? Do you see them?"

Molly's impatience was contagious. Amanda slipped on her jacket and stepped outside for at least the fortieth time in two hours. Molly was right beside her.

She studied the road leading to the hotel with no real expectation of spotting the small caravan. "Do you think they'll show up faster if we wait outside?"

Molly grinned. "You never can tell, and I'd rather be where I can see everything."

Amanda's eyes swept the vicinity. There really wasn't much to see. Very little snow remained at the end of April. Spring rains had alternated with falling night temperatures to create slushy conditions on the slopes. The roads were clean to the blacktop.

"The big season is over," she murmured.

"Yeah. And now we get ready for summer."

The enthusiasm in her sister's voice made Amanda laugh. "You never get tired of it, do you?"

"Why should I? There's always something to do. This summer, Daddy is hiring my friends and me as junior counselors, not just baby-sitters, because we're finally teenagers. We can do lots of things with the kids, like nature walks—they love going in the woods—and swimming and volleyball. And maybe we'll take them white-water rafting. If Daddy comes. I can teach them all kinds of stuff. And we get paid! It'll be great."

Molly's excitement caused Amanda to focus on the youngster's eager face. *Molly thinks she can do anything. When I was her age, I was afraid of everything. Until I learned to ski.*

"Why are you staring at me like that? Is my hair a mess? I want to look good for Daddy."

Amanda continued to look at the beautiful girl, her thoughts tumbling together until they finally made sense. A bubble of excitement ran through her. She knew exactly what she was going to do with her investments.

She put her hands on Molly's shoulders. "Pops is going to be a new man when he sees you." She looked closer. "Good job, sis. I bet he won't notice the eye shadow and mascara!"

Molly grinned from ear to ear, but sounded defensive. "I can use makeup. I'm almost thirteen. All my friends wear it. And I'm sorry I had to use your stuff, but I don't have any yet."

Amanda hooted with laughter. "You are priceless, Mol."

A calculating gleam came into her sister's eye. "You can tell Mommy that, in New York, all the girls wear it."

"I have a better idea."

Molly looked at her first with surprise, then with such eagerness Amanda would treasure the moment. "We'll talk to Mom and Pops, and then if you want to, we'll go shopping together. I'll teach you how to use cosmetics the right way."

"Just like when you were a model in *American Teen* magazine?"

"Not quite yet. But by the time you're ready, you'll know exactly what to do."

"Yes, yes, yes!"

Amanda laughed again at Molly's zest for life. And then had to find her balance as the young tornado grabbed her hands and led her in a crazy dance.

"You're the best sister, Amanda. I love you."

She pulled Molly into a hug. "And I love you, Popcorn Girl," she whispered.

"AND WHEN I SAW my girls hugging each other like that, I knew I was home again."

Zach leaned back in his chair, content, as his uncle regaled everyone in the dining room with his homecoming. There were only a handful of guests, but all the long-term staff members were there.

"I tell you, it was a sight for sore eyes. And my eyes are pretty darn sore from being cooped up all this time. But these girls of mine, they knew how to welcome me back.''

Zach yawned, glanced at Amanda and caught the appeal in her eye. He stood up and ambled toward her.

"We're giving you the rest of the day off, Unc. And as many days as you want to take. But Amanda's a working girl. We've got to prepare for the final hearings at the state capital next week.''

"I know all about those hearings. It's a lot of foolishness is what it is.''

Zach grinned. "You're preaching to the choir, Uncle Ben.''

Ben smiled back. A slightly lopsided smile. "I know it, son. You've done a great job, you and Mandy. But I still own forty-nine percent of this mountain, and I want to hear what you're going to say before you go to the statehouse.''

His uncle was back! Maybe not in full force. But in full mind. And that was more important.

"You'll hear every word, partner.'' He snagged Amanda around the waist and left the room. In the connecting hallway, he heard Ben's voice.

"They're a beautiful couple, Lily. In love. So when's the wedding?''

"You keep your nose out of it, Benjamin Porter. If there's an announcement to be made, you'll be told. Until then, mind your own business.''

Their voices faded as he and Amanda walked to the office. He looked at her. A blush suffused her face.

"What's the matter, sweetheart? If my uncle's embarrassing you, just tell him we have an August-first date and he'll shut up."

Tears glistened when she turned to him. "I can't marry you yet, Zach. Not until you trust me completely."

He was stunned. Shocked. After their wonderful time together, working and playing, in the past few weeks, he'd assumed they'd both brushed aside that earlier conversation. "Look at me, sweetheart," he said. "I love you and I trust you. You've been killing yourself for the business. No one's worked harder. All those meetings, trips to the statehouse, lobbying. You don't have anything to prove anymore."

A horrible thought popped into his head. "Unless you don't trust me?"

"Of course I trust you, and I believe in you," she protested. "But I still have something to prove to myself."

"You have nothing to prove," he almost shouted. "Stop punishing yourself. You're the best thing that's ever happened to me, Mandy. My life would be empty without you. So I don't want to hear any more about it. And that's that."

She smiled and hugged him, and didn't say a word. But somehow her silence spoke eloquently. His mind raced. He'd have to do something to put this matter to rest. After all, he was the one who'd erected the wall in the first place, and he'd be the one to tear it down.

AMANDA STOOD at the entrance to the hotel dining room hoping it could accommodate the large turnout. She rose on tiptoe trying to spot any vacant seats, then turned to greet another arrival. When David Webster, their state rep, had asked Zach and her to host this meeting today, two days before the gambling issue came to the floor of the statehouse, they willingly obliged. David wouldn't have coordinated such a gathering unless he had something important to announce. Amanda's instincts said that she, Zach and their committee workers had come to the end of their campaign. She crossed her trembling fingers and wished for a happy outcome. Her heart warmed when she saw Ben walking from table to table with only the use of a cane. He was in his element, chatting with each of his cronies. These were his neighbors, people who lived and worked in the mountains, some in the ski business, some not. But they'd all turned out this afternoon. Seemed that no one wanted to miss hearing what their state representatives had to say.

The noise level in the room seemed too loud. Heads turned constantly to check out other attendees. Everyone was anxious, Amanda realized. But no one more than she. She wanted to win this fight. She *needed* to win.

When David Webster arrived with a cadre of other elected officials from a host of state districts, the tension increased dramatically as private conversations died away.

"Come up front with us, sweetheart," Zach said

quietly in her ear. "You're as much a part of this as I am."

He squeezed her hand, and her nervousness lessened. She blinked and felt a tear drop. No matter the outcome, she reminded herself, she and Zach were a team. She just wanted him to know that she could pull her fifty percent.

She and Zach, as well as the presidents of the Chamber of Commerce and ski association, escorted David and his party to the makeshift dais. Ben didn't wait for an invitation to speak.

"David Webster," he called. "My friends and I are sitting here wondering what the fuss is about today. If you've got something to say, let's have it."

"I've got something to say, Ben Porter, and you're going to like it. So sit down and let me do it my way."

Instantly, the atmosphere changed from suspicion to curiosity, laced with excitement.

Leave it to Pops. In thirty seconds, he changed the entire tenor of the place. Out front. Direct. Just like Zach. They were all together now. Her family under the same roof. Their minds on the same things. It had been a long time since they'd been a unit. A long time because of her.

But that was changing. Amanda's hands clenched in her pockets. David's announcement wasn't the only one set for today. She had a doozy of her own, and although she hadn't planned to say anything yet, she couldn't pass up the opportunity to have a perfectly targeted and captive audience.

She watched Zach adjust the microphone, heard him welcome everyone to the Diamond. And then heard him say, "Please stay seated after David's discussion, because I have another announcement you'll all be interested in."

What was he talking about? He didn't know about her surprise. He couldn't know. She hadn't told anyone. And he hadn't discussed anything with her. She raised her brow in inquiry. He responded with a wink and a gorgeous, sexy smile. And heat in his smoky-gray eyes. Even in the crowded room, she started to squirm.

David Webster started to speak. "The powers that be in the gaming industry have indicated that the best locations for successful gambling ventures are places with nothing else to offer. Places like Las Vegas, which was carved out of the desert. Places like Atlantic City, once an impoverished area with nothing else going for it. Our mountains, our sports industry, offer too much competition. Our roads aren't six-lane freeways, and our weather is unpredictable. We are not a choice location."

Cheers erupted before he could continue.

"We could've told them all that right away."

"Yeah, why didn't anyone ask us?"

The comments came fast and furious.

"You did," Zach replied. "All the meetings, all the committees, all the lobbying. And now it's over. Am I right?"

David nodded. "It's all over, folks. The issue will

not come to the floor of the legislature, since there's no real support for it. There's no point.''

Amanda postponed her relief and scanned the crowd. Some people would be disappointed not to make a killing on their properties, but most would feel secure about their current livelihoods. She met Zach's searching gaze and smiled. He'd know how she felt. She wanted no misunderstandings now.

Zach approached the mike and motioned her near. Everyone settled down again.

''As I mentioned before, folks, I have my own announcement to make. So instead of the news traveling slowly from phone to phone, I thought I'd give it to you all at once.''

As one, the whole crowd sat forward, including Ben and Lily. Ben didn't look too happy. Probably didn't know anything about what his partner was going to do. Zach really knew how to get everyone's attention.

''Amanda, will you join me up here?''

''Me?'' she whispered, pointing at herself. She didn't know what he was doing, either. So how could she help him?

He nodded and crooked his finger. She went to his side, and he put his arm around her before turning to the audience again.

''Friends,'' he said, ''there's going to be a wedding at Diamond Ridge. And you're all invited. It's on August first at two o'clock. And I don't even know what day of the week it is. But that's when Amanda and I are getting married.''

She couldn't speak. He was crazy. A lunatic. What was he doing? And he wasn't finished yet.

"Because she's the most wonderful, loving, trustworthy partner a guy could have."

And he kissed her. Full-blown. In front of everyone.

"That's my boy," called a familiar voice. "Knew he'd get it right."

Cheers, catcalls and whistles. Amanda felt the heat rise to her face. "Zach," she whispered, "what are you doing?"

"I'm marrying you. And that's that."

"But, but…"

"There are no buts. So, my beautiful Amanda, will you marry me?"

She looked into the face she loved, into the eyes that shone with love for her, into the smile that lit her life. He loved her. He trusted her. He'd called her the best partner a guy could have. He must trust her. And Lord, she wanted a life with him. She wanted to live!

"Yes," she said. "Yes and yes. I accept." She scanned the room. "Sam Johnson, do you still need a partner?"

"Hell, yes!" the lawyer replied.

"Well, you've got one." She turned to Zach and laughed at his dumbstruck expression.

"Wow," he said. "Well done, Mandy."

"I'm not done yet." She took the mike and smiled. "Hi, everyone. Thanks for your cheers. Hi, Pops, Mom. He surprised me, too. Sort of. Anyway, it seems it's a day for announcements. I've got one of my own, and it involves all of you.'' Was that her voice? Shaky and squeaky? She certainly didn't sound like a confident New York lawyer. But it wasn't every day that a girl's marriage announcement was made without her knowledge!

She took a deep breath and waited until everyone quieted. ''I've been back at the Diamond for almost five months now, and I've done a lot of thinking. About our lives here, about sports, and about how skiing literally changed my life years ago when I was a young teenager. Changed it for the better. Definitely for the better.

''So I have set up the Ben and Lily Porter Scholarship Fund for youngsters who would never otherwise have the chance to challenge the mountain and challenge themselves. We'll have—''

The sound of loud applause made her stop. She looked at her mother and at Ben. Surprise. Tears and smiles. She blew them a kiss.

''We'll have high-school kids from New York City and from the school districts in Vermont.'' She gave a few other details. ''The fund is well seeded—I guess I didn't have any trouble with that—but I need an outside advisory board and some volunteers during the week of ski camp.''

She looked into Zach's grinning face.

''Your dowry?'' he asked.

She returned his smile and nodded. ''Most of it. I kept out a college fund for Molly and for our...um...children. If you want.''

"If I want? You crazy woman. Of course I want. But more than that, I want *you*. I love you, Amanda. And I'll say it to you every day of our lives."

She leaned into him, her arms around his waist. Her entire life had changed—no, she had changed—because of one man. Because she let love in.

"I love you, Zachary. And I will love you every day of our lives."

"I'm counting on it, sweetheart."

EPILOGUE

ON THE AFTERNOON of August first, Zach stood on the vast back lawn of the hotel, which had been temporarily transformed into an outdoor chapel. He stood in front of the two hundred guests who were seated in rows on either side of a center aisle. His eyes were glued to a spot behind them where Amanda would appear and begin her journey down that aisle toward him. Lily and Ben had escorted him down that same path moments earlier, before returning for Amanda.

He focused on Molly, walking slowly toward him, a dazzling maid of honor and totally delighted with herself. He looked at her closely and saw the woman flowering within the girl. The Mona Lisa smile, the slight sway of her hips. When did that happen? He shook his head. Ben would be beating off the boys after his younger daughter before too long.

Molly reached his side, grinned and stepped back to stand slightly to the left of him. The music swelled. Zach's gaze panned back up the aisle and remained riveted.

Suddenly, she appeared. Amanda. Like a princess. A fitted bodice, a full skirt, a veil of mist preserving her for his eyes alone.

He forgot to breathe.

How lucky he was to be given this woman. He closed his eyes for a moment, collecting himself. He'd been so afraid of pain he'd lived only half a life. Until Amanda. Where once he'd spurned commitment, now he looked forward to the relationship of a lifetime. His life had changed because of one woman. Because he'd let love in.

He watched as Ben and Lily led their daughter down the aisle. When the trio stopped halfway, Zach walked toward his bride, hoping the love in his heart was visible to her. As he drew closer, she lifted her face toward him, and beneath the veil, her blue eyes shimmered.

"Bless you both," his uncle murmured as he relinquished his position next to Amanda. Zach barely heard him.

"Take care of each other," Lily whispered.

He nodded and placed Amanda's hand on his arm. Her skin felt cold for a warm August day. He lifted her hand to his mouth and kissed her fingers. "I love you," he whispered.

She caressed his cheek in reply, before taking his arm again.

Together, they walked to the front of the congregation and began the most important partnership of all.

Harlequin proudly brings you

STELLA CAMERON
Bobby Hutchinson
Sandra Marton

in

MARRIED
IN SPRING

a brand-new anthology in which three couples
find that when spring arrives, romance soon
follows…along with an unexpected
walk down the aisle!

February 2001

Available wherever Harlequin books are sold.

HARLEQUIN®
Makes any time special ™

#1 *New York Times* bestselling author

NORA ROBERTS

brings you more of the loyal and loving, tempestuous and tantalizing Stanislaski family.

Coming in February 2001

The Stanislaski Sisters

Natasha and Rachel

Though raised in the Old World traditions of their family, fiery Natasha Stanislaski and cool, classy Rachel Stanislaski are ready for a *new* world of love....

And also available in February 2001 from Silhouette Special Edition, the newest book in the heartwarming Stanislaski saga

CONSIDERING KATE

Natasha and Spencer Kimball's daughter Kate turns her back on old dreams and returns to her hometown, where she finds the *man* of her dreams.

Available at your favorite retail outlet.

Silhouette®

Where love comes alive™

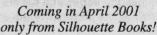

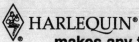
HARLEQUIN®

makes any time special—online...

eHARLEQUIN.com

shop eHarlequin

- ♥ Find all the new Harlequin releases at everyday great discounts.

- ♥ Try before you buy! Read an excerpt from the latest Harlequin novels.

- ♥ Write an online review and share your thoughts with others.

reading room

- ♥ Read our Internet exclusive daily and weekly online serials, or vote in our interactive novel.

- ♥ Talk to other readers about your favorite novels in our Reading Groups.

- ♥ Take our Choose-a-Book quiz to find the series that matches you!

authors' alcove

- ♥ Find out interesting tidbits and details about your favorite authors' lives, interests and writing habits.

- ♥ Ever dreamed of being an author? Enter our Writing Round Robin. The Winning Chapter will be published online! Or review our guidelines for submitting your novel.

HARLEQUIN®

AMERICAN *Romance*

New York Times Bestselling Author

Kasey Michaels

launches Harlequin American Romance's
brand-new series—

TEXAS SHEIKHS

beginning in April 2001 with

His Innocent Temptress

TEXAS SHEIKHS: —
Though their veins course with royal blood,
their pride lies in the Texas land they call home.

*Available at
your favorite retail outlet.*

HARLEQUIN®
Makes any time special®